Dara

By Carol Martin

Corporate Publishing
Published under the pen name Carol Martin

ISBN: 978-0-9747108-4-6
First Edition

This novel is an original work of human authorship. Portions of this manuscript were developed with the assistance of artificial intelligence tools for drafting, editing, and refinement in accordance with industry best practices. Final content reflects the author's voice and editorial control.

This novel contains mature themes and language intended for adult readers

Dedication

For the light that finds us, before we know we need it…

For the one who writes stories, long before we understand them…

About This Story

Dara is a story about brilliance, and the cost of it.

It explores the tension between intellect and identity, beauty and perception, power and worth. It examines what happens when beauty and genius occupy the same space, and how quickly the world reduces one to appearance and the other to utility. What happens when genius wears a face the world cannot categorize?

Dara embodies unspoken fears:

that we are seen, but not known.

Admired, but not understood.

Desired, but not loved.

This novel questions the paradigms we inherit, about power, about beauty, about intelligence, about worth. It asks whether autonomy is freedom, or exile.

There is an ancient line that says light shines into darkness, and the darkness does not overcome it. Whether one approaches that line as literature, philosophy, or faith, its implication remains unsettling: truth is not manufactured. It is revealed. Truth does not bend to narrative.

At its core, this story is not about scandal or ambition.

It is a story of recognition. Of discovering that what we thought we
were searching for had already begun searching for us.

About the moment when a person realizes they were never truly lost, only walking without light.

Dara is simply a mirror.

And what it reflects may be uncomfortable.

Because redemption is not reserved for the weak.

It is required by the strong.

Epigraph

There are truths that wait for us,

Longer than we wait for them

Chapter 1

"The man who paid me was old enough to be my father …" - Dara

An elderly Christian woman once told me, *"If the mountain was smooth, you couldn't climb it."* My mountain was jagged, treacherous, and unapologetically steep. My story is provocative, and for some, it will be uncomfortable. This may not be the story you're ready for.

I won't lie. I wish I could rewrite my past. But I can't. My experiences, as flawed and messy as they were, shaped the person I've become. My hope is that by sharing my story, I can bring light to others who feel trapped in the same darkness. The people who brought light into my life didn't care about my profession, appearance, or sharp tongue. They saw beyond all that. They recognized my intellect and unique ability to read people's intentions. It is an ability that often hurt me more than it helped. Because it showed me who people really were.

Society is quick to praise physical beauty over the beauty of a sharp mind. Knowing this, I invested heavily in my appearance, leveraging it as my ticket to success. It was my way of fitting into a world with little room for me. It became my escape plan.

But I was an outlier, intellectually and physically. When you have the "girl-next-door" look, people often dismiss your intellect. Born with an excess of both intelligence and charm, I thought I could navigate the world on my own terms. After all, aren't we taught that brains or beauty can guarantee success? I learned how wrong that was. Success, I've learned, is less about talent and more about the choices we make and the people we choose to let in.

My mother, with the best of intentions, dragged me to church as a child. There, I heard stories about women like me. It seems the Bible had much to say about prostitutes and even more about the self-righteous who judged them. I remembered a story about a woman at a well, drawing water at the wrong hour, meeting a man who spoke to her as if she were something more than the sum of her mistakes. He didn't ask her to justify herself. He didn't take from her. He simply saw her and somehow knew her better than she knew herself.

I needed someone like that. Someone who looked at me without hunger or judgement. Someone who felt my past was not the most interesting thing about me. Someone who knew me better than I knew myself. I reluctantly found people with whom I felt safe.

Prostitutes, I realized, were rebels. Women who broke the rules society imposed on them. Their plight resonated with me. They weren't just scorned; they were ignored, used, and discarded. Yet, deep down, I understood the paradox of redemption. Those who deny their need for it cannot be saved. Yet, some who see the need may still find redemption elusive.

My story is one of redemption. If my past or words offend you as I share my journey, then this isn't the story for you. Carl Jung once said, *"Everything that irritates us about others can lead us to an understanding of ourselves."* Jung was a psychologist who understood the shadows we avoid. If you recoil from my world, ask yourself why. Perhaps it's easier to turn away than to confront what makes you uncomfortable before you see a part of me in you.

I ran and wouldn't look at myself too. I ran from solutions, from people who wanted to help and from myself. I chased problems and justified my actions, all the while seeking a redemption that seemed just out of reach.

Then, I met those rare individuals who saw not who I was, but who I could become. They met me where I stood, parched and desperate, waiting at the metaphorical well I didn't yet understand. They weren't afraid to engage with the likes of me. And in their willingness to listen, I found an oasis in my desolate world.

I wasn't the typical call girl, and my story isn't typical. I was just a lonely girl who thought she could quench her own thirst.

My name is Dara. This is my story.

Chapter 2

"The only way to find out how far you can go is by risking going too far." - Dara

The touch of gray at his temples lent him an air of authority. His flat torso, firm build, and biceps that pressed subtly against his dress shirt told a story of dedication to the gym. When I complimented his physique, he casually admitted to working out which was a typical response. He wasn't supposed to turn me on. He was just another date. But sometimes, in those fleeting moments, I lost myself.

I had a knack for dissecting the world, peeling back its layers. The corners of my lips curved upward, playing along as my date absorbed my compliments. Flattery was the currency of the evening, just as analysis was the lifeblood of my education. By day, I was a scholar. By night, I honed a different kind of craft. One that required intellect as much as allure. Passion was dangerous. It clouded judgment. Successful men craved a challenge, and I knew how to provide just enough without crossing the line.

There was a part of me, the calculating part, that felt as though I carried a fragment of Elliot Keene's brilliance in my DNA. I read about Keene once. He was a brilliant mathematician who worked in wartime intelligence during World War II. The kind of guy people mentioned with a half-smile and a lowered voice. A math professor once noticed my last name on a paper and asked if I was related to him. I laughed it off. Keene was officially childless. At least, that's what the biographies said. Still, the idea lodged itself in me like a splinter.

Perhaps my analytical thoughts had trickled down through some distant, infamous ancestor of his. A genius turned rogue, their legacy diluted yet potent enough to spark my love for patterns and logic. My family name, abandoned long ago, no longer mattered. It was just a ghost left behind by my father, whose departure carved a mistrust of men into my soul. All I had now was my mind and a body more noticeable than my lineage.

When the sun set, I swapped textbooks for silk and intellect for allure. My nights were a balancing act of survival and ambition. I sold moments of my time to fund a future I couldn't afford otherwise. In those quiet moments before the mirror, I often wondered if my choices made me weak. But the mirror offered no answers, only the reflection of a girl piecing herself together with fragments of resilience.

Every night, I became someone else. Carol, a carefully crafted alias. It was a mask I wore to navigate the tightrope between survival and self-respect. I had learned an uncomfortable truth: no one helps you once you're screwed. Before sex, people help each other undress. Afterward, you dress alone. The lesson is that once you're screwed, you're on your own.

My date leaned closer, his laugh rich with charm. The soft glow of candlelight bathed our table, isolating us in a bubble of warmth amidst the dimly lit restaurant. The waiter, a distinguished man with kind eyes, mistook me for his daughter. My date found it amusing, joking about his youthful charm. The waiter's gaze lingered on me for a moment longer before he left, his smile dimming as realization set in. I had seen that look before, judgment, pity, or perhaps a mix of both.

I scanned the room, pretending to admire the ambiance. In reality, I was cataloging exits, scanning faces, and playing my aloof card to deflect personal questions. But tonight's client was persistent, his interest genuine, a rarity. Narcissists were easy to handle. They talked endlessly about themselves, requiring little effort from me. But this man floated somewhere between charm and sincerity, and I couldn't yet determine where he'd land.

"Why does a successful attorney need an escort?" I asked, letting my question hang like bait.

"Why does a college student need to be an escort?" he countered without missing a beat.

"Tuition."

"Touché." He smiled, but I didn't let him off that easily.

"You didn't answer my question."

"I'm a lawyer. Redirecting questions is part of the job." He leaned forward, his grin disarming.

"Well, I get to decide if you screw me. How's that for redirection?" I didn't smile. His composure wavered for just a moment.

"Your profile said you were feisty."

"Is that why you picked me?"

"No. I've used your agency before, but you're the first escort to list Mensa membership as a credential. How smart are you, really?"

It was the first genuine question of the evening, and I filed it away for later.

"That's funny. I thought men only cared if our sexually transmitted infection tests were up to date."

He didn't flinch. My intrigue shifted from his physique to his thoughts.

"And birth control," he said, meeting my gaze. "But I'm not convinced you think men are that shallow. Now you're redirecting the question."

I leaned in slightly, letting my voice soften. "Maybe I just like knowing the kind of man who thinks with his genitals."

He chuckled, sipping his drink to mask his discomfort. I had struck a nerve, and I wasn't about to let it go.

Our conversation turned into a verbal chess match, each move designed to test the other's limits. He confessed to hiring escorts to avoid the complications of relationships. I pushed, probing deeper, and his responses danced between honesty and evasion.

"You're the first escort who's ever wanted to know the reasoning behind using a high-end agency," he said, his tone calm, measured. "Most of the girls are content to be eye candy when I need one."

"I'm not that kind of girl," I replied, my voice steady, my gaze unwavering.

"Well, that's pretty obvious." He leaned back slightly, his expression thoughtful. "You still haven't answered my question. Do you know other languages or something? How high is your IQ to qualify for Mensa membership?"

"Does it matter?" I asked, tilting my head slightly. "Why do you need an escort service? I'm just curious."

I leaned forward, propping my elbows on the table and resting my chin in my hands. The gesture was deliberate, calculated to disarm, to draw him in. I needed him to drop the polished façade, even for a moment. It worked.

He paused, his hand drifting to his napkin as he dabbed at his lips, an unnecessary gesture that betrayed his nerves. After a deep breath, he began to speak, his voice slower now, less rehearsed.

"My wife left me for someone else years ago," he admitted. "Our children are grown. I'm alone, and I have a large firm, one of the biggest in the region. I attend functions where I need a companion, someone who can impress my high-paying clients."

"And sometimes you just need sex," I added, my tone neutral, my words cutting through his explanation.

"And sometimes I just need sex," he admitted with a small shrug, "with no strings attached." He hesitated, then leaned forward, his eyes meeting mine with a flicker of something genuine. "But I picked you because I'm tired of casual girls without independent thought. I figured you'd be…interesting. Plus, I have foreign clients. If you speak other languages, that's an added bonus."

I studied him, my brow furrowing slightly as the corners of his lips curved upward in a faint, almost self-deprecating smile. It wasn't the full truth. I could feel it. There was something more to his choice, something he wasn't ready to admit.

But for now, I decided to let it go. Sometimes, rolling with the partial truth was enough to get what I needed. It was time to decipher what he wasn't saying.

"You're tired of bimbos," I said finally. "You want companionship without risking your success. A disposable relationship has value to you. That's why you're here."

"I didn't say that."

"You didn't have to."

"You escort for tuition."

"I didn't say I was any different," I replied, a wry smile playing on my lips. "I'll be eye candy in front of your friends all day for a fee and play the game. I'll even engage in intelligent conversation with them because, apparently, they've caught on to the fact that you always have airheads on your arm. I'll bet they first thought you were dating gold diggers, and you probably just let them imagine the rest. I doubt you've ever told them you hire escorts, though it does protect your success in many ways. Not to mention your ego."

His mouth opened slightly as if to interject, but I pressed on, not giving him the chance. "I suppose you're taking a calculated risk that I might pass for a legitimate girlfriend. But if I'm going to bed with you, I'd at least like to know who I'm crawling into bed with."

"Otherwise, you'd just be another prostitute?" he said, his tone equal parts intrigue and challenge.

"I have my standards," I shot back, holding his gaze.

"Interesting assessment," he said, leaning forward slightly. "Now, how high is your IQ?"

He was certainly persistent. It was my turn to smile. I lowered my tone. "Mensa recognizes scores above the 98th percentile on standard intelligence tests. Personally, I think Mensa membership is just intellectual narcissism."

"Then why put it on your bio?"

I shrugged lightly, letting the moment linger. "Mental masturbation, mostly. Flash a Mensa card, and it grabs the attention of men who are either egotistical or looking for a challenge. Intellectual narcissists pay well. Is being in the top two percent good enough to hold my own at one of your cocktail parties?"

He laughed, the sound low and genuine, catching me off guard. "I thought geniuses were supposed to be socially awkward."

"I have a broad set of skills," I replied smoothly, then sipped from my glass in an attempt to hide my smile that he'd mistake for a smirk.

"I bet you do. You think it makes you more appealing to high-class men?"

"Let's just say I know how to market my assets," I said, my voice dropping slightly, my words deliberate. "I'm a high-end escort. Do you really think I care about *appearing* smart?"

"Well, in case you haven't noticed," he said, his eyes flicking over me with an unmistakable hunger, "you already have very good assets without marketing your IQ."

"I'm after a niche market," I said, leaning forward. My gaze trailed over him, deliberate and slow, then settled back on his eyes. He probably thought I was admiring him, a narcissist certainly would. In truth, I was testing the waters, gauging whether my intellectual sparring was working. It was.

"I get it. Other escorts rely on looking pretty. You prefer to attract professional men," he said.

"Professional men with money," I corrected.

"At least you're honest."

"Like I said, I have tuition to pay."

He paused, swirling the wine in his glass as if contemplating his next move. "So, tell me, what's your plan? Beyond the tuition, I mean. You're obviously not planning to do this forever."

I studied him for a moment, weighing how much truth to reveal. "I'm not just paying for tuition," I said, my tone softer, more thoughtful. "I'm buying time. Time to figure out what I want to do when this chapter of my life is over. You can't build a future on student loans and hope."

He leaned back, his expression unreadable. "Fair enough. But with that IQ, you've got to have something bigger in mind."

I smirked. "And I thought you just wanted me for my looks."

He chuckled, shaking his head. "Don't sell yourself short. You're clearly more than just a pretty face."

"Noted," I said, letting my voice take on a playful edge. "But if you keep saying things like that, I might start to believe you actually care."

"Would that be so bad?" he asked, his tone shifting to something more serious.

"That depends," I replied, sitting back and crossing my legs. "Are you the type of man who keeps things professional, or are you looking for something… messier?"

For the first time all evening, he didn't have a quick response.

He exhaled sharply through his nose, a mix of frustration and resignation. "You're intriguing but exhausting at the same time, you know that?"

"Funny, I've been called worse," I said, flashing a sly smile.

Eye candy had its standard rates, but the unspoken rule was clear, clients expected something extra for their tip that would end the date. It was up to the girls to negotiate the boundaries while keeping everything technically legal. Charm was as much a currency as beauty, a skill I had perfected in a previous job as a waitress. It wasn't just about appearances; honesty, strategically deployed, and intrigue were the real tools of the trade. These qualities didn't just attract wealthy clients; they kept them coming back.

I imagined this man could be an investment. He seemed to have the kind of wealthy friends who might also appreciate my services. Repeat customers were the golden ticket in this business. They spared you the exhausting effort of breaking in new clients each time. But I hadn't yet decided if I wanted him as a regular. His motivations were still a puzzle I wasn't sure I wanted to solve.

His eyes gave him away. They darted with thoughts he didn't voice during dinner, layering our exchanges with an unspoken complexity. He checked his phone often. It always unnerved me until I could untangle those hidden threads. The physical game was easy. It was the mental one that required finesse, patience, and practice. I was an eager student; men like him were my case studies.

After dinner, he took me to meet his friends at a show, a cluster of professionals with polished veneers and easy laughter. He had gifted the tickets to some of his clients, a calculated move, no doubt. One of them spoke with a Russian accent, and I caught myself listening closely. I loved languages, the subtle nuances of dialects, and the stories they told without words.

As the house lights dimmed and the play began, I decided to test him. My hand drifted to his thigh, the motion deliberate, but casual enough to seem spontaneous. His reaction was immediate, a sharp side glance, equal parts nervousness and intrigue. I couldn't tell if he was worried his colleagues might notice or simply be thrown off by an escort making the first move. Probably both.

He sat stiffly, his body language a mask of indifference, but I could feel him squirm as my hand moved higher. His friends were engrossed in the performance, oblivious to the quiet drama unfolding beside them.

"Not now," he whispered, his voice clipped and commanding.

"What if I want it now?" I countered, my tone playful yet with a deliberate edge. Pushing boundaries was my personal flaw.

"I have a hotel room reserved for later." His response was dismissive, and I felt a flicker of irritation. Dismissal never sat well with me. I needed to see how much control he really wanted.

"Great," I said, standing abruptly. "Let's go."

The theater aisle stretched before me, and I walked it like a runway, each step calculated. My dress shimmered under the dim light, the high slit revealing just enough leg to be provocative without being overt. His friends glanced over, curious but polite. I knew he wouldn't risk an awkward pause. Men like him couldn't afford to look inferior.

He apologized to his party, concocting some excuse about an emergency, and took my outstretched hand as I paused in the aisle. As we exited, the house lights began to dim further, casting us in shadow.

"What are you doing?" he hissed once we were in the lobby, his tone suddenly sharper.

I smiled, enjoying the shift in power. "They'll be fine on their own. Besides, a call girl would sit passively at your elbow. This way, it looks like I'm your real girlfriend."

"You're not my girlfriend," he said, his voice laced with annoyance.

"Exactly. Jeesh, do you pay attention?"

He ran a hand through his hair, exhaling heavily. He looked around briefly, then back at me. "You're impossible."

"And yet, here you are," I said, my tone light but deliberate.

He shook his head, and for a moment, I thought I saw a flicker of amusement behind the frustration. As we stepped into the crisp night air, I knew I had thrown him off balance and I liked it that way.

He hailed a cab, and we slid into the back seat.

"This isn't exactly the schedule I had in mind," he said, his tone tight with irritation.

"I've already seen that play," I replied, crossing my legs deliberately. "Do you want me or not?"

The driver's eyes flicked to the rearview mirror, curiosity written in his glance.

"That's what you get paid for, isn't it?" he shot back.

The driver looked again, his brow subtly furrowing.

"No," I said evenly, locking eyes with my date. "I get paid to impress your friends. Seeing me naked? That's extra."

"I'm only leaving with you to avoid making a scene," he countered, his voice low.

"Leaving *is* making a scene," I said, leaning back against the seat with a small, knowing smile. "You always want to leave clients wanting more."

"My clients are different."

"Not really," I said, letting the silence stretch for a beat. Then, with precision, I added, "We both screw people for money."

His jaw tensed, and for a moment, he was silent, processing. That was when I struck. Leaning over, I kissed him. Hard.

He hadn't expected it, which was precisely why I chose that moment. Timing was everything. Flooding his brain with dopamine was like slipping a leash on a restless dog. If you knew how to handle the response, you were in control.

It wasn't a polite kiss, not the kind exchanged in public or for show. It was deep, deliberate, and demanding. At first, he resisted, caught off guard, but I pressed forward, my tongue teasing his until he relented. The shift was palpable. His body leaned into mine, his hand moving instinctively from my hip to my thigh. His attitude softened with his posture.

I felt the rhythm of his breath change, growing deeper, rougher. My own breathing stayed controlled, measured. When I felt his heart rate quicken, his hand beginning to grip my leg with intent, I broke the kiss abruptly.

His surprise was evident as I pulled back, smoothing the fabric of my dress as if nothing had happened. I smiled, trailing my fingers along his greying temples, my touch soft but deliberate.

He tried to lean in, his lips parting as if to reclaim the moment, but I tilted my head away, the smile never leaving my face. A teaser before the main course makes the meal more savory.

"Not yet," I said quietly, my tone calm but firm as I pressed a finger to his lips.

The rest of the cab ride passed in charged silence. For me, it was over in moments. For him, I knew, it must have felt like an eternity.

He had spared no expense. The VIP suite was a study in opulence, the kind of space designed to make anyone feel important. The sitting area exuded understated luxury, with plush furnishings draped in fine fabrics. The adjoining bedroom was equally lavish. A king-sized bed framed by ornate draperies and illuminated by a crystal chandelier that sparkled like starlight. Double doors adorned with intricate gold patterns separated the bedroom from the sitting area. Beyond those doors, a marble-clad bathroom gleamed, its elegance quietly boasting wealth and attention to detail.

I kicked off my shoes, the soft carpet cool against my bare feet. My date glanced at his watch, an action that felt more reflexive than intentional. The cool air kissed my legs beneath the smooth fabric of my dress, the sensation heightened by the quiet intimacy of the room. The plush pillows on the couch seemed to beckon indulgence, but I knew better. This wasn't a place for comfort. It was a place for power dynamics.

In this line of work, walking barefoot in a sleek dress in the presence of an attractive, paying client wasn't just an act. It was a calculated maneuver. The atmosphere alone could arouse a natural response, the body's erogenous zones quick to react, flooding with hormones and desire. But desire was dangerous. Desire blurred lines and softened edges. I couldn't afford that, not here, not now.

I allowed myself a slow turn around the sitting room, taking it in as though I were just another guest in awe of the extravagance. Then, reaching behind me, I unzipped my dress with deliberate slowness, letting it glide from my shoulders to the floor in a silken whisper.

Without a word, I turned and walked toward the double doors leading to the bedroom, leaving my dress pooled behind me. I stopped in the doorway, the frame accentuating the curve of my half-naked body.

"Where are you going?" he asked, his voice calm but tinged with curiosity.

"Shower," I replied, glancing back over my shoulder. My lips curved into a knowing smile, the kind designed to linger in a man's mind.

I stepped fully into the doorway, letting the light from the bedroom fall over me. With a measured pace, I reached behind my back to unhook my bra. I watched his face as I revealed myself, studying the subtle shifts in his expression. His pupils widened, his breath audibly catching for a fraction of a second.

My breasts, unrestrained, were one of my better assets, not too large, not too small, just ample enough to invite attention without overshadowing the rest of me. The cool air teased my skin, drawing my nipples to attention. I ran a hand briefly over them, the sensation a fleeting indulgence. I held his gaze as I stood there, offering him just enough to whet his appetite without sating it.

Then, with a playful smile, I turned on the ball of my foot, executing a fluid pirouette before sliding my fingers to the waistband of my underwear. I peeled the delicate fabric away, stepping out of it as I sauntered toward the bedroom, leaving him to decide whether to follow.

At the edge of the bed, I tossed the underwear back toward the sitting room, hearing the faint rustle as it landed near the doorway alongside my discarded dress. I imagined him still sitting there, momentarily frozen, grappling with whether to remain in his seat or cross the threshold.

By the time I reached the bathroom, I was completely bare. The stockings came off last, one by one, each movement deliberate, purposeful. I stood there, naked, feeling utterly in control.

Nakedness had always been my armor. Stripped of fabric, the dynamics shifted. No matter how clothed the man before me might be, he was exposed. His desires, his vulnerabilities, his soul were laid bare. I learned early that power doesn't always wear a suit; sometimes, it lies in disarming truth, in being the mirror they never expect. But that armor comes at a cost. Because when you wear your nakedness like a weapon, you forget how to be seen without it.

But for now, this was my moment, my stage. And I had learned how to own it.

While the shower warmed, I leaned over the sink and splashed cool water onto my face. The droplets felt sharp against my skin, grounding me momentarily.

He soon appeared at the doorway, his silhouette framed by the soft glow of the bathroom light.

"You don't waste any time," he said, his voice calm but clipped.

"And you can't take a shower with your clothes on," I replied, meeting his gaze. His eyes held something I couldn't quite place, a depth that felt out of sync with the moment. His mind was somewhere else and not on me, meaning he had another agenda I had yet to figure out. That was a problem. A red flag. An unspoken one. Especially when a naked woman stood in front of him.

"Time is money?" he quipped.

I inhaled deeply, letting the air fill my lungs as my mind began its relentless calculations. My brain always did this, picking apart inflections, tones, and the spaces between words. I rarely cared what men *said*; my attention was on what they didn't. The atmosphere should have been charged with erotic electricity at this moment. But it wasn't.

By now, he should have been under my spell. The dopamine rush from the cab should still have him wanting more. Lust should have dilated his pupils and softened his edges. But his tone didn't match the script. It wasn't sensual; it wasn't even curious. It was measured, detached. Businesslike. It was out of place.

His choice of idiom wasn't the problem. It was how he said it. The upward lilt at the end of his sentence, that faint questioning rise, stuck in my head like a splinter. *Time is money?* Linguists call it upspeak, or high-rising terminal, a way of turning a statement into a question, intentionally or not.

My brain screamed at the mismatch. The inflection didn't belong in this moment. It carried a hint of superiority, the kind that thrived on having the upper hand and demanded submission. Narcissists. They're either the worst clients or the easiest to manage, no in-between. That was the next red flag. A spoken one.

The revelation snapped through my thoughts like a live wire for a fleeting moment. *Fuck.*

I kept my face calm, my expression neutral. But inside, my mind was already recalibrating.

I brushed past him, the heat of his presence barely registering as I exited the bathroom and entered the bedroom. My hands moved mechanically, picking up my discarded stockings and underwear, each piece a silent protest. I could feel his eyes on me, watching every movement, but he didn't say a word.

It wasn't the usual kind of gaze. My instincts still screamed that his thoughts were somewhere else, far removed from the naked woman in front of him. Something about his demeanor continued to set off warning bells, a quiet alarm in the back of my mind that refused to be silenced.

If he wasn't fully focused on me, it meant one of two things: I wasn't going to get paid top dollar for my time, or something was seriously wrong. Either scenario wasn't in the plan. My pulse quickened, a brief spike of panic surging through me before I forced my brain to recalibrate. I couldn't afford to lose my balance. Not here, not now.

Fine.

I let the stockings fall back to the floor and slipped on my underwear. The sound of elastic snapping into place was sharp in the stillness. Behind me, I heard him exhale deeply, the sound weighted with something I couldn't yet define.

"Did I offend you?" he asked finally, his tone measured, probing.

"Offend?" I echoed, not turning to face him.

"Yes. Apparently, I've upset you."

I straightened, meeting his gaze with a cool, even stare. "What did you mean?"

He hesitated, the briefest flicker of uncertainty crossing his face before he recovered. He probably was thinking that I was either a crazy escort or a mind reader who saw right through the unarticulated thoughts go through his brain. "I have to get back to my colleagues before the show ends. One of them holds the key to some deals I'm working on. If we'd stayed, I could have spent more time with you afterward. But now, I have to leave. Time is money. That's all I meant."

"Liar," I said flatly.

His words had a grain of truth. I could hear it in his tone. But the rest of it? A carefully calculated excuse designed to shift the blame onto me. Classic. He was adjusting, molding the narrative to make me feel at fault. My mind filed it away with precision: another notch in his narcissistic armor.

He straightened his shoulders, his demeanor slipping further into defensive arrogance. "I don't have time for showers and all-nighters. That's all."

"You think I'm angling for an all-nighter because the tip is higher?" I shot back, my voice sharp. "And it's *my fault* I dragged you away early?"

"Who's really the liar here?" he countered, his tone suddenly laced with challenge. "Am I playing you, or are you playing me?"

I stepped closer, narrowing the space between us. My voice dropped, low and deliberate. "I have sex on my terms."

He nodded, a hint of tension leaving his posture. "Agreed."

The word hung in the air, a fragile truce between two people locked in a game neither fully trusted the other to play fairly.

I stood there, wearing only sheer panties, feeling the weight of his gaze. His arousal was unmistakable, evident in the tension in his body and the way his pants betrayed him. I closed my eyes for a brief moment, willing the analytical hum of my brain to quiet. When I looked at him again, his lips curved into a faint grin, calculated, yet revealing.

He was turned on, that much was clear. But what intrigued me was *why*. Confrontation seemed to fuel his desire. My mind couldn't help but parse the details, his posture, the deliberate set of his shoulders, the way his eyes followed me. He wasn't just reacting to me; he was measuring me, calculating something unspoken. He was trying to size up more than my physique.

I knew how the body worked as chemistry took over. Add the right cocktail of hormones, testosterone, dopamine, maybe a touch of oxytocin, and desire would eclipse rational thought. It was my job to ensure the balance tipped toward lust and nothing more. Lust was fleeting, uncomplicated. It bypassed the emotional pathways that led to attachment, steering clear of drama and entanglement.

But his demeanor gave me pause. He was used to control and accustomed to power. And money, he had plenty of it. Yet there was something else in his eyes, something distant. My instincts warned me there was more at play here than his attraction to my body. Screwing me physically was one thing. I hadn't yet met a man who wanted nothing from me at all. A man trying to penetrate my thoughts was something else entirely and far more personal. I took a deep breath, forcing my mind to focus.

"You're afraid to touch me," I said, my voice low, laced with challenge.

His pupils widened just slightly, a tell I knew too well. Men often reacted to the unexpected boldness of dirty words. It was a subtle but reliable crack in their composure. The challenge was a reasonable test of his primary desires.

He chuckled, a soft sound that didn't quite reach his eyes. Then came the smile, deliberate but a fraction of a second too late. That delay was all I needed to know. My brain hummed with satisfaction. He might have an agenda. But he was still a typical man. *Got him.*

"That's what you think?" he said, his voice steady but betraying a sliver of defensiveness.

"Hmm." I let the sound linger, a note of curiosity and provocation. "I wonder why?"

I hooked my thumbs into the waistband of my panties, sliding them down again, slowly. They pooled at my feet as I stepped out of them, my movements fluid, unhurried. His eyes followed every motion, his breath catching just slightly. I was drawing him in again by tapping into his most primal desires.

I crossed to the bed, climbing onto it with deliberate grace, my movements slow enough to keep his attention fixed. "Oh, you want me," I said, glancing back at him over my shoulder. "That's not the issue. You're afraid of staying with me all night. You're glad we left early. Now you have an excuse." Not all of that was true, but I at least knew he wasn't an immediate danger.

He hesitated, his lips parting as if to speak, but no words came. Instead, he adjusted his stance, unconsciously shifting the tension in his body. His hand brushed against his pants, the movement revealing more than he likely intended.

"Like I said," he began, his voice quieter now, "I have to get back." But his body told a different story. His pulse thrummed visibly at his neck, his breathing shallow and quick. His gaze narrowed, locked onto me as I stretched out on the bed, every movement designed to draw him further into the moment. His pupils constricted, then wavered. He was weighing his options.

This was my domain, my stage. I had spent years perfecting the art of seduction, learning how to override reason and draw men into a haze of desire. His power dynamic was slipping, his instincts betraying his logic. Primal instincts are powerful.

I let him watch, let the chemicals swirl in his brain, clouding his judgment. He wasn't in control anymore. And for now, that was exactly where I needed him to be to figure out the rest of his story and maybe enjoy finding out while getting paid.

"We'll make it quick," I said, my voice calm and calculated. Some would say hypnotic.

I stretched out on the bed, my body relaxed but poised. His pupils now widened as he watched me, his gaze sharpening with intent. I could see the tension in his neck, the faint throb of his pulse in his temple. His breathing quickened, matching the rhythm of his escalating desire. He was focused now, all hesitation gone.

"I have time for a quick one," he said, his tone softer, more vulnerable than before.

"Then take your clothes off," I replied, a quiet challenge in my voice.

I watched him as he began to undress, his movements deliberate, almost ritualistic. There was always something fascinating about this moment, the shift in power, the unveiling. He took a steadying breath as he pulled off his shirt, revealing a chest and abdomen that hinted at discipline and effort.

He unbuckled his belt, then slid his pants down, stepping out of them with practiced ease. Shoes and socks followed. The air between us thickened as I spoke again, my words laced with suggestion.

"I've been wanting to see it all night," I said.

He glanced down briefly before removing his last barrier, standing fully exposed. His eyes drifted from my face to my body, lingering on my curves as I shifted slightly, letting the soft light catch the lines of my form. I moved my hips just enough to draw his attention, a subtle reminder of the leverage I held.

He reached for a condom without hesitation, a routine we both understood. My rules were non-negotiable.

This was business, after all. But I couldn't deny there was something I enjoyed in moments like these, the power, the raw connection, the brief escape from everything outside the room. I pushed aside the thought of his age, the whisper in my mind that he could have been old enough to be my father. I'd built walls to protect myself from those thoughts.

He settled onto the bed, his focus unwavering. "Time is money, remember?" I teased, letting a sly smile play on my lips. At any other time, I might have drawn things out and enjoyed the slow unraveling of tension. But tonight, my instincts told me this required a direct approach. No foreplay, no distractions. Then, unceremoniously, he crawled onto the bed with me. He wasted no time. The man between my legs was at least twice my age. He was fit, good-looking, somewhat charming, and I pushed the age contrast from my mind. I always did. Again, it was a necessary barrier I had created. This wasn't about romance. It was business. In many ways, it was also my classroom, my lab.

As we moved together, I kept my eyes on his, watching the subtle shifts in his expression, the unguarded moments that spoke volumes. There was something primal during these interactions, something beyond words. Vulnerability, even when fleeting, opened a window to the soul.

He didn't last long. It was quick, as I'd expected. His breaths were labored, his chest rising and falling as he soon collapsed onto the bed beside me. He was breathless and sweaty. For a few moments, we lay in silence, the sounds of our breathing filling the room. The rush of hormones began to subside, his gaze shifting as his mind returned to reality.

"You've got to go," I said finally, breaking the quiet.

He nodded. "The show will be over soon."

"Yes, it will," I replied, a note of finality in my voice.

He began to rise, but I placed a hand on his arm. "Wait."

"What?" he asked, his brow furrowed in confusion.

"This is my favorite part," I said, my voice soft, almost playful.

He followed my gaze, looking down at his body as his man parts began to return to their resting state. I watched as it receded. The corpus cavernosa of erectile tissue began to shrink his manhood as its contents drained from the length of his once rigid shaft. The tension drained from him as well, leaving behind a quiet vulnerability. I watched, my expression unreadable, as he removed the condom and discarded it as it was about to fall off his member, which had quickly become flaccid.

"Figured you preferred the other part, when a man gets excited," he said, half-joking, his tone uneasy.

"I do," I admitted with a small smile. "But this is better. Watching the aftermath. It's a reminder. No matter how strong, every man bows to a woman in the end."

He shook his head, an uncomfortable smile playing at his lips, his posture shifted, his arms instinctively moved to cover himself. Suddenly, he looked exposed, and my observation made him feel even more naked. I called it the Adam and Eve moment. A flicker in their eyes when they become aware they are naked. A brief moment of shame as innocence dies quietly. It is a moment of clarity of our vulnerability and mortality.

I, on the other hand, didn't feel that way at all. The vulnerability in the room was his, not mine. The story of Adam and Eve, the first knowledge of nakedness. I got it. The loss of innocence, the awareness of oneself. I always *got* it, even if no one else seemed to. But I had built barriers to that idea as well, realizing I would pay for that barrier in my future self.

"What's your name?" he asked, turning away as he began to put on his clothes.

"Carol," I said, my tone even. "What's yours?"

"John."

I tilted my head slightly, studying him. "John isn't your real name, is it?"

He smirked, not looking at me. "No. And Carol isn't yours, is it?"

"Of course not."

We both paused, our eyes meeting for a brief moment. His gaze flickered over my still-flushed body, and I could feel the lingering warmth of my own pulse, hormones slowly settling. Bedding a man still does something, even if we try to build walls against it. The moment hung there, suspended between us, brief, transactional, yet strangely personal.

"I've got to go," he said, breaking the silence. "You can use the room as long as you want. Check-out's tomorrow morning. I'm not coming back."

His words were clipped, practical. He bent down to gather the last of his clothes, barely sparing me another glance.

"I'll just shower," I replied, rolling onto my side as he headed for the door.

He didn't clean up. He didn't say goodbye. He didn't even bother to look back as he left the bedroom, though I caught the briefest glance as he crossed into the sitting area to put on his shoes.

Some men wanted conversation. Others needed to be heard, held, or distracted from whatever burden they carried. Then there were men like him who needed none of those things. Or perhaps needed something they didn't know how to name. Whatever it was, I'd given him what he came for. Maybe that was enough.

The shower was long and indulgent, the warm water washing over me in steady streams. I let it cascade over my hair, down my shoulders, and across my body, cleansing more than just my skin. Post-sex showers were always invigorating, a moment to reset and reclaim myself. I shower not only to clean the skin but to pretend, just for a moment, that the water can wash away more than sweat.

As the water poured down, I ran my hands over my breasts, torso, and hips, lathering soap in slow, methodical motions. My fingers brushed against my thighs, the cool slickness of the soap contrasting with the warmth of my skin. Tilting my head back, I let the water engulf my hair, its weight pulling me into the present.

I smiled. Mortality often found me in moments like this. My beauty wouldn't last forever, and I knew it. One day, the edge I used to navigate the world would dull, and I'd have to rely more on my intellect, something that often intimidated men, whether they admitted it or not.

I rinsed the soap from my hair, forcing my mind to let go of its wanderings.

When I finally emerged from the bathroom, wrapped in a towel, I knew instinctively that I was alone. The room was still and quiet, the air carrying that faint, lingering scent of intimacy. I dressed slowly, taking my time before stepping into the sitting area.

My eyes scanned the space, taking in the neatness of it, the way it felt untouched despite the charged moments we had shared. Then, I saw it.

A small, folded stack of cash sat on the table, neat and deliberate. I didn't count it. I didn't need to. Its thickness told me it far exceeded my standard fee, the silent acknowledgment of a tip for the extra service.

I smiled as my thoughts crystallized into a single, daring realization: *"The only way to find out how far you can go is by risking going too far." The idea is that you'll never know your limits unless you're willing to push beyond them, and I was still trying to figure out those limits.*

The agency would send my fee in a check later; the cash was a gesture, understood without needing to be discussed. The unspoken agreement was part of the system. The agency was there to protect us, but this? This was between him and me.

As I stepped closer, something else caught my eye. A folded piece of hotel stationery lying next to the cash. A note.

Chapter 3

"Often, the things we want most are found beyond our fears." — Dara

"What's up, Dara?"

I looked up to see Susan heading toward me, her blonde hair catching the light as she moved. Susan was a classic bombshell, by her own admission and to her advantage. She slid into the chair next to me with a warm smile.

"Homework," I said, glancing at her before returning to my laptop.

Susan scanned the escort agency's lobby, her restless energy evident. I loved Susan. She was doing her best as a single mom, banking on her looks while she still could. She didn't overthink our work. It was a way to build a better life for her kid.

"You waiting to see Jill?" she asked.

"Yeah. She's got my check and next week's schedule."

"Same here." She leaned closer, curious. "What kind of homework?"

"Psychology."

"I thought your major was... bio-something?"

"Biochemistry," I corrected.

Susan scrunched her nose. "Pretty sure psychology and biochemistry are two different things."

"I'm a double major. Biochemistry and neuroscience."

Susan raised an eyebrow. "A psychology class is a neuroscience thing?"

"Not exactly. Neuroscience is less about psychology and more about neurobiology and chemistry. Psychology deals with behavior, but neuroscience is about how the brain's wiring and chemistry make that behavior happen. There's some overlap, and biochemistry helps bridge it."

"And then what? Med school?"

I shrugged. "Maybe. Research. I haven't decided yet."

Susan nodded toward my laptop. "What's this video about? Line dancing?"

I smirked. "There's more neuroscience in this video than you'd think. Watch." I tilted the screen toward her. "See that cowboy? The one with the awkward moves?"

"Yeah, nerd cowboy. Not much of a dancer," Susan said.

"Exactly. Now watch what happens when this other guy joins."

Susan's eyes lit up. "Whoa. Hunky cowboy has some serious moves. Sexy."

"Let's call him hunky cowboy," I said, smiling.

"Mmm. I'll die happy if he's on my schedule next week."

"Now watch the girl next to them. See how her movements change when the better-looking hunky guy joins the dance line?"

"She's good. Sexy hips."

"Notice how she only glances at nerd cowboy once. But when the hunky cowboy starts dancing, her focus shifts. Her hips match his rhythm, and she moves closer."

"Like they're making out on the dance floor," Susan teased.

"Exactly. It's all chemical. Hunky cowboy's movements triggered a dopamine release. Dancing and attraction both activate pleasure pathways. She's dosing herself with feel-good hormones just by syncing with him."

Susan grinned. "So, hunky cowboy's rocking her world, huh?"

"Pretty much. The other girls on the dance floor? They're more reserved, holding back. However, this girl knows how to let go, which reinforces those pleasurable chemical reactions."

"The other girls are missing out."

"They might have barriers, psychological, emotional, who knows. Human interaction is complicated, but it's often just chemistry at work."

Susan raised an eyebrow. "You're saying love and lust are just formulas?"

"Not just formulas, but they're a big part of it. Moderate doses of dopamine and oxytocin help us bond and feel good with a partner. Too much, though, and you risk addiction, jealousy, or worse. It's all about balance."

Susan sighed, leaning back. "Well, my love formula must be broken. Last night, I was lying naked on a hotel bed, waiting for my date's little blue pill to kick in. It took forever, and he wasn't even that old."

"His testosterone levels are probably low," I said. "That pill is a PDE inhibitor. It doesn't actually cause the erection. You still stimulated him. Otherwise, the pill wouldn't have worked."

"A PDE, what?"

"It blocks the chemical that breaks down another chemical that causes the erection."

"Let me get this straight," Susan said, folding her arms. "You're saying the pill doesn't make it happen?"

"Not directly. Erection starts with nitric oxide, a neurotransmitter released by nerve endings. That triggers a cascade of reactions, but another chemical, PDE, breaks it down. The pill stops PDE from interfering."

"So, PDE is the party pooper?"

"Basically. Without the pill, the 'go juice' fades too quickly."

Susan rolled her eyes. "Great. Now I'm studying chemistry. Who knew getting a guy hard was so complicated?"

I laughed. "It is. But hey, you're the one making it work. The pill doesn't do anything without stimulation. The guys still has to be aroused to start the reaction."

Susan grinned, shaking her head. "Girl, I need to go to college. Oops, there's Jill."

Right on cue, the agency door opened, and Jill stepped out, clipboard in hand. Susan looked up, her usual swagger returning. I closed my laptop, still smiling.

"Dara?" Jillian McMaster called from the office door.

"Gotta go," I said, standing up.

Susan gave me a quick fist bump. "I'll be sitting here filling out my college application," she joked.

"You'd be great."

"I'll major in sex ed and teach 'em how to get their equipment working," she said, giggling as I walked away. Her laughter followed me into Jill's office.

"Your check is on the desk, and here's next week's client list if you're available," Jill said as she sat down.

"Did the guy from last night ask for me again?"

Jill raised an eyebrow. "You still have Friday night off, right? There's a convention that needs pretty girls to hand out brochures. Easy work for good money if you're interested."

"He did, didn't he?"

Jill hesitated. "He's powerful. Out of your league in ways you don't see, Dara."

"You let me meet with him last night, though. Who is he?"

"You know I can't tell you that," Jill said, her tone firm but calm. "He specifically requested you after looking at your bio. I understand the date was cut short. What happened?"

"Was he bragging or complaining?"

"Neither," she said. "With him, I never know. Sometimes, he just needs someone on his arm for an event. Other times…" she trailed off, letting the implication hang.

"What did he say?"

"Nothing bad. Just that he didn't spend the night. You usually push for an all-night booking with high rollers. What happened?"

"I think he enjoyed himself," I replied evenly. "If he requests me again, you should book it. He pays well."

"I need to think about it."

"Think about what? He's a client. He asked for me. I have tuition to pay, Jill."

"Again, he's powerful, Dara. I'm hesitant to mix you two too much."

"What the hell does that mean?"

Jill leaned back, sighing. "That must've been one hell of a tip for a quick booking."

"I could see two clients in a night and make just as much. But yes, it was quick money for the time we spent."

"You like him."

"He's interesting. Plus, seeing one client for the night is more efficient than juggling two."

"He's complicated. You always like complicated."

"Hormone cascades are complicated, Jill. This is just business. And I know some clients pay you extra to schedule me. If he's asking, I'm doing it. We both make money."

Jill exhaled slowly, then waved a hand. "Fine. Pick up your check and schedule. I'll think about it. Send Susan in on your way out."

I grabbed the envelopes off her desk and headed for the door. Just as I reached it, I stopped and turned back.

"Jillian," I said, a teasing edge in my voice, "you're such a tight ass."

"I beg your pardon?"

"You know what I mean. Have you ever had something stuck up your ass?"

"Dara, what are you getting at?"

"Nothing goes up a tight ass unless there's a reason, Jill. And no matter the reason, you need grease. It's not natural otherwise."

"And you are suggesting I'm the tight ass here?"

I stepped closer, holding up one finger at a time. "Let me break down the three reasons you let something up your ass, Jill. First, you're getting paid. Second, you're getting pleasure, or third, someone else is getting paid to do it. Like a doctor's appointment. Either way, it requires lubrication. Nothing goes up there for no reason, and nothing goes up there without preparing your ass."

Jill stared at me for a moment, her expression unreadable. "No one is greasing my ass, Dara. I'm not trying to screw you over, either. And don't consider that paycheck some kind of lube. I'm just trying to protect you. You're young."

"I appreciate that, Jill. But I'm not worried about me."

"Then what?"

"Why are you protecting *him*? Is it money or pleasure, or does he know something about you no one else does? He seems to be all up in your business."

"You think he's screwing with me?"

I smiled faintly. "I'm just saying, Jill, getting it in the ass can be a fine thing if you're prepared. But it can get really painful and messy if you're not. Be careful who's in charge of the grease."

Jill shook her head, a small smirk breaking through her frustration. "See, Dara, this is why someone has to look out for you. You got a mouth on you, and you're too damn fearless."

"The things we want most are often found beyond our fears," I replied, heading for the door.

"Send in Susan. I'll be fine."

"Love you, Jill. Mean it."

"Love you more, Dara."

As I opened the door, Susan was already grinning. "Were you two talking about anal?"

Jill gave her a pointed look. "Dara thinks I'm treating her like a kid."

"You're not my mother," I called over my shoulder as I walked away, flashing Jill a quick middle finger she couldn't miss. It wasn't anger. It was love. Just my own way of showing it.

My apartment is right across the street from the University. My roommate Leslie was still in her pajamas when I walked in. I loved Leslie. She was everything I wasn't: sweet, idealistic, and hopelessly romantic.

"You've been crying," I said, setting my bag down.

"Just a little," Leslie admitted, her voice soft.

"You're not even dressed. You'll be late for class," I said, tilting my head at her disheveled state.

"Where were you?" she asked, dodging my observation.

"I had to pick up my check from work. What's going on?"

Leslie hesitated, then sighed. "Jake. I think I'm going to break up with him."

I sat down on the couch beside her. "What did he do?"

Her voice cracked. "He's cheating on me."

"Oh, Leslie," I said, trying to keep my voice calm. "You've been with him a whole six months."

She put her head on my shoulder, and I fought the urge to roll my eyes.

"I know," she whispered. "I thought he was the one."

"How many times do I have to tell you, Leslie? *The one* will chase you. You need to stop chasing them."

"He *did* chase me."

"He asked you out. That's not chasing. He has a reputation, remember? He wanted to get laid."

"I thought he loved me," she said, her voice cracking again.

"Six months, Leslie. You barely know him."

"I'm saving myself for marriage," she said, folding her arms defensively.

"Yes, I know the saying. *Why buy the cow if you can get the milk for free,*" I said, finishing the familiar line for her.

"Well, I'm not going to be one of those cows."

"Good for you, Leslie. That's who you are, and I respect that."

She looked at me suspiciously. "But?"

"No buts," I said gently. "It's actually less complicated that way. If a guy really loves you, he'll pursue you for *you*. He'll wait."

"So, you think I'm doing the right thing breaking up with him?"

I paused. "I don't know. It's less complicated insisting a guy commit to you before you take him to bed. But on the other hand, guys like Jake… they think with their dicks."

Her eyes widened slightly. "You're saying if I gave it up, Jake would stay?"

"No. Guys like Jake are still going to be Jake. It's not about what you do or don't do. Either way, you're still left sorting through emotions. The question is how much of yourself you want to give."

"I thought we were right for each other," she said, her voice barely above a whisper.

"You were in love, Leslie. He was in lust. Lust isn't a very deep emotion. And the truth is, you always fall in love too fast. You worry so much about giving a guy your body too quickly, but it's your *heart* you need to learn not to give away so easily."

Leslie leaned into me, her breathing steadying as my words sank in.

I finally got Leslie out the door and, on her way, to class. It wasn't easy. Her tearful dilemma had left a mark on my mind, lingering like a heavy mist as I sat at my desk. I had studying to do before my next course, but my thoughts kept drifting back to her.

If I were wired differently, Leslie would be my girl. That thought, as crude as it was, made me pause. Sometimes, I hated myself for thinking in sexual terms. But that's the world in which I lived. A world where power and control were intertwined with sex. You start to think in the language of the environment you inhabit.

I learned early that language and control are inseparable. Words can bend emotions, shape outcomes, and build illusions. I often hoped Leslie could learn from my mistakes or successes, depending on how you measure success in this messy department.

As a teenager, I teased boys because I could. I learned how easily I could manipulate them, how much power lay in a smile, a laugh, a carefully timed glance. I was the opposite of Leslie. Where she blended love and sex into one ideal, I separated them with ruthless efficiency. I read situations too easily, used foul language too often, and wielded my looks and smarts like tools in a trade.

For all my supposed blessings, my girl-next-door appearance, my sharp mind, those gifts often felt more like curses. I understood how the world worked far too early. During my formative years, I shared Leslie's values. Deep down, I think I still do. But those values became buried, suppressed by the need to control my environment. And control always seemed to hinge on emotional or sexual leverage. It was simply how the world worked, and I adapted.

It wasn't my fault that sex and emotions held so much power. I didn't invent the rules. I just learned how to play the game. Before I realized it, I was in too deep, trading my cherished values for knowledge, my innocence for control. I guess, in a way, I sold my soul for this understanding. It was the realization of Adam and Eve all over again. What scared me was that I wasn't ashamed enough to cover my nakedness.

Leslie was who I wanted to be. For her, love and sex were inseparable, beautiful and pure. For me, they were separate currencies, tools of survival. I envied her ability to believe in something so simple, so honest. And I worried I'd literally screwed myself out of ever finding that kind of clarity.

What I think in my head is never what comes out of my mouth. No one knows how much of a performance I'm putting on. I pretend to be a sex object, but in truth, I'd rather be lost in a library. It's a shame, really, that this world so often values the superficial over the substantial. Survival sometimes demands a show.

You'd think logic and reason would rule the world, but they don't. While many things drive the world's engine, the sensual, the emotions, desires, and impulses really lubricate the gears. I learned early on that there's truth in the cliché: men think sexually. But women aren't that much different. The only real distinction is that women often think more about the consequences of their sexuality.

Either way, sex starts in the brain, not the body. Leslie doesn't fully understand that. I probably understand it too well. The difference between a drug addict and everyone else is simply which chemicals we crave. They all cloud judgment and command attention in their own way.

Leslie's brain was addicted to romance novels, to an idealized version of love and happily-ever-after endings. She'd built a utopia in her mind that left her vulnerable to heartbreak. Words on a page had become her reality.

Me? I recognized the nonsense faster. Where Leslie saw tragedy in her illusions shattering, I saw opportunity.

"I looked up the name *Dara*," the professor said as he walked into the classroom. "In Gaelic, it means 'oak tree.'"

I blinked, surprised. I'd slipped into class early to review my notes, completely unaware of his arrival. Sitting in the back row, I hadn't noticed when he entered from the front. I glanced around. It was just the two of us in the room.

"And why would you be interested in the origin of my name, Professor?" I asked, not looking up from my notes.

"You can call me Aiden," he replied casually.

"And what does *Aiden* mean in Gaelic?"

"The closest is *Aodh*, the Celtic god associated with fire and light."

"Interesting," I said, turning back to my notes.

"You didn't answer my question."

"You didn't ask a question. You made a statement," I countered, allowing a small smile to slip through.

He nodded, leaning against the desk at the front of the room. His arms folded, and I caught a glimpse of his stubbly beard, a clear attempt to add maturity or scholarly gravitas. It didn't quite work; he still looked too young to be a professor.

"Fair enough. Maybe I was probing for a response," he said, watching me.

"I'm sure," I replied, keeping my focus on my notes.

"It was a compliment," he said, his voice quieter and leaning forward a bit.

I felt his gaze lingering and could picture him shoving his hands into his pockets, unsure whether to continue as I let a bit of silence settle between us.

"Small talk?" I glanced up, one eyebrow raised.

"Yes," he admitted, a crooked smile forming. "I was hoping to engage you in conversation."

I looked at the clock, then at my watch. I realized checking my watch was a reflex. "Thirty minutes early," I muttered, mostly to myself. *Great. I didn't realize I was this early.*

"Am I interrupting?" he asked.

I sighed louder than I intended and closed my book. I then looked up. "Dara originates from Hebrew. It means 'nugget of wisdom.' A descendant of Judah, known for wisdom."

"That's fascinating," Aiden said, leaning forward again with a smile. "I understand you're a science major?"

"Statement or small talk?"

"Small talk," he said with a nervous chuckle.

"Neuroscience and biochemistry," I said, trying not to smirk.

He shifted his stance slightly as though trying to find a balance between casual and confident. "Are you okay with small talk?"

"I can do small talk." My lips threatened to curl into a smile, but I held back, curious to see if he would read it as a smirk or see through his own attempts at charm.

"So," he said, shrugging again, "are you wondering why I'm asking?"

"You're asking why a science major is taking an English course?"

"Something like that. A course on 'The Origins of Language' doesn't seem to fit neatly into your curriculum. I'm curious." He tried to adjust his tone, leaning into his role as professor, though it felt more like a defense mechanism than confidence.

"I felt a soft science like English would fit best into my elective requirements," I replied evenly.

He raised an eyebrow. "Soft science? I don't think I've heard English referred to that way before."

I allowed myself a small, deliberate smile. "The hyoid bone in the throat is the only bone in the human body not connected to another bone. Its suspension in the neck muscles forms the foundation for speech. That's hard science. Language guides thought and shapes our perception of the world. That's pretty scientific, too. Without a command of language, how can we communicate science? So, calling English a soft science doesn't feel like much of a stretch."

He let the thought hang in the air for a moment, then said, "I'm impressed."

"Don't be."

"Why not? You're acing this course, except for that 95 on the last midweek test. Shocking."

"I was busy the night before," I replied, glancing back at my book.

"Didn't realize Tuesday nights were hot nights for college students," he quipped.

I nodded slowly, keeping my expression neutral. A few students began trickling into the room, breaking the moment. Aiden stepped away, his posture stiffening as he moved to greet them. One student approached with a syllabus, and he engaged her in conversation, though I noticed his eyes flicker toward me briefly before focusing on her. I sensed that although he was speaking to the student, his thoughts had not left our conversation yet.

As my own thoughts drifted, I realized what he'd said about Tuesday nights was true, though not in the way he thought. For me, Tuesdays weren't wild nights of partying or adventure. They were something else entirely. Something far more important.

Aiden's voice faded into the background as my mind drifted to my first Tuesday night with George, my longest-running regular client. It had been three years since I'd nervously knocked on the door of a VIP suite, dressed in my sexiest outfit. I was new to the escort business then, eager to make a good impression. Jillian had told me George specifically requested me. Flattered, I wanted to exceed expectations, even if my shoes pinched and I felt more awkward than alluring. I had picked out a revealing outfit.

When the door opened, I was greeted by a distinguished older man, his temples dusted with gray. He wore a tailored suit and nodded politely, his movements measured.

"You must be Carol," he said, calling me by my work alias.

"Jillian gave me this room number," I replied, my voice more tentative than I liked.

He studied me for a moment, his gaze steady. It wasn't the appraisal I was used to. No lingering over my curves, no telltale quickening of breath.

Instead, his eyes carried a faint sparkle that suggested amusement or relief rather than lust. It threw me off balance. It was my first indication that my relationship with George was going to be…different.

"Greetings, young lady. Pleased to meet you," he said, stepping aside to let me in.

As I entered, I noticed he didn't bother with the usual rituals: no peeking into the hallway to ensure discretion, no locking the door twice, and no rushing to close the curtains. His composure unsettled me.

The suite was elegant, far more luxurious than any I'd seen before. A faint scent of tobacco hung in the air, and a polished pipe rested on the side table next to a folded newspaper. The view from the window was breathtaking, with the sun setting over the city skyline.

"Make yourself comfortable," George said, moving to put away his pipe and paper.

Instinctively, I walked toward the bed to do just that. Back then, I thought the quickest way to calm my nerves was to take control of the situation. I reached for the zipper at the back of my blouse, ready to start the routine I'd practiced in my mind. But before I could lift the fabric over my head, I felt the zipper sliding back up as he prevented me from undressing. I froze.

"That won't be necessary, my dear," George said softly, his hands firm but gentle as he smoothed the back of my blouse so that I'd remain decently clothed.

I turned to look at him, confused. "You said to make myself comfortable," I said, trying my best doe-eyed expression.

He tilted his head slightly, a hint of a smile on his face. He looked at me the way a man might look at a daughter, not a body. Then, to my surprise, he pinched my cheek gently, like I was a small child, before gesturing to my shoes.

"You might start by taking off those heels if you like. They look terribly uncomfortable," he said, walking back to the chair by the window. "You can even let your hair down if you want, but please keep your clothes on. I'm not that kind of customer."

His calm yet authoritative tone left me at a loss. I couldn't decide whether to bolt or play along. As he settled into the chair, he gestured to another chair beside him. "Join me. Tell me a little about yourself," he said, crossing his legs and folding his hands casually.

I hesitated. "You realize you hired an escort, right?"

"Ah, there's the misunderstanding," George replied. "I didn't hire an escort. I reimbursed Jillian for your time this evening. What I'd like is to get to know Carol, not an escort."

"I get it," I said, straightening my blouse. "You're one of those do-gooders who thinks he can save a prostitute."

"Far from it, my dear. I spoke with Jillian about you. She said you were headstrong, not the type to let anyone dictate your path."

"So, what are you looking for? A challenge?" I asked, feeling a mix of irritation and curiosity.

"A woman of your intellect should never forget who she is because of what men expect her to be," he said, his voice steady. "I'm not looking for a project or a challenge. Humor me, no strings attached. Just relax for a moment."

"You'd be better off hiring a therapist," I quipped.

George chuckled. "I'm not here to work through my problems, nor am I here to save you. I just think I'd like to get to know you. Maybe we could even learn to be friends."

His words unnerved me. "You don't know me," I said, my tone sharp.

"Perhaps not yet. But sometimes the narrative world and the objective world intersect in surprising ways," he said, adjusting his newspaper and setting it aside.

I looked at the door, considering my options. But something in his voice anchored me. He wasn't like anyone I'd met before. He was calm, sure of himself, but without a trace of arrogance. Strangely, he felt safe despite the awkward situation. My indecision of what to do next allowed the silence to linger longer than I expected. Then, his voice disarmed me even further.

"They're tight, aren't they?" he asked, nodding toward my shoes.

"Damn tight," I admitted, kicking them off with a sigh.

"Good," he said, gesturing again to the empty chair beside him.

"Fine," I muttered, sinking into the seat.

George smiled, folding his hands in his lap. After a moment of silence, he asked, "Do you use profanity often?"

"All the time," I said, watching his reaction.

He nodded slowly, his expression thoughtful. "I see."

And then we just talked. It was a real conversation. My mom was the last person I had that kind of conversation with. We never said who we truly were; maybe that's why we could share our thoughts honestly. Even though we didn't know each other, I soon knew how he took his coffee with too much sugar. He knew I dreamed of something beyond my work as an escort. We traded truths without names. At the end of the evening, we learned everything…and nothing.

And that was the beginning of it all. That was the beginning of my Tuesday nights. My sanctuary.

As I sat there, recalling that first Tuesday night with George, Aiden glanced over his shoulder at me. His eyes held that same sparkle, a look that felt like he truly saw me.

In the narrative world I'd built to fund my education, George was the only one who seemed to see past the façade. But that world wasn't my *real* world, at least not in my mind. In my objective reality, Aiden was the only man in that moment who saw *me*, Dara and not the construct or act.

George once said that sometimes the narrative and objective worlds touch. I thought about that now, and it felt absurd. Those two worlds could never meet. At least not in my plan.

The thought stirred something deep and painful. In that moment, I missed my father and hated him all at once. A tear welled up in my eye, blurring my vision. I wiped it away quickly, just before Aiden turned back toward me.

Chapter 4

"This is the secret everyone knows, but doesn't know." – *Dara*

"Hi, George," I said with a genuine smile as I walked into our usual suite. Tuesday nights were the rare times my work smile felt real. I placed two takeout cups on the counter and emptied a bag of creamers and sugar packets onto the table.

"Good evening, Carol. Any trouble at the front desk?" George asked, removing the pipe from his lips.

"It was a new guy, but he didn't hesitate to give me the key," I said, kissing his forehead before handing him a coffee. I tossed the hotel key onto the bed, kicked off my shoes, and sank into a nearby chair. The weight of the week lifted slightly as I propped my feet up and leaned back.

"I already fixed your coffee. Two sugars and a cream, just the way you like it," I added.

"And from that little shop on Main. Thank you, Carol. That was kind of you," he said, settling into his chair as I stirred sugar into my own cup. He set his pipe aside and folded his newspaper.

"How's work?" I asked, arranging my cup on the table beside me.

"The usual," he said, his voice measured.

"Still not going to tell me what you do after all these years?" I teased, popping the lid back onto my coffee.

"You're still not going to tell me which university you attend?" he countered, setting his paper beside the hotel key.

"And let me guess, next you'll ask if today's the day I'll tell you my real name." I grinned over the rim of my cup.

"As soon as you tell me, I'll stop calling you Carol," he said with a twinkle in his eye.

I laughed. This back-and-forth had become our routine, one I looked forward to every week. George knew me better than anyone without really knowing me at all. He was the only steady presence in my life, a comforting thought and a sad one, given he existed solely in this world I'd built to survive.

"No new secrets today," I said lightly. "How's the wife? Did you make out with her this week?"

"She's going to have her hormones checked and only because a bridge club friend is doing the same. Libidos do decline with age, my dear. She's more concerned about her hot flashes, though."

"George, I keep telling you. Just bend her over the kitchen table. That's all she needs."

"Now, Carol," he said, feigning disapproval. "That wouldn't be proper. And your language, young lady. We've talked about this."

"Yeah, yeah. But you spanked her on the ass like I told you, didn't you?"

He coughed, slightly embarrassed. "I did."

"And?"

"Well... she smiled," he admitted.

"Progress!"

"She also liked the love notes you suggested I leave for her. I've not done that in years."

"You move too slow, George. We talked about this months ago."

"It took a while to fix my... little problem."

"Erectile dysfunction isn't a 'little' problem," I said. "And it took you months to even admit it to me. The first urologist gave you meds for an enlarged prostate because you couldn't bring yourself to tell him the truth. You're too modest, George."

"I was raised in a time when such things weren't discussed. I still don't know why I told you."

"I have a way of dragging things out of people. And why worry about etiquette? You spend every Tuesday with a prostitute."

"You're not a prostitute, Carol. You shouldn't say that. How's school?"

"Jill told me an anonymous client wanted to pay my tuition again."

"And how did that work out?"

"Don't play coy, George."

"What? Sounds like a nice deal."

"I pay my own way in life. But thanks for trying."

"I don't know what you're talking about," he said, sipping his coffee.

I recognized the look he gave me over the rim of his cup. He knew that I knew he always tried to pay my tuition.

"What?" I said.

"You should work on your profanity, Carol."

"I think my profanity's pretty good."

"You know what I mean. You're about to graduate and enter the real working world. You should think about professionalism."

"You've known me since I first entered this business, George. It's easy for someone like you to think the best of people when you're loaded."

"What gives you the impression I'm loaded?" he asked with a nervous chuckle.

"You've been my regular every Tuesday for nearly three years. I've seen your car, sometimes with a driver waiting for you. You wear custom shoes and high-end suits, and I've caught glimpses of patent diagrams when your briefcase popped open. Whatever you do, it's expensive, and I'm not a low-budget escort. You pay Jillian serious money just to chat every week."

"Cheaper than a therapist," he said. "Do you know how much my wife pays her therapist? Tuesdays with you are a bargain."

"And your wife still thinks you're at that cigar club you told me about."

"Every Tuesday. Men only. They won't tell, and she's busy playing cards. It's my night out."

"And you spend it with me."

"You need men in your life who want more than sex. But you already know that," George said.

"Even men who don't want sex still look at me with a certain kind of lust. You just... twinkle."

"Maybe I should get checked for cataracts. Lust is shallow, Carol. Look for love. Love and time are more valuable than money."

"And yet you spend your time paying for an escort to chat."

"I spend money on things of value."

"I'm not charity."

"No, you're not. What I mean is that you have value. Spending time with you is worth it."

"You're still not trying to keep me off the streets?"

"You don't need me to do that. It's just nice spending time with you."

I rested my chin on my hand, studying him. His gaze was steady and genuine, his touch never inappropriate. He'd been the closest thing to a father figure I'd ever had, and I was starting to dread what would happen when I graduated. Our worlds were never meant to meet, and Tuesday nights were the only part of this life I knew I'd miss.

"You graduate soon, Carol. Work on your language. You're too sharp to limit yourself. Maybe you'll find a real boyfriend who's good for you and sees your value."

"I suck at boyfriends too, George."

Leslie was still up when I walked into the apartment. She didn't need to say anything. It was written all over her face.

"You broke up with the dick, didn't you?" I said, dropping my bag by the door.

"Yep. Clean break," she replied.

"You're not crying."

"I think I'm getting tough, like you."

"I'm not tough," I said quietly.

"You're tougher than me," she said, her tone light but sincere. "Want to talk about it?"

"Not really."

I sat down beside her on the couch. Sometimes, silence said more than words ever could.

"You want milk and cookies?" I asked after a moment.

She smiled faintly. "How was your first breakup?"

"I thought you didn't want to talk about it."

"Dara."

"Fine," I said, leaning back. "Technically, I've never had a boyfriend to break up with."

"But, you—"

"*Escort* is the word you're looking for," I said, cutting her off gently.

"I know, but don't you... you know?"

"Have sex with them? Not all of them. Sometimes, I'm just eye candy for events or conventions. They're not boyfriends, though, and they're not even close. Don't get the two ideas confused."

"Well, you're more experienced with men," she said, fiddling with the edge of a pillow.

"And you've had more relationships," I countered.

She glanced at me. "You've had a boyfriend, haven't you? Off-duty, or whatever you call it?"

"Not really," I said, shaking my head. "I didn't even get laid until I was twenty."

"Dara," she said, almost scolding.

"Seriously. His name was Greg. Back seat of a car in the community college parking lot. I made him wear a condom. He had premature ejaculation in the process, so technically, I'm not sure it even counted."

Leslie snorted, trying not to laugh. "What happened to Greg?"

"Embarrassment? Conquest achieved? Who knows. It was over before it started. The relationship *and* the sex."

"Well, if he didn't stick around, it wasn't love."

"Wonder where you've heard that before?"

She rolled her eyes. "I know. You're right."

"We've been roommates for three years. You'll be fine," I said, nudging her shoulder lightly.

"I wish I'd known you four years. I forgot you did your first year at community college."

"My mom was sick," I said simply.

"I remember you told me she'd passed away when we met. I didn't want to pry further."

"It's fine," I said. "I was able to take care of her. The community college was close by. My mom made me promise to finish school. It was important to her. She wanted me to come to college here."

"You've never mentioned your dad," Leslie said carefully.

"He was a bum," I replied bluntly.

"I'm sorry."

"Don't be. He left when I was little. Mom raised me alone. He didn't even have the decency to visit when she was sick."

"You don't talk to him?"

"No way. He moved to another state ages ago."

Leslie hesitated before speaking again. "I hate to bring this up, but… we graduate this year. Do you have any family to invite?"

"I was an only child. Mom didn't have siblings, and her parents died before her."

"What about your father and his family?"

"I vaguely remember him from when I was little. I had photos. Once, out of curiosity, I looked him up on social media. Saw him with his new family."

"You could invite him," she offered hesitantly.

"Fuck him and his new family. I don't know them, and I don't want to."

"No boyfriends? No family at all?"

I hesitated, then leaned in slightly. "Well, just between you and me, I think there's this one guy who's got his eye on me."

"Dara, could I see you after class?" Professor Aiden Strach asked as the students shuffled out of the room.

I closed my schedule book, having spent the last few minutes of class reviewing my client bookings. It was my final class of the day, and I had just accepted a booking for a guy who was into light bondage. I usually avoided those kinds of requests, but Jill assured me this client only wanted to be tied up and tickled. It wasn't too kinky. It paid well, and the logistics didn't seem too complicated.

Lost in thought, I realized Aiden was still waiting for me. The room was nearly empty.

"Yes, Professor?" I said, looking up.

"Aiden," he corrected with a slight smile.

"Right, Aiden. You needed to see me?"

"I wanted to tell you that I enjoyed our conversation earlier this week."

"And?" I prompted.

"And?" he repeated, raising an eyebrow.

"There's going to be an 'and,'" I said.

"How do you know that?"

"If you were about to use the word '*but,*' it would be to prepare me for bad news. '*But*' as a preposition tends to signal something unfavorable. However, you're smiling and not using that transition, so I'm betting on '*and*' as a conjunction used to convey something you want to share, not something you dread. Though, you're clearly nervous. You are about to say 'and' would be my bet."

He chuckled, scratching the back of his neck. "Are you always this analytical? That's the most I think I've heard you speak in class."

"I felt bad for being short with you earlier this week. It wasn't my intention to be rude."

"You weren't rude," he said quickly. "I just enjoyed talking with you. You're... relaxing to talk to, actually. Why do you think I'm nervous?"

I smiled, wondering if I should tell him. I nodded after a moment of thought. "Well, your pulse rate is up. I can see your carotid artery pulsing in your neck. Your heart rate's hovering around 100, give or take. You're already blushing and fidgeting which are things you don't do when interacting with students during class. Plus, you're leaning forward, and your pupils are dilated. Classic signs of interest and nervousness." I smiled, trying to hide the spark of amusement in my eyes.

"Well, you've got me figured out," he said, laughing softly. "Now I've forgotten what I was going to say."

"You were saying you enjoyed our conversation," I reminded him.

"Right. I enjoyed our conversation, and I was intrigued by your thoughts on English as a soft science. I was wondering if you'd like to join me for coffee?" He said, seeming to force out the question at the end before he lost his nerve.

"Now?"

"If you're free."

"Actually, I'm tied up after class or rather, I have to tie some things up," I said, struggling to keep a straight face.

"You mean loose ends to tie up?" he asked, tilting his head.

"Something like that," I replied, biting back a smile.

"So, I got nervous for nothing, and now you've figured out that you interest me. That's... embarrassing."

"I didn't think professors dated students," I said, raising an eyebrow.

"I don't. We wouldn't call it a date. Just a chat. Besides, you won't be a student for much longer. You graduate soon, don't you?"

"I'm flattered," I said, sidestepping the comment.

"Are you free this weekend?"

"I don't have my work schedule yet."

"Oh. What kind of work do you do?"

"Customer service," I said vaguely, tilting my head.

"Retail?"

"Public relations."

"Nice," he said, nodding. "Okay. Maybe I could ask again sometime? Is that okay?"

"I should have my schedule by the weekend," I said.

"Great. Is it that obvious I'm nervous?"

"I think it's cute," I said, letting the faintest smile touch my lips.

"Here's your schedule, Dara," Jillian said, sliding the paper across the desk. "The light bondage guy from yesterday liked your work. Wants to do it again. He's not on your schedule next week, though. I told him I'd have to check. What the hell do you *do* to these guys?"

"They love me," I said, scanning the list.

"Certain ones love you."

"What's that supposed to mean?" I asked, looking up.

"You scare some men off."

"Really? Who?"

"Well, like the Irish guy from last month."

"He's not one of your top-tier clients."

"So?"

"He's a union boss."

Jillian raised an eyebrow. "And how would you know that?"

"The ring he wore, the things he talked about. It was all about him. He wasn't corporate. Wanted to be, maybe, but he was trying too hard. The Texans call it *all hat, no cattle.*"

"It wasn't anything you said that scared him off, Dara. I think it was... physical."

"He didn't think I was pretty enough?"

"On the contrary. He thought you were gorgeous."

"Then what?"

"It's what he didn't say. He was complimentary, sure, but every request after that was for girls he could dominate. My guess? He sensed he couldn't manipulate you."

"He suffers from premature ejaculation."

Jillian smirked. "Probably. In my experience, guys like him can't handle sexually mature women. You're too street smart for him."

"Teach me, Obi-Wan," I said dryly, glancing back at my schedule.

"For what it's worth, he avoids any girl with experience. He loves shy, inexperienced types. You weren't the only one he ghosted."

"He's a coward," I said, shrugging.

"He's macho."

"Like I said."

Jillian laughed and handed me a check. "Let me know if you want to take on bondage guy again. How's the rest of the schedule look?"

I frowned, pointing at a name. "Wait. John Taylor. The attorney?"

"Yeah, I thought about it," Jillian said, leaning back in her chair. "He insisted. Begged, actually. Plus, he referred another high-roller Russian client your way. Don't screw it up."

"What's it like?" Leslie asked suddenly, breaking the quiet. She was curled up on the couch with a book while I was settled in my favorite chair, studying.

"What's what like?" I said, looking up and closing my book.

"Having sex with so many men."

"Leslie—"

"When you first told me what you do, I kind of already knew. The long hours and phone calls weren't hard to figure out."

"And you promised not to bring it up again," I reminded her. "It's a secret that stays in this college town and never leaves."

"And I've kept it. For two years, I haven't asked for details."

"I need to study. Finals are coming up."

"I'm your best friend. I could learn something from you."

"Trust me, Leslie, you don't want my lessons on men or sex."

"I'm just curious about how it works," she pressed. "Do you have to force yourself? Do you like some of them? Does it pay well?"

I sighed and set my book aside, took a deep breath, and rubbed my eyes, knowing Leslie was not going to let up. I looked at her a bit then took a deep breath. "The agency screens clients well. What I do is as old as time, but it's not simple. The ancient Greeks had a system for it. At the bottom were the *pornai,* basically owned by pimps, simply trading sex as a commodity. At the top were *hetairai*. These were educated women paid as much for their intellect and companionship as anything else. The hetairai class weren't required to have sex, but the understanding was that it was an option."

"And you're like the *hetairai*?"

"Something like that, or at least I like to think of it that way," I said. "We're not required to have sex, but if we do, the money is significantly better. And most of the men are pleasant enough."

"Do you ever fall in love with them?"

"Love?" I smiled faintly. "Prostitutes are mentally tough, Leslie. You build walls. You have to separate who you are from what you do. Without that, you lose yourself. Some of the men are interesting, sure. Maybe, under different circumstances, I'd have gone to bed with a few of them for nothing. But mostly, it's business. There's a difference. Sex has nothing to do with love, Leslie."

"Have you ever had bad dates?"

I hesitated. "A Russian guy recently. Not awful, just... crude. A client referred him to me as a favor. It wasn't fun, but I got through it."

"You just take the money and block it out?"

"Basically. But the client who referred him, an attorney. He's different. I'd see him again. I dated his Russian client as a favor."

"Is that when you stay out all night? When you'd like to see them again?"

"I didn't stay all night with the attorney. He's... interesting though. I'm just trying to figure him out. When I can't figure a man out, it's stimulating to me. Let's see how it goes after this weekend."

"Maybe it'll turn into something more. Like in the movies."

"That's not happening. He's good for a roll in bed and some cash, nothing more. I keep personal and business separate." I hesitated, wanting to change the subject. "Speaking of personal, I think my professor wants to ask me out this weekend."

"Oh! Now that sounds interesting."

"It is. I'll play it differently with him as he's in my real world, not my work world. I've vowed to clean up my act. After all, we graduate soon."

Leslie set her book down and leaned forward. "Okay, forget the men. Tell me a sex secret. Something no one else knows while I've got you talking."

I rolled my eyes, hoping she'd get off the subject I was trying to change.

"I could make cookies," she pleaded. She then gave me a puppy-eye look.

"Cookies," I said, opening my book.

"I'll bake you some."

I laughed, then closed my book again. "Alright, one thing. But it's not what you think. I'll tell you a secret everyone really knows but doesn't know."

Leslie's eyes widened. She was sitting at the edge of the couch like an eager student.

"Most people think sex is purely physical," I said, taking a deep breath. "It's not."

"Go on," she said, leaning closer.

"Sure, it feels good physically. But the real secret? It's not about the body. It's about something deeper. Vulnerability, connection, power. When you're with someone, you give a part of yourself to them, and they give a part of themselves to you. That's not simply physical; it's... spiritual."

"Spiritual?"

"There's a reason people say *the two shall become one flesh.* It's not just a poetic metaphor. There's something unseen, something real, that happens during sex. A connection in a world we can't see."

"You really believe that?"

"I don't just believe it. I feel it," I said. "There's this moment, during intimacy, where you step into a realm beyond the physical. It's fleeting but powerful. That's why sex sells. That's why it drives humanity. It's not just about pleasure. It's about power, intimacy, and connection. It's both magic and a weapon."

Leslie stared at me for a moment. "That's pretty deep, Dara. You make it sound like it is some kind of magic."

"Well, it can heal or destroy, depending on how it's used," I said quietly. "That's the power of it. Don't be like me, Leslie. Don't take it lightly. Don't make the choices I've made. I've got to have faith that my choices don't destroy me."

"Having faith should make it easier to make it through," she said softly.

"Faith doesn't make it easier," I replied. "It just makes it possible. Faith is walking through the fire believing there's something worthwhile on the other side."

"You think you have faith the fire won't harm you?" Leslie asked.

"I'm just hoping it's worth the burn."

Chapter 5

"Vorovskoy Zakon" – Dara

"You're early for class. And on a Friday, no less," Aiden said, his tone light with surprise.

"I am," I replied, glancing up from my notebook.

"Did you do your homework?"

"I did. I studied the language found in the late Bronze Age Hittite Code, perused some early Greek literature from the Byzantine Empire, and found the biblical writings from around the 1st century quite fascinating."

His eyebrows lifted. "Impressive. Reviewing literature leading up to the 1st century was certainly part of the assignment. I wanted the class to appreciate the breadth of early texts. But I was actually talking about your *other* homework. Checking your schedule?"

"Oh, *that* homework." I paused, debating how much to reveal. It was my last chance to deflect his interest, but the pull of his curiosity, and my own, kept me engaged.

"Well?" he prompted, his tone teasing yet expectant.

I relented. "I checked. Tomorrow night works."

"Perfect. Dinner?"

"I thought it wasn't a date," I said, giving him a playful smirk.

"Just dinner," he replied, feigning innocence. "Two academics discussing ancient literature. Purely scholarly."

"A private tutoring session, then?" I asked, playing along.

"Whatever works," he said with a grin. "But I'll surprise you."

"Where to on a Friday night?" Leslie asked, looking up from her book.

"Work," I replied, grabbing my purse.

"Tell me."

"Leslie, you promised you wouldn't ask too many questions about my work."

"We kind of broke the ice on that subject, don't you think?"

I sighed. "Some Russian guy."

"I thought you weren't seeing that Russian guy again."

"This is a different one. The one I told you about was older and referred by an attorney client. This guy's much younger. Some other Russian."

"Are the Russians having a sale or something? Why all in the same week?"

I smirked. "The agency's briefing file didn't explain that part. Most of the names are fake anyway, but we get photos. At least I know what to expect."

"When can I expect you back? Is this one of those all-night things?"

"No. Just a dinner date. I'm meeting him in front of some restaurant. Quick and easy."

"You and foreign men," Leslie said with a mock shake of her head.

"He's younger. I suspect he'll be more of a gentleman."

"So, the older Russian was that bad, huh?"

"Not bad, just... awkward. Younger should be easier," I said, smoothing out the fabric of my dress.

Leslie tilted her head, giving me a once-over. "Well, you look gorgeous."

I checked my watch. He was late. I checked my watch again and glanced at the bustling restaurant inside, buzzing with diners. The air buzzed with chatter and clinking silverware. Finally, a sharply dressed man in his late thirties approached, his confident stride matching the description I'd been given. Would he know my work name?

"Carol?" he asked, his accent thick and unmistakably Russian.

"Sasha?" I said, tilting my head.

"We must go," he replied curtly.

"I thought we were having dinner."

"There is a hotel down the street."

"Wait. We didn't book a room," I said, narrowing my eyes.

"No need. I have it taken care of," he said, his tone dismissive.

"You don't understand. My agency handles bookings if you're not a regular," I said, stopping mid-step.

"I understand," he said sharply, placing a firm hand on my arm to pull me forward.

"I need to check in with my agency," I insisted, pulling my arm free. He stopped abruptly, his gaze hardening.

"You do not want to go to the hotel?"

"I'm not that kind of escort."

"I think you are."

"Unless I know you, I'm not going to a hotel room with you."

"You are mistaken. I do not want a whore. We need to speak and not here," he said coldly as he looked around.

"Who are you?" I demanded, taking a half step back. I caught myself glancing around, and he seemed worried about talking to me in public.

He glanced around again, then grabbed my arm and guided, almost pushed, me into a narrow alley just a few steps off the main sidewalk. Cars passed nearby, their headlights slicing through the growing dusk. We were still in public, but the relative privacy sent a shiver down my spine.

"You know this man, yes?" he asked, pulling out a photo.

It was the older Russian client. The one from the previous week, set up by the attorney that I had mentioned to Leslie.

"Maybe," I said, keeping my voice steady.

"Let me refresh your memory," he said, producing another photo. The older Russian and I were in the hotel room in that photo. Naked.

My stomach churned. "How did you get that?"

"What did you tell him?"

"I don't know what you're talking about."

"Who do you work for?"

"I work for the escort agency," I said, holding his gaze.

"Lie," he hissed, stepping closer. His cheap cologne filled the narrow space between us. His eyes were sharp, predatory.

"Look, Sasha, I'm just a working girl. I don't know who he is in real life. We go out to eat, I go to a hotel room, they pay me. That's it."

"Just a stupid prostitute who knows nothing," he muttered, his lips curling in disdain.

"That's me," I said, forcing a calm I didn't feel.

"Must I persuade you to remember?" he said, his tone a low threat as he leaned in closer.

"You don't need to threaten me," I said evenly. I wanted to tell him the Russian wasn't even a good lay but didn't want to set him off. "I assure you, my encounter with him was like a dozen others. Uneventful. There's no reason for me to lie when sleeping with men is literally what I do. There was nothing more. Honestly, he wasn't memorable."

I watched his eyes closely. The sharpness in them softened ever so slightly, his jaw relaxing just a fraction.

"You're a pawn," he said, almost to himself.

"I'm not even a pawn," I replied, my tone flat but measured.

He studied me for a moment longer, then pulled a small card from his pocket.

"This is my card. If you recall anything from that night, you will call me. Do you understand?"

I took the card, its off-white surface blank except for a single number.

"I understand," I said, tucking it into my purse as I watched him retreat back toward the street.

"You're back early," Leslie said, looking up from the couch as I headed straight for the kitchen.

"It was a quick date," I replied, opening the cabinet to grab a glass.

"Is something wrong?" she asked, her tone shifting with concern.

"Date just ended early," I said, busying myself as I pulled a bottle from the cabinet and began mixing a drink.

"The date didn't go well, did it? I can tell. Do you still get paid if it ends early?"

"It's pre-paid through the agency," I said, stirring the drink with more focus than necessary. "The guy was just... creepy. I'll deal with the agency about it later."

The next afternoon, I met John for lunch. The attorney. I glanced at my watch, tapping my fingers on the edge of my purse. The lunch crowd was bustling into the restaurant, a steady stream of chatter and clinking cutlery spilling out each time the door swung open. I considered heading straight to the bar to wait when I spotted him approaching.

"Hello, Carol," John said, his tone light but his eyes scanning me like a chessboard. He looked every bit as poised as that first night at the play.

"What the fuck, John?" I shot back, crossing my arms.

"Nice to see you too," he replied, unbothered. "Lunch?"

"I've lost my appetite," I said, my voice clipped.

"You seem upset. I booked this to make up for leaving our date so early last time."

"Your Russian friend roughed me up last night. What the fuck, John?"

His expression faltered for a split second. "What friend? I wanted to thank you for going out with him."

"Not the older Russian that you referred to me. A younger Russian. Sasha. Ring any bells?"

John's gaze darted away briefly, betraying his thoughts before he composed himself. It was all I needed to know before he spoke. "I don't know what you're talking about."

"He had a photo of me and your older Russian client in the hotel room. Naked." My voice was low but seething.

"Let's go to the bar," he said, motioning toward the door.

We walked inside. He tipped the bartender generously, ordered drinks, and led us to a quiet corner table. His posture was taut, his eyes scanning the room like a hawk.

"You're nervous, John," I said, leaning back in my chair.

"What did Sasha say?"

"Interesting deflection," I said, leaning forward, my tone sharp. "You're not really asking what Sasha said. You want to know what I told your older Russian friend."

John's jaw tightened. "Fine. What did you tell him?"

"I repeated the words on the note you gave me. *Vorovsky Zakon.* Just like you asked." I kept my voice steady, but my blood simmered beneath the surface.

His eyes narrowed, leaning in closer. "You said those exact words?"

"Yes. I found your note after our first date between you and me. The note said you'd consider it another favor if I'd accept a date with your older Russian client. It also said to thank your friend with that phrase at the end of the evening. That he would appreciate it. 'Vorovsky Zakon.'"

"Good."

The bartender brought our drinks, interrupting the moment. John took a sip, his movements measured, his thoughts racing.

"Now let's go back," I said quietly. "Who is Sasha and why does he have naked photos of me? You set that date up, John."

"That's a mystery," he said, his smile forced.

"To hell it's a mystery. I looked it up, John. *Vorovsky Zakon.* The Thieves' Code. Russian mob culture." I let the accusation hang in the air. "I thought it was some weird inside joke. Maybe a reminder for him to keep the date discreet. Clearly, it wasn't."

"Where's the note?" His voice hardened, his eyes narrowing.

"Oh, now you care about the note. Suddenly, it matters." I studied him. "Something's changed, hasn't it? Why does it matter now?"

"Nothing's changed. This is news to me. I'm sorry if Sasha frightened you."

"Don't fuck with me, John. You needed someone smart enough to say Russian phrases without messing them up, didn't you?"

"You're overreacting. Sasha works for a competing client. Nothing dangerous."

"Competing clients? What kind of lawyer are you? And don't tell me it's nothing. Your entire demeanor says otherwise."

John took a long sip of his drink before lowering his voice. "Just keep your mouth shut, and everything will be fine."

"Leave me out of whatever this is, John. That's all I ask."

"This is the last time you'll see me," he said flatly. "You don't know who I am, and I don't know who you are. The agency protects us both. That's why I use your agency. Agreed?"

"Agreed," I said, though every fiber of me screamed otherwise.

As we stood, a voice called out from behind us. "Dara?"

I turned sharply. Aiden.

"Professor?" I said, plastering on a smile. "What are you doing here?"

"I was passing by and stopped in to make dinner reservations," Aiden said, his gaze flicking to John.

"John. I'm like her uncle," John said, extending a hand with exaggerated pleasantries.

Aiden shook it, his expression polite but reserved. "Nice to meet you."

"Dara is a bright young lady," John said, emphasizing my real name and looking me in the eyes as he said it.

"Yes, she is," Aiden replied, his eyes lingering on mine with a softness that unsettled me more than I cared to admit. His gaze had no lust, no calculation, just genuine warmth. He nodded, then excused himself to complete his reservations, apologizing for the interruption.

John turned back to me as Aiden walked to the bar. "Let's go," he said.

John and I were silent as we walked to the door. I glanced over my shoulder once to see Aiden making what was obviously reservations for our first date. I bit my lip momentarily. We soon stepped onto the sidewalk, the air thick with unspoken tension. John stopped and leaned in. "Remember, keep quiet, Dara. This is for your own good." He glanced through the window at Aiden. His eyes still deceived him.

I leaned in closer to him, forcing him to turn his gaze away from Aiden. "Listen to me, motherfucker," I said, my voice low and firm. "If you try anything, anything at all. At any level of my life or anyone I know, just remember Monica Lewinsky."

"What?"

"She kept the dress, John. She outsmarted the most powerful man at the time, the President of the United States. Don't think for a second, I don't have something just as damning. Don't fuck with me."

His hand brushed my elbow in an attempt to guide me toward his car, but I yanked it away. A few passersby glanced in our direction, their curiosity piqued.

"Young lady, I think you should stick to screwing men the old-fashioned way," he hissed.

"I screw men on my own terms. Remember? Now, leave me out of this," I said, staring him down. "And stay away from anyone I care about."

"Goodbye, Dara," he said, his tone dripping with finality.

I flipped him off as I walked away, my pulse pounding in my ears. It wasn't much, but it felt like a small victory, for now.

"I'm sorry I interrupted your reservations," I said, leaning slightly forward later that night.

Aiden tilted his head and smiled. "I thought you were going to apologize for being with another man."

I smirked. "I wasn't worried about it. Hope you didn't mind how I played it off, though. It's pretty obvious he's not a love interest, not that it matters what it looked like. He's an attorney and associated with the marketing agency I work for. He's clearly much older than you."

"No worries. But how old do you think I am?" Aiden raised an eyebrow.

"Aiden, you're obviously not much older than I am. I'd say we're about the same age."

He chuckled. "Actually, you'd be right. I usually keep that under wraps. It's interesting that you're the only student who's noticed. I thought I was pulling it off."

"You mean getting away with how young you actually are."

"Exactly." He leaned back, running a hand through his hair. "I went straight from high school to college, took maximum credits, summer school, the works. Grad school only took two years. This is my first teaching job."

"That explains why your credentials don't list a PhD. I thought a doctorate was required to teach at the university level."

"Typically, yes. My grad school grades were strong, and I worked closely with the department head. When a slot opened, they took a chance on me under the condition I finish my PhD."

"You stood out."

"I had connections." He hesitated, then added, "Speaking of connections, so your... uncle is an attorney?"

I frowned slightly. "He's not my uncle. He just knows the owner of the marketing agency where I work. It was a business meeting."

"I see. What about your real family?"

"I don't have any," I said simply, tracing the rim of my coffee cup.

Aiden's expression softened. "None?"

"My mom got sick while I was in high school. I waited tables for a couple of years. She insisted I go to college. We compromised, and I started at the community college nearby so I could stay close to home."

"She needed you."

"She did. But she passed away during my first year."

"I'm so sorry."

I nodded, offering a small, tight smile. "Thanks. After that, I transferred here. I promised her I'd finish at the university."

"That's a lot to carry." His voice was low, earnest. "So, no siblings?"

"No. And my dad. Well, I call him my mother's baby daddy. He lives in another state, and we're estranged. That's putting it kindly."

"Why? If you don't mind me finding out more about you."

"He walked out when I was little. I barely remember him. Never visited, not even when Mom was sick. I've seen his social media. He has a wife, some bland-looking kids, and zero mention of me. As far as he's concerned, I don't exist. And honestly, I'm fine with that."

"You've never tried to reach out?"

"Hell no," I said quickly, then caught myself. "I mean, heck no." I winced and shook my head. "Sorry, I'm trying to clean up my language. Bad habits from my upbringing, I guess."

He smiled gently. "You don't have to censor yourself for me."

"I'm not. I'm trying to censor myself for me. I don't want to sound like a low-life. I guess I inherited something from him after all."

"What, the language?"

"That, and nothing else. He's a bum. Apparently, he'd been in Naval intelligence. I stalked him a bit online. Found some old photos and pieced together his new life. But I don't want to know more."

"Still, he's your father. You might have half-siblings—"

"Fuck him," I said, then immediately closed my eyes. I took a deep breath and reopened them, meeting Aiden's gaze. "Sorry. I mean, screw him. I don't need family. I don't want it. I'm alone, and I like it that way."

His gaze lingered on me for a moment, his expression unreadable. "I don't think anyone really likes being alone, Dara."

I forced a smile, but the weight of his words lingered, heavy and unsettling.

Monday morning, I waited in the office, my mind racing. The moment Jillian walked through the door, I fell into step behind her, following her across the waiting room and into her office.

"Good morning, Dara," Jillian said as she unlocked her door.

I didn't waste any time. "Who the hell is John?" I said as soon as the door clicked shut behind me.

She glanced at me briefly, her expression calm as always, before taking her seat behind the desk. "Good morning to you too. I take it your weekend date didn't go well."

"It wasn't a date." My voice was sharp.

"He paid for a date," Jillian replied, unfazed, as she settled into her chair.

"Yeah, and he used it to tie up loose ends. He's playing games, Jill. He set me up in some kind of blackmail scheme."

Jillian raised an eyebrow, folding her hands neatly on her desk. "John is a reputable attorney, Dara."

"With some very disreputable clients," I snapped.

"You're overreacting. He doesn't know who you are any more than you know who he is."

"He knows exactly who I am. We ran into my professor at a restaurant."

Jillian's lips quirked into the faintest smirk. "You mean your boyfriend?"

"Jill." I shot her a glare.

"Office gossip," she said with a shrug.

"John, or someone who doesn't like his client, set me up. There are naked photos of me and the old Russian guy. I can't figure out which side of this mess it came from, but John knows who I am. You're supposed to protect me, Jill."

Her expression hardened slightly. "I have a reputation to uphold, Dara. I protect my escorts, yes, but I also protect my clients. You know this. And let's be clear: John isn't blackmailing you. If he's blackmailing anyone, it's the Russian guy. So, what are you worried about? You're not the target."

"Oh, I'm just collateral damage in a mobster's scheme? That makes it okay?" My voice rose, frustration bubbling over.

"I'm saying, if this is true, you're not the focus. Escorts are always just bystanders in these sorts of things. This isn't the first time someone's tried to use the agency for their own agenda. Private investigators, blackmail setups. It's not unheard of."

"Well, your 'setup' sent Sasha, the younger Russian, after me last night. He threatened me, Jill. The date *you* arranged."

"Sasha?" Jillian frowned. "That doesn't sound like him."

"If that's even his real name. Only you know the truth about these players in this Russian mess. Maybe *you* should be worried."

Her eyes narrowed. "What are you implying?"

"John wanted me in bed with the old Russian. Why?"

"It was a favor for a high-paying client. That's all."

"John left me a note after our first meeting. He told me to say something in Russian to the old guy at the end of the date. I thought it was some weird inside joke. Turns out, it spooked him. Next thing I know, there are naked photos of us. And Sasha cornering me about my time with the old guy."

"You know Russian?" Jillian leaned forward slightly.

"He wrote it phonetically. I just repeated it. The phrase was *Vorovskoy Zakon*. The 'Thieves Code.' It's part of Russian mob culture."

Jillian's brow furrowed. "That… doesn't make sense."

"No kidding. Then Sasha shoves me into an alley, flashing those photos and demanding to know who I work for. I told him the truth, your agency. I assumed he already knew that unless *you're* hiding something."

Jillian's calm exterior cracked slightly, but her voice remained steady. "This isn't the first time a client has tried to use the agency for ulterior motives. I'll look into it."

"Do that," I said, turning toward the door.

"Dara." Her voice stopped me. "Why don't you take a vacation for a few days? Let things settle."

I turned back, narrowing my eyes. "John says it's nothing. You say this isn't the first time. Yet you're both concerned enough to tell me either to stay away for my safety or to skip town. Why?"

"Because I care about you," she said firmly. "You're right about one thing. I need to protect you. These are powerful men, Dara. Let me handle this. In the meantime, take a break. Lay low."

I hesitated, studying her for a moment. "I'll think about it," I said, my voice clipped.

I walked out, letting the door slam harder than I meant to, or maybe I did mean to.

"What are you doing?" I asked, sinking onto the couch next to Leslie. She was eating popcorn, her eyes fixed on the TV.

"Watching TV," she said, popping another kernel into her mouth.

"The news?"

"There's a documentary I've got to watch for class after this." She tilted the bowl toward me, and I grabbed a handful of popcorn.

The screen suddenly shifted to flashing blue lights and yellow crime scene tape. A photo of a woman appeared on the screen. My hand froze mid-air, a piece of popcorn suspended between my fingers.

"Turn it up," I said, my voice sharper than I intended. I stared at the photo on the screen superimposed over a crime scene.

"Why?" Leslie asked, glancing at me.

"Just turn it up. Louder."

She grabbed the remote and turned up the volume.

"Susan Hampton survived the attack by jumping out of a two-story hotel window. Susan, who worked for a prestigious modeling agency, is currently listed in critical condition…"

Leslie looked over at me, her brow furrowed. "Do you know her?"

I pressed a finger to my lips, gesturing for her to listen. She turned back to the screen.

"Russian oligarch Dmitri Krushnic was found dead in the hotel room. His body was riddled with bullets, according to police sources. Krushnic reportedly ran international trade businesses from his home in the U.S. and was credited with aiding Russian privatization after the dissolution of the Soviet Union. He was also a known associate of former Russian President Boris Yeltsin. The FBI has been called in to assist with the investigation…"

"What's all that about?" Leslie asked, her eyes darting from me to the screen.

I didn't answer. My mind was already spinning. "I need to call Jillian," I said, standing abruptly.

"Who is Susan?" she asked, setting the popcorn down. "She works at the agency, doesn't she? Does she… do what you do? And who's that guy?"

"Shh," I said, holding up a hand as I dialed Jillian's number. Leslie fell silent but didn't take her eyes off me.

The phone rang once before Jillian picked up. "Hello?"

"Jill, it's Dara."

"I already know," Jillian said briskly. "Susan is fine. I'm on my way to the hospital now."

"I'll meet you there," I said, already grabbing my bag.

"No. Listen to me. Leave town."

"What? Jillian—"

"I'm serious, Dara. The FBI will probably show up at my office tomorrow looking for a list of all the escorts Dmitri hired through the agency. As you've probably figured out, he's the older Russian you dated in the photos."

"How many are on that list?"

"A few. He liked our girls. You weren't the only one."

"Did John have anything to do with this?"

"Who knows? Either way, I'll have to cut him off."

"Are we in trouble?"

"No. Officially, the agency only hires models. We've been through this before. We have built-in protections; frankly, their biggest fear is my client list."

"What happens now?"

"They'll interview the girls he's been with, in the past few weeks. It'll take time for them to track everyone down."

"My name is on that list."

"Exactly. Which is why you need to disappear for the rest of the week."

"Won't that look suspicious?"

"It's not the authorities I'm worried about."

I paused, the weight of her words settling over me. "Got it," I said softly before hanging up. My mind raced.

"What's going on?" Leslie asked, her voice rising with concern.

"I need to leave town for a while."

"Tonight?"

"No. It's too hot to leave tonight. I'll go to class tomorrow, keep everything normal. Then I'll leave quietly tomorrow night. It'll look like I'm just taking a vacation during the break."

"Are you involved in this somehow?" Leslie's voice was tinged with fear.

"Don't worry. I'll be fine," I said, trying to sound more confident than I felt.

"You're not going to tell me where you're going, are you?"

"No. If anyone asks, you can honestly say you don't know. It's safer that way."

"When exactly are you leaving?"

"Tomorrow night."

"You're staying for another day?" Leslie's eyes widened. "Why?"

"I have a regular Tuesday client. I can't miss it. If I disappear immediately, it looks like I'm running."

Leslie's face fell, her concern deepening. I forced a reassuring smile and squeezed her hand before retreating to my room, already planning my next steps.

"George, I need to tell you something," I said the next evening, setting a large coffee from Mom & Pop's on the table next to him, light and sweet, just how he liked it.

"Let me guess. This is about the Russian hit job," George said, picking up his coffee without missing a beat.

"How do you know about that?"

"It's not every day an international scandal blows into town, let alone one that might brush up against Jillian's agency. Why am I not surprised you're in the middle of it?"

"The Russian was a client."

"A regular?"

"No, and that's just it. I was with him only once at the request of another client. A client who said he was the Russian's attorney."

George arched an eyebrow. "Aren't you violating your own privacy policies by telling me?"

"He's dead, George. What's he going to do, sue me?"

"You didn't bump him off, did you, Carol?" he said, taking a long sip of coffee, his tone laced with dry humor.

I sighed. "The attorney set me up with him weeks ago. Booked a date between me and this Russian guy I now see all over the news, Dmitri. Someone took photos of us in the hotel room. It was a setup. Then someone bumped him off on another date with a friend of mine."

"Blackmail? Hidden cameras? Thank goodness you weren't with him when the Russian mafia got to him."

"How do you know it was the Russian mafia?"

"Just a hunch. I'm more worried about you."

"A younger Russian guy tried to intimidate me afterward," I said, leaning forward. "He wanted to know what I told Dmitri. That's how I found out about the photos."

"The Russian mafia has fingers in everything, organized crime, international markets, even government. What kind of trouble are you in?"

"The attorney, John, or whatever his name is was entertaining Dmitri when we met. I was John's date that night. Afterward, John left me a note, asking me to meet Dmitri and deliver a specific phrase in Russian at the end of our date. He said Dmitri would appreciate the gesture. He didn't."

"You slept with both of them?" George's brow furrowed.

"George." I gave him a look.

He held up a hand. "Spare me the details, child. What else is so special about this note?"

"It was handwritten. If tested, John's DNA would be on it. It's my way of connecting him to Dmitri's death." I reached into my bag and pulled out a plastic-wrapped note, placing it on the table in front of George.

"You bagged it?" He looked at the note, then back at me.

"It's evidence. The attorney's DNA and his instructions are on it."

"This could be incriminating. Are you planning to use it to connect him to the murder?"

"Only if I have to. I want you to keep it safe."

George picked up the bag, examining it. "What do you want me to do with this, Carol?"

"I don't know. I just know I don't want to be caught with it. I don't want it destroyed either. It's my insurance."

"You threatened the attorney, didn't you? He knows you can tie him to the murder."

"Why would you think that?"

"Because I know you, Carol."

I sighed. "So, what should I do with it?"

"Who else knows about this note?" George asked, setting the bag down carefully.

"Jillian."

"You told Jillian?" His voice carried a note of concern.

"I trust her. But I don't trust her enough to give her the note."

"But you trust me?"

"You're all I've got, George. And I don't think this puts you in any danger. I'd never do that to you. I just have nowhere else to go, and no one would suspect you have it."

"Did it occur to you to give this to the police?"

"Not preemptively. Prostitutes don't exactly have stellar credibility with law enforcement."

"Carol," he said, shaking his head slightly.

"Will you keep it safe?" I asked softly.

George leaned back, studying me. "Why trust me? I'm just a regular client."

"You're more than that," I said. "You've been my Tuesday-night regular for three years, meeting secretly together. You correct me when I swear, you won't let me wear provocative clothes around you, and you give me advice like a father would. You've never taken advantage of me, not once. If I can't trust you, George, who can I trust?"

He paused, his eyes searching mine. Finally, he picked up the bag, holding it firmly. Leaning forward, he touched my chin gently, lifting it so our eyes met. "It'll be safe. But are you safe?"

"Jillian thinks I should leave town for a few days."

George leaned back in his chair, nodding slowly as he took another sip of coffee. The room was silent for a long moment.

"She might be right," he said finally. "Let's make sure you're safe too."

Chapter 6

"I have issues with people who need to be seen at church rather than being the church." - Dara

I took a final sip of coffee and slipped my shoes back on. George tidied up his papers while I turned my cell phone back on. It rang almost instantly.

"Hello?" I answered, bringing it to my ear.

"Dara, where are you? I've been trying to call you," Leslie said, her voice breathless.

"I just turned my phone back on. You know I have a Tuesday meeting. I was about to leave the hotel. What's wrong?"

"Someone broke into the apartment. The police are here."

"What? Are you okay?"

"Yes. No one was here when I got home, but the place is a mess."

"What did the police say?"

"They asked what was stolen, but I couldn't find anything valuable missing. They're finishing their report now. Dara... does this have something to do with you?"

"Probably. Text me when the police leave," I said, then hung up and tossed the phone onto the bed. I rubbed my temples, trying to collect my thoughts.

George walked over and pulled me into a hug. His embrace was warm, steady, and comforting. It was never inappropriate, always safe. I rested my head against his chest, and he gently kissed my forehead.

"It's okay, my dear. We'll figure this out," he said softly.

"That was my roommate," I said, my voice barely above a whisper. "Someone must've been looking for that note at my apartment. It has to be."

I grabbed my phone and started dialing.

"What are you doing?" George asked.

"Calling Jillian. She knows the attorney's identity."

Before the call connected, George reached out and gently took the phone from my hand. He ended the call, handed the phone back, and gave me a sad, knowing smile.

"Don't bother. She won't tell you."

"Damn it, George. What the—"

"Carol," he interrupted, narrowing his eyes. His tone was enough to stop me mid-sentence.

I rolled my eyes, exhaling sharply. "What the heck am I supposed to do?"

"Let me take care of it," he said calmly. "In the meantime, I'll drive you home."

"No," I said, quickly stuffing my phone back into my bag and tossing the coffee cups into the trash. "I can't let you drive me. I have to keep my business and personal lives separate. I can't let clients into my real life."

"Carol," George said, his voice steady but firm. "You trust me with your note. You can trust me to get you home."

"It's not personal, George. It's a boundary," I said, my voice rising slightly. "I've worked hard to keep those two worlds apart. I can't blur the line now."

He sighed, his expression softening. "I think it's too late for that. This is your real life, Carol. We've been prying into each other's real lives every week for years."

"It's not real," I said, my voice cracking slightly. "It's a routine. A game we play. I don't need to know who you are publicly. I already know who you are privately, and that's enough. Who a person is in private is who they truly are. That's all that matters."

My words trailed off, and I threw my hands up in frustration. George stood there quietly, letting me vent, his face calm and understanding. A tear slipped from the corner of my eye before I even realized it. George wiped it away gently.

"What do you need from me, my dear?" he asked softly.

"Just keep the note safe," I said, my voice trembling. "That's all I need from you."

"That's it?" he asked, tilting his head slightly.

"You've been the only constant in my life, George. The only thing I can rely on. Public or private, you're all I've got right now."

"I'm sorry if I'm all you have," he said, his voice tinged with sadness.

"It's not your fault. It's just the way things are. When I walk away from this life, I want to walk away from all of it. That means keeping my private life separate as much as possible. Even from you one day. You understand, don't you?"

George nodded slowly. "I understand, my dear. And I want you to be free of this life. It'll be bittersweet when it happens, but I'll be proud of you."

"I know," I whispered, wiping another tear from my cheek.

His steady presence eased the turmoil inside me, even if just for a moment.

"Hello?" Jillian answered her cell phone, her smile widening as she glanced at the caller ID.

"I want you to fire Dara," George said, his tone steady but firm.

Jillian sighed, leaning back in her chair. "I offered to do that years ago, George."

"You and I both know that would have just pushed her into the streets. You know her. She wouldn't have changed. She would have been worse off."

"Why now?" Jillian's voice softened, a trace of concern slipping through her professional demeanor.

"You know she's in danger, Jillian. More than she realizes. Her value to you…as you put it, is over."

"If I fire her, I lose the ability to protect her or you, for that matter," Jillian countered, her sharpness returning.

"She's about to finish school. Her tuition is paid. She's done with this life. It's time."

Jillian hesitated, twirling a pen between her fingers. "If I fire her, you lose your little influence over her, George. And let's be honest, she doesn't let anyone have much influence."

"This isn't about control or manipulation. I've never needed that with her. Besides, I've always used my real name, even if I have to call her by an alias. Everyone knows me as just George."

"That's precisely why you use your real name with her," Jillian said with a wry chuckle. "You know she overanalyzes everything. Using your real name makes her think it's an alias. You and Dara are cut from the same cloth. Always two steps ahead of everyone, always analyzing. But friend or no friend, my clients don't dictate what I do with my employees."

"You know I'm not one of your clients, Jillian. I'm your friend. And you're hers, whether she realizes it or not. Your real clients? They have everything to lose if their identities get out. I don't care about that, and you know it. You also know I don't need anyone's protection."

Jillian tapped the pen on her desk, weighing his words. "So, you want me to fire her for her own good?"

"We agreed to this plan all along," George said, his voice softer now. "I know it's earlier than we planned, but she's so close to graduation. She'll stay in school; you know she will. And firing her spares you the burden of keeping up the lie."

Jillian closed her eyes briefly, exhaling through her nose. "And then what, George? What happens after that?"

"I'll take care of her," George said without hesitation as he looked out the window watching Dara get into a vehicle.

"You always do," Jillian said, her tone resigned but tinged with admiration.

"Thanks for picking me up, Aiden," I said, glancing at him. His smile caught the glow of passing city lights as we drove. "I didn't have anyone else to call."

"Why is a girl like you stranded late on a Tuesday night?" he asked.

"I had to meet someone, and then my roommate called. Our apartment was broken into while she was at her evening class."

"Wow. That's serious. I'm glad you called me," he said, his tone earnest.

"I hated to bother you. I didn't want to inconvenience the friend I was meeting," I said, watching the headlights of cars trailing behind us. The light from the street reflected off Aiden's wavy hair as he turned onto another block.

"I'm happy to help. Gives us more time together outside of class," he said, glancing at me with that twinkle in his eye.

"At least there's no class tomorrow," I said.

"For you, maybe. I've got office hours all week."

"Turn here," I said, checking the rearview mirror. Aiden turned without hesitation.

"I thought you said your apartment was near the university."

"It is. Turn again."

"You sure?" he asked, briefly glancing my way before making the turn.

"Yes. Then take a right at the next corner. Quickly."

Aiden hesitated but followed the directions. "Dara, that's three right turns. We're just circling the block. What's going on?"

"I think someone's following us," I said quietly.

"Following us? Don't you think that's a bit paranoid?"

"Then the car several lengths behind us is having a very peculiar case of déjà vu. It's made all the same turns."

Aiden frowned and adjusted his rearview mirror. "Are you sure?"

"Drop me off at the next light. Circle the block and meet me on the other side. I'll cut through the store on the corner."

"Dara—"

"Just do it, Aiden," I said firmly. Before he could respond, I opened the door as the car slowed at the light and stepped out. I kept my gaze forward, avoiding any direct glances at the trailing car, but I caught its reflection in a nearby storefront. The car slowed and parked as I walked into the store.

Peeking between a rack of clothes, I saw a man exit the vehicle and jog across the street toward the entrance. My pulse quickened. He was alone.

I quickly darted deeper into the store, zigzagging through aisles to stay below the sightline of the shelves. Glancing back, I caught a glimpse of the man's head as he stepped inside. Without hesitation, I headed for the opposite exit.

The moment I emerged, Aiden's car pulled up. I jumped in and slammed the door.

"Go," I said, urgency sharpening my voice.

Aiden stepped on the gas, his expression a mix of concern and confusion. "What was that all about?"

"Nothing," I said, forcing my breathing to steady. "You're right. I was just being paranoid."

"Dara, you're back! And you've brought someone?" Leslie said, glancing between me and Aiden as I stepped into the apartment.

"This is Aiden. Aiden, this is my roommate, Leslie," I said. Aiden extended his hand with a warm smile.

"You look familiar," Leslie said, shaking his hand. She tilted her head, studying him.

"I'm a professor at the university," Aiden said.

"Client?" Leslie asked, her eyebrows arching as she glanced at me.

"Friend," I said firmly, shooting her a warning look.

"Client?" Aiden repeated, his voice laced with curiosity.

"She means my public relations side job…marketing. You know, handing out brochures and things like that. He just gave me a ride," I explained quickly, trying to deflect.

"I'm sure she appreciates it," Leslie said, her gaze lingering on Aiden.

"Did the police say anything?" I asked, steering the conversation in a different direction.

"They just took a report. Nothing seemed to be missing," Leslie replied.

"It's not as much of a mess as I expected," I said, looking around the apartment.

"I cleaned up a little. You shouldn't be here," Leslie said, her voice tinged with concern.

"I can't just leave you."

"What were they looking for?" Leslie asked.

I shrugged, avoiding her eyes as Aiden began straightening a chair and putting a few items back into an overturned drawer.

"We can handle that, Aiden," I said.

"I don't mind helping," he said. As I bent down to assist, our hands brushed. We exchanged a smile, and I tucked a strand of hair behind my ear.

For the next hour, we worked together to tidy up the apartment. Aiden's lightheartedness made the situation feel a little less heavy, and even Leslie started warming up to him.

"He's cute," Leslie whispered to me as we neared the end of our cleanup.

"Stop it. He might actually be boyfriend material," I whispered back.

"So, where are you going to stay?" she asked.

"I'll stay here. Whoever broke in didn't find what they were looking for," I said.

"How do you know?"

"I'm guessing."

"But they could come back."

"You'll be here. I'm not leaving."

"They're not looking for me, Dara. You said that yourself."

"I can't leave you."

"Well, I'm thinking about staying with my new boyfriend," Leslie said casually.

"Leslie?" I said, incredulous.

"I already called him. I told him I was too scared to stay alone."

"You're unbelievable," I muttered just as Aiden emerged from the bathroom.

"So, where are you going to stay?" Leslie asked loudly, making sure Aiden could hear. I motioned for her to lower her voice, but she ignored me.

"Not sure," I said softly, glaring at her.

"You're not staying here? It looks fine now," Aiden said, joining us.

"I'm heading to my boyfriend's place. Dara doesn't want to stay alone," Leslie said, feigning concern. "Or rather, I'd be afraid for her to stay alone. She can get paranoid."

"I'm fine," I said, narrowing my eyes at Leslie.

"Dara probably needs a few days away from the apartment. Don't you think, Aiden?" Leslie said, ignoring my look.

"I agree. You're welcome to stay at my place," Aiden said.

"I'm not that kind of girl. Plus, I wouldn't want to impose. I'll just check into a hotel for a few days," I said quickly.

"She *is* that kind of girl," Leslie teased, grinning mischievously.

"What Leslie means is it wouldn't look appropriate," I said, shooting her another pointed look.

"I understand, but it wouldn't be inappropriate. I have a guest room. I live in a small farmhouse just outside the city. It's a short drive and no trouble at all," Aiden offered.

"Then it's settled," Leslie said cheerfully.

I furrowed my brow at her again, but Leslie just smiled knowingly.

"Fresh linens are on the bed, and the bathroom is down the hall," Aiden said, gesturing toward the cozy guest room after arriving at his place.

"Got it," I said, stepping into the space.

"My bedroom is at the opposite end of the hall. It has its own bathroom, so consider the hall bathroom entirely yours," he added.

"Thank you. You didn't have to do this," I said, turning back to face him.

"Someone breaking into your apartment is traumatic. A change of scenery can help," he said with a reassuring smile.

"Well, we've technically only had one date," I said, feeling the awkwardness creep in.

"I'm happy you considered it a date," he said, a glimmer of amusement in his eyes.

"It just feels... a little awkward, that's all," I said.

"I understand," Aiden said with a reassuring smile. "I'll do my best to keep things comfortable."

"I mean, it's not you. I'm just not used to certain social situations with men."

"Staying overnight, you mean?"

I looked down for a moment, then back at Aiden. "I've never really had serious boyfriends," I admitted.

"I can't see why not. You're beautiful, kind, and incredibly bright," he said, his tone genuine.

"You're being too kind. Honestly, I think all that just intimidates potential boyfriends."

"And tonight, I also learned you're quite clever."

"Clever?" I tilted my head.

"Dara, I'm not prying, but it's obvious there's something going on that you're not sharing," he said, his voice gentle but perceptive.

"What makes you think that?" I asked, my tone defensive.

"It's none of my business, and you don't have to explain anything. But the signs are there. You called me for a ride, said someone broke into your apartment, spotted a car following us, and insisted we lose them."

"Oh, that," I said, brushing it off.

"There's more?" he asked, raising an eyebrow.

"Of course not," I said quickly. "I guess it did seem paranoid."

"I chalked it up to nerves about the break-in. But your roommate was pretty eager to ditch you."

"She just wanted to stay with her boyfriend," I said, shrugging.

"You don't strike me as someone who's afraid to be alone. At least, not unless there's a good reason. And you kept checking behind us the entire drive here."

"You're right. The break-in really shook me up," I said softly.

"And country roads can feel dark and isolating," he said, nodding. "I get it. None of it is my business, but I'm glad you trusted me enough to call."

"I didn't know who else to call," I admitted, avoiding his gaze.

"Well, I'll make breakfast in the morning," he said with a warm smile. "A little fresh air and space should clear your head."

"Thank you, Aiden," I said, feeling a rare sense of relief in his kindness.

Breakfast in the country has its charm. From the table, I could see the distant city skyline framed by chirping birds and soft morning light. Aiden had gone all out: bacon, eggs, toast. It was simple but thoughtful. He then dashed off to the university, promising to return after lunch. For now, the farmhouse was mine, along with a strong cell signal and a call I needed to make.

"Jill, are you screwing me?" I said as soon as she answered.

"Dara? No F-bombs? Who is this, really?" Jillian said, her tone teasing.

"I'm trying to reform."

"It's very becoming of you," she said with a laugh. "Now, what's got you so worked up?"

"My apartment was broken into, and someone followed me from my Tuesday night appointment. You wouldn't happen to know anything about that, would you?"

Jillian's voice tightened. "What are you implying, Dara?"

"You're the only one who knew where I was Tuesday night. You're the only one who had both my appointment address and my home address. Someone broke in while I was out, and I was also followed from my date. Just seems like a coincidence, Jill."

"Why would I tell someone about your appointments? If I wanted to have you followed, I wouldn't need the hotel address. I could just give them your college address."

"Exactly, Jill. And, my apartment was trashed."

"Dara, you know how tightly I protect my client and employee records. I have no reason to risk your safety or the agency's reputation."

"Then explain what's happening. I'm being followed, Jillian. My life feels like it's spiraling out of control."

She sighed. "We both know this is fallout from the Russian hit job."

"Did you cut John off?"

"I haven't heard from him since we spoke last. And while I don't have answers about your apartment, I do have something to put your mind at ease about being followed."

"What do you know?"

"George told me."

I froze. "George? How would he know anything?"

"When you told him about the break-in, he sent his driver to follow you. He wanted to make sure you were safe."

"To keep tabs on me, you mean?" I asked, my frustration rising.

"You know George better than that. He wasn't sure about the guy you called to pick you up and didn't want to take chances."

"To protect me?"

"To protect you," Jillian confirmed. "Knowing George, he probably plans to hire a professional to watch over you discreetly, would be my guess."

I sighed, leaning back in my chair. "He told you this?"

"He worries about you, Dara. You know he's tried to pay your tuition for years, and you won't let him. He's also helping cover Susan's hospital bills."

I softened. "Susan's bills?"

"He knows she's your friend. That's the kind of man he is."

"He hovers, Jill. Not once in three years has he treated me like an escort. Not that I'm complaining. But it's like he's trying to be some father figure since he knows I have no family."

"You've accused me of hovering too," Jillian said.

"You're my boss. It's different. But George… I just don't know what his deal is."

"You trust him, though."

"I do. He's been the only constant in my life these last few years. But I still have my rules, Jill. I have to keep my escort life separate from the one I want to build after graduation. I can't afford a father figure. As much as I like George, he's still part of the life I want to leave behind."

"Good luck with that, Dara. This business has a way of lingering, no matter how clean the break."

I hesitated. "The police picked up the list of escorts who dated the Russian, didn't they?"

"They did."

"How long is the list?"

"Shorter than I expected. He saw the same few girls repeatedly. Expect a call soon."

I exhaled sharply. "I don't know if I should hate you or love you for getting me into this business."

"You want the truth of what I think about you and the business?"

"When have you not been brutally honest?"

"You're one of the best in the business, Dara. But you're also the one person with no business being in it."

I laughed bitterly. "We just make men look good. Sometimes, we go to bed with them."

"You connect with people on a deeper level, Dara. That's a rare gift."

"Pretty sure that wasn't in the job description."

"It's not. That's why you don't belong here. You're destined for greater things."

"How's Susan?"

"She's awake but still in the hospital. I don't know when she'll be released."

"Maybe I'll sneak into town to visit her."

"Be careful. I'll let you know if I hear anything about your apartment."

"Thanks, Jillian. I know I give you a hard time."

"I can take it, Dara. Just stay safe."

"How was your day?" Aiden asked as he walked in, balancing a bag of takeout.

"Thanks for bringing food. I wasn't in the mood to go out," I said, clearing space on the table. "I just lounged around all morning. It's so peaceful here; I half expected to see chickens out back."

"No chickens," he said with a grin. "But I rushed back. I know it sounds cliché, but I missed your company."

"It *is* cliché, but I'll allow it," I teased, pulling open the takeout bag.

"On our first…" Aiden gestured in the air, searching for the word.

"Date?" I offered, arching a brow.

"You seem okay with that word."

"A date is fine. I just didn't imagine myself dating a professor. But I feel better knowing we're the same age. At least *you* have a job."

"You sound a little old-fashioned."

"That's me. Miss old-fashioned."

"I like that," Aiden said, settling into a chair. "An old-fashioned girl next door. Someone who cares about appearances, values wholesomeness, and doesn't have a string of exes. A girl who's saving herself for marriage and worried about the appearance of impropriety… I'm lucky to spend time with someone like that."

I let out a short laugh. "Yep, that's me. The *wholesome* girl next door." I rifled through the food trays.

Aiden studied me, his expression soft. "I know almost nothing about you, except your mom passed away, and you're not a fan of your dad."

"There's not much more to tell."

"I don't believe that," he said, picking at his food. "You're more complex than you let on. Let me guess. You eat healthy, drive safely, and go to church on Sundays?"

"I try to eat healthy, my driving's terrible, and I went to church as a kid. But I became disillusioned pretty quickly with all of the above." I popped a bite into my mouth, mulling over my words. "There's something about people acting one way in church and the opposite outside it. Worse, some even use scripture to justify their actions. There should be a special place in hell for those kinds of people. That's why I might not be as 'wholesome' as you think. Though that's probably the wrong attitude."

Aiden raised an eyebrow. "Sounds like you have issues with your church."

"I have issues with people who go to church to be *seen* at church rather than *be* the church."

"Wow. And you're opinionated." He sat back, clearly impressed. "The girl next door I'm interested in has some stories."

"Let's just say I'm more focused on the future. As far as I'm concerned, the past doesn't exist."

"That's fair. So, you eat well, can't drive, don't trust people, and refuse to talk about your past. What's something that would completely shock me about you?"

"You really want to ruin the image you have of me?"

"Well, you're so perfect. Sweet, attractive, incredibly smart. There's got to be a flaw somewhere."

"Why would you want to know my flaws?"

"Because when you care about someone, you've got to love their flaws too."

I narrowed my eyes playfully. "Okay, but don't say I didn't warn you. This will shatter your perfect little image of me."

"Go ahead. Shock me."

"Sometimes I use profanity. And not just 'hell' when referencing biblical Hades."

Aiden's lips twitched into a smile. "That *is* shocking."

"See? I'm not as wholesome as you think."

"Clearly not," he said, grinning. But I like you even more now." There was a moment of silence that settled between us. I guess we both were reflecting in our own way. Aiden broke the silence as I caught myself staring away from him and out the window at the countryside. "Want me to show you around?"

The cool breeze carried the faint scent of wildflowers as Aiden and I strolled through the yard. The sky above the country home stretched wide and endless, painted in soft hues of orange and pink from the setting sun. His yard wasn't perfectly kept. There were patches of overgrown grass mingled with a few budding plants, but it had a charm that suited him.

"It's peaceful here," I said, breaking the comfortable silence. "You've got quite the view."

"It's not much, but it's home," he replied. "I like the quiet. Helps me think."

I smiled. "Seems like it fits you, academic, thoughtful, and a touch mysterious."

He chuckled softly. "Mysterious? I think you've been reading too much into me, Dara."

"Maybe. Or maybe I'm right."

He didn't reply, just smiled in that quiet, knowing way of his. As we passed a line of trees, I noticed his hand brushing close to mine. It was subtle at first, like the movement was accidental, but when he shifted closer, his fingers lightly grazed mine again.

I glanced up at him, catching the nervous flicker in his eyes before he quickly looked forward. His touch lingered, tentative, waiting for my reaction.

Instead of pulling away, I let a small smile curl at the corner of my lips. Without saying a word, I slid my fingers between his, intertwining them with his. His grip tightened slightly, and I felt the warmth of his hand steady and reassuring as we held hands.

A strange feeling settled over me, something I hadn't expected. It felt real. Honest. His hand in mine wasn't part of an act or a transaction. It wasn't calculated or forced. It was just a simple gesture, genuine and unspoken.

For the first time in years, a man's touch didn't feel like an exchange of power or control. It felt… natural.

"You okay?" Aiden asked, glancing over at me with that gentle twinkle in his eye.

"Yeah," I said, my voice softer than I expected. "I'm okay."

And as we walked on, his hand in mine, I realized that, for once, I wasn't just pretending to be okay.

"How's your sleepover?" Leslie asked, her voice teasing through the phone.

"I was about to ask you the same thing," I replied, adjusting the phone against my ear.

"He slept on the couch," Leslie said.

"At the new boyfriend's place?"

"Yeah. He snores. But he's nice."

"Sounds like a gentleman if he slept on the couch."

"I was kind of hoping for more."

"Wait, is this my 'saving-herself-for-marriage' roommate on the line?"

"I don't mean *that.* But, you know, second base would've been a nice icebreaker."

"Look at you, turning into a party girl."

"You're rubbing off on me."

"Well, that's your first mistake."

"Did you get to second base with Professor Aiden?"

"Never even stepped up to bat. It was…nice, though."

"*Nice?* You didn't even make out?"

"Of course not. He has a guest room."

"Ugh, I'm living vicariously through you now, Dara. You're disappointing me."

"He made breakfast. Then brought back dinner. We talked."

"That's it?"

"He showed me around his property. There's an old barn, and he's pretending to fix up a garden."

"Okay, you're officially a corny romance novel. Next, he'll be carving your initials into a tree."

"He did touch my hand."

"Thrilling. You know he has the hots for you, right?"

"He was sweet. He thinks I'm wholesome. But yeah, he does have that look in his eye."

"You could cure that."

"When he touched my hand, it was like he was testing the waters. So, I just grabbed his. We walked around holding hands. We're taking things slow."

"Wait. That's it? No bed?"

"Leslie, taking him to bed would ruin it."

"You're right. You'd probably scare him."

"Not sure if that's a compliment."

"Are you going to tell him?"

"Tell him what?"

"What you do for tuition."

"I've gotten pretty good at keeping those two lives separate."

"Just saying. But if he finds out from someone else…"

"I know. I'll deal with it before things get too serious. What about you? Anything from the police?"

"Nothing new. I figure if my new boyfriend doesn't warm up soon, I'll head back to the apartment by the weekend."

"They're probably done with the break-in investigation. But they might look into it further if they connect me to Dmitri before he was killed."

"You think they'll call?"

"Any day now."

Chapter 7

"Sometimes the loudest messages are the silent ones." – Dara

Aiden texted: *"Ready for our date?"*

I smiled despite myself. Straightforward and sincere, so very Aiden.

"Sure, I'll be ready in a few minutes," I replied.

Thirty minutes later, I slid into a chair across from him at a cozy café nestled on a quiet side street. The aroma of freshly baked pastries mingled with the scent of coffee, wrapping us in a comforting warmth. Aiden's eyes lit up as I sit down, and a quiet, inexplicable joy fills me.

"You look beautiful," he says, his words earnest and unembellished.

I blush, ducking my head slightly. "Thank you. This place is charming."

"I hoped you'd like it," he says, leaning back with a grin. "They have the best scones in town. And no crickets like at the farm."

His playful tone coaxes a laugh out of me. "The farm is nice, but I could do without the nighttime orchestra."

As we chatted over tea and pastries, I felt the tension I didn't even realize I was carrying slowly dissolve. His openness is disarming, and his attention is unwavering in a way that felt both comforting and new.

"So," I say, curious, "what made you want to become a professor?"

His eyes light up, and he leans forward slightly. "The first time I saw a student truly grasp something. When you can see the light bulb go on in their mind. That moment of understanding is... addictive."

"I can see that," I reply, nodding. "There's something about helping people see things in a new way. That's part of why I got into neuroscience."

Aiden tilts his head, intrigued. "What sparked that interest?"

I take a sip of tea before answering. "I was always fascinated by the things people didn't say. When I was a kid, I noticed how people's words didn't always match their body language or intentions. I guess you could say I became obsessed with understanding those unspoken dynamics. It led me to study language first. I love language and how language shapes thoughts and conveys meaning. But eventually, I wanted to know how the brain works behind it all."

Aiden raises an eyebrow, a playful smile tugging at his lips. "Loving language but focusing on what's not said? That's an interesting contradiction. Sounds very Sherlock Holmes of you."

I laugh, shaking my head. "I guess it does. I've always been more interested in discerning meaning than taking things at face value. Truth is often found in questions, not answers. Puzzles intrigue me."

"Your intellect must've stood out early," he says. "Your grades in my class are perfect, and I've seen your record. Were you one of those kids who skipped grades?"

"Not exactly," I say, shrugging. "But they did test my IQ in middle school. It was high enough that they recommended advanced programs. That's where I really fell in love with languages. Languages made sense to me in Latin, French, and ancient Greek. I learned that language doesn't just express thought. It shapes it."

"Latin and ancient Greek?" he says, mock-stunned. "Okay, now I'm feeling underqualified to sit here with you."

I smile, warmed by his genuine interest. "Don't sell yourself short. You're the one sparking light bulbs in classrooms."

"And here I thought I was the intellectual in this dynamic," he teases, leaning back. "But I must admit, your ability to read between the lines, and people, is impressive."

"I just pay attention to patterns," I say modestly. "But it's part of what drew me to neuroscience. Understanding what's happening in the brain when people communicate, or fail to, could change so much. Interpersonal communication is complex."

Aiden studies me for a moment, his expression thoughtful. "You know, Dara, you make me feel like I've been approaching things from the wrong angle. Maybe it's not just about what's said, but what isn't."

"Sometimes the loudest messages are the silent ones," I reply, meeting his gaze.

We fall into a comfortable rhythm, our conversation flowing as naturally as the quiet stream of people coming and going around us. For once, I'm not dissecting every word or gesture, not questioning his intentions. And in this simplicity, I enjoy the moment for what it is.

"By the way, I need to visit a friend in the hospital tomorrow," I said. The words tasted wrong in my mouth, too ordinary for what they meant.

I push open the hospital room door, and the sight of Susan makes my breath hitch. Her face is pale, drawn tight against the pillow, with dark shadows under her eyes. The rhythmic beeping of the monitors seems to echo the ache in my chest.

"Hey, you," I say softly, stepping toward her bed.

Her eyelids flutter, and recognition lights up her weary face. "Dara? You came."

I take her hand, careful not to disturb the IV taped to her fragile skin. "Of course I did. How are you feeling?"

She tries to smile, but it wavers. "Like I got hit by a truck," she murmurs.

I swallow the lump in my throat, guilt pressing hard against my ribs. "Susan, I'm so sorry. This is my fault."

Her head shakes weakly, her eyes steady on mine. "No, Dara. Don't do that. None of this is on you."

"Did you..." I hesitate, lowering my voice. "Did you see who did this?"

Susan's gaze darts toward the door before returning to me. Her voice drops to a whisper. "I'm not sure. But the accent…Russian, I think."

A chill prickles at my skin. A professional? A foreign hitman? The pieces shift and click into place, and the picture forming in my mind terrifies me.

"The police have been asking questions," she continues, her voice tinged with fear. "About you. About our work."

I tense, my grip on her hand tightening. "What did you tell them?"

"Nothing specific," she says, her voice trembling. "But Dara... what have we gotten mixed up in? They asked if you'd been with Dmitri too. You must have, or they wouldn't have asked. How are you involved, Dara?"

My stomach twists, a nauseating churn of dread and determination. "I don't know," I admit, my words quiet but firm. "I saw him once. Before you did."

Sunday Morning – Across town

"Good morning, everyone," George greeted warmly, standing in a world far removed from the one Dara navigated every day. His rich baritone resonated through the small Sunday School class. "Today, we're in Luke 7:41-43 and we'll keep reading further if we have time. It's one of my favorites. Would someone read the passages for us?

A woman in the front row raised her hand, her Bible already open. George gave her an encouraging nod, his expression contemplative as she began.

"'A certain moneylender had two debtors. One owed five hundred denarii and the other fifty. When neither could pay, he canceled both of their debts. Now, which of them will love him more?' Simon answered, 'The one, I suppose, for whom he canceled the larger debt.' And Jesus said to him, 'You have judged rightly.'"

As she finished reading, the room grew quiet, the weight of the words settling over the group. George let the silence linger, allowing the lesson to resonate. His thoughtful gaze moved across the room, landing momentarily on each face.

"Thank you for that beautiful reading," he said, his voice warm and steady. "This parable invites us to reflect on the relationship between forgiveness and love. But before we dive into the discussion, let us pray."

George bowed his head, and the room followed suit. "Heavenly Father, we gather here today with open hearts, seeking to understand your boundless grace. Teach us to forgive as you forgive, to release burdens that bind us, and to love deeply, even when it feels undeserved. Amen."

The collective "Amen" echoed softly, a shared breath of reverence.

George looked up, his kind eyes meeting those around him. "Now, let's talk about this parable. What stands out to you about the moneylender's actions?"

The woman who had read earlier raised her hand again. "He forgave both debts, even though one was much larger."

George smiled and nodded. "Exactly. The moneylender didn't measure forgiveness by the size of the debt. It was an act of grace, freely given. Sometimes," he paused, his voice softening, "the hardest debt to cancel is the one we owe ourselves. Forgiveness begins within, and it can be the most challenging and freeing gift we give. And while the lender didn't measure forgiveness by the size of the debt, the one with the largest debt understands most about the depth of that grace."

The class ended, and the room was emptying, voices murmuring as people filed out. George stood at the front, tidying his notes, when he caught sight of a tall, broad-shouldered man lingering near the back. Their eyes met, and a quiet intensity passed between them in an unspoken exchange. The man nodded, and George returned the gesture with a flicker of recognition.

Once the room cleared, the man approached, his presence commanding without being overbearing. George motioned him toward a quiet corner, away from the door.

"You wanted to see me?" the man asked, his voice low and measured.

George nodded. "I need to coordinate with a couple of our federal contacts. It's sensitive."

The man, a retired FBI agent named Randy, crossed his arms and smiled knowingly. "You know them better than I do, George. Half the tools the NSA uses were built on your patents; signal work, pattern detection, things they don't put on brochures. I think you have a higher security clearance than I do."

George smirked faintly. "The U.S. intel community gets skittish because I profit from the technology. I try not to call in favors, even with my clearance and longstanding relationships."

"They get skittish because they're never quite sure who else has access to your tech."

"They know I have access keys to monitor any nation that poses a national security risk."

"Intercept capabilities they both love and hate, I'm sure. You think they don't trust you?"

"My colleagues in the intel community trust no one," George said, his voice dropping slightly. "They'd pull my clearance in a heartbeat if I stepped out of line. I just don't want anything to appear personal."

Randy raised an eyebrow. "Keep your friends close and your enemies closer, huh?"

"I'm their friend," George said, his tone steady. "But they're cautious. They turn a blind eye if they think I'm cozying up to foreign governments, so long as it serves national interests. But like you said, those access keys I own are their greatest asset and their biggest fear."

Randy let out a dry laugh. "Sounds like a love-hate relationship. But why bring me into this? You're the one who got rich off the intel game, not me."

"I need the FBI in my corner," George said plainly. "This needs to be clear-cut business, not personal. The FBI will want my intel, but this situation requires some inter-agency coordination."

Randy leaned in slightly. "You're asking the Bureau to look the other way?"

"No, Randy. I'm saying we can help each other. The agency tracks me. It's their job and I want the Bureau in the loop before I visit an old acquaintance."

"Who's the acquaintance?" Randy asked, his tone sharpening.

"An attorney who was Dmitri Krushnic's lawyer. The Feds are already watching him due to the recent Russian mob hit. They'll flag me when I meet him because of his ties to foreign nationals and suspicions over his connection to Dmitri's assassination."

"And you want me to find out which FBI agents are monitoring him so they don't misinterpret your involvement?"

"Exactly. I'll inform the agency beforehand to keep everything above board. But they don't always loop in the Bureau, and I don't want things tangled. We both know how this works."

Randy shook his head, his skepticism evident. "Forgive me, George, but this sounds like overkill. Are these precautions really necessary?"

George's lips twitched into a faint smile. "You don't trust your Sunday school teacher?"

George strides past the secretary in John Mitchell's law office; his steps are decisive and unwavering. The young woman starts to protest, but George silences her with a raised hand, his gaze locked on John's office door as he pushes it open.

John looks up from his desk, his expression flickering between surprise and amusement. The tension in the air feels almost tangible, a live wire crackling between them.

George wastes no time. His voice is sharp, cutting through the room like a blade. "I'll get to the point, John. Dara is off-limits. And good luck untangling yourself from the mess you've made with the Russians."

John leans back in his chair, a smug chuckle escaping his lips. "Dara? You do know she's an escort that goes by the name of Carol. I didn't peg you as the call girl type. You've always been so a squeaky clean guy."

George's voice drops, icy and controlled. "You know nothing about her or my relationships. What you *do* know is how often you get in over your head. Let me make this simple: Dara stays out of whatever game you're playing. Am I clear?"

John's smirk deepens, his tone dripping with faux curiosity. "I must admit, you've surprised me, George. I never imagined you'd care about someone like her. Showing up here? That's a new move for you. It's been a while."

"My caring is irrelevant to you," George snaps. "What's relevant is that you keep your distance. Understood?"

"Crystal," John replies smoothly, his voice laced with mock sincerity.

George narrows his eyes. "You're no longer on my payroll, John. You lost that privilege long ago. You have a history of overstepping boundaries. It's why the intel community will no longer hire you either."

John shrugs, feigning nonchalance. "You and Jillian just never appreciated my methods. But barging in here, accusing me of schemes without proof? Come on, George. I'm a prominent, honest attorney."

George lets the silence stretch, his unspoken thoughts heavy in the air. "John," he says finally, the name laced with quiet menace. "I think you know I'm not someone you want to annoy."

John's expression tightens briefly before he masks it with a grin. "Ah, yes. The man with all the intel toys. The man who made a fortune from secrets. Always thinking you know everything and that includes everything about me. But here's the thing, George. You don't scare me. I've done nothing wrong."

"Good," George replies, his voice steady and cold. "Then you won't have any trouble continuing to do nothing wrong. Stay away from Dara and any of Jillian's girls. I'm not asking."

John holds up his hands in mock surrender, his grin never wavering. "Crystal clear, George."

As George stands up, he sees an ashtray on John's desk full of cigarette butts. George takes it and empties the cigarette butts into the trash. "You should clean up, John." George discreetly palms a single butt, fresh, still faintly warm as he then replaces the ashtray.

John never sees it. George then turns to leave, his steps as measured and resolute as when he arrived. John watches him go, his smirk faltering ever so slightly as the door swings shut behind him.

Chapter 8

"But words and silence are two sides of the same coin, aren't they? Both tell a story." – Dara

The office is dim, shadows stretching into the corners like waiting predators. Sasha sits behind the desk, his face partially obscured by the gloom, his posture unnervingly casual. The faint hum of fluorescent lights buzzes overhead. John hesitantly enters, his heart pounding, and sits opposite Sasha. The air between them feels charged, electric with unspoken threats.

"John, my friend," Sasha purrs, his accent curling around the words. "We need to discuss the arms deal."

John forces a smile, though his palms are damp. "Of course, Sasha. What would you like to know?"

Sasha leans forward, the light catching his eyes, which seem to glint with something predatory. "We obviously knew about your little... arrangement with Dmitri. The blackmail."

John freezes, his carefully neutral expression cracking for just a moment before he regains control. "I'm afraid I don't know what you mean," he says, his voice calm but strained.

Sasha's lips curl into a cold, predatory smile. "Oh, I think you do. Poor Dmitri. His greed made him sloppy. And his sloppiness became your opportunity, didn't it?"

Realization crashes over John, his throat dry. The mob killed Dmitri. His fears about Sasha confronting Dara were true. They know about the blackmail. They know *everything*. Did they know about the note? He shifts uncomfortably in his seat, tugging at his tie.

"I... I can explain," John stammers.

Sasha raises a hand, silencing him with a gesture. "No need. What's done is done. But understand this, John. You work for me now." Sasha leans closer, his voice dropping to a whisper. "You don't want to end up like Dmitri."

"Of course," John manages, his voice trembling. "Whatever you need."

Sasha nods, his expression sharpening. "Good. I'm glad we understand each other. Now, about your role. You were the intermediary between Dmitri and the U.S. arms company, correct?"

"Yes, but only as an attorney handling contracts," John says quickly, trying to downplay his involvement.

Sasha chuckles, the sound low and humorless. "John, let's not pretend you were just a hired pen-pusher. Dmitri's weaknesses were well-known; his greed, need for secrecy, and penchant for young women. You saw it all, and you exploited it."

John's face pales. "I may have... negotiated for a larger fee, but I was just facilitating—"

Sasha slams his hand on the desk, cutting him off. "Facilitating? You set him up. You had leverage. You were preparing to use it. And you thought no one else noticed."

John's eyes dart around the room, panic evident. Sasha smiles, leaning back in his chair, exuding a terrifying calm. "We intercepted the photos you intended to use. You should have been more careful about whose hands you let in on your schemes."

The truth, unspoken but undeniable, hangs in the air. John swallows hard, realizing just how deep he's sinking in.

Sasha's voice drops again, icy and deliberate. "Now, about this Dara girl. Handle her, John. And any other loose ends."

John blinks, his mask of professionalism faltering. "Dara? The escort? She's just—"

"A liability," Sasha interrupts, his tone like a knife. "She knows you set up the date and the photos. If she connects you to this, that thread could lead to the arms deal, and to us."

John's hands twitch in his lap. "It's not that simple. She's not a typical... escort. People are watching her. Important people. She's got connections."

Sasha's eyes narrow, a flicker of curiosity breaking through his calculated exterior. "Connections? Interesting. Perhaps there's more to her than you're letting on. Either way, this only proves she knows more than she should."

John hesitates, fear etched in his face. Sasha's gaze bores into him, reading the secrets John can't risk sharing: the note with his DNA, George's involvement, the thin ice he's already skating on.

"Deal with her, John," Sasha says finally, his voice as cold as steel. "Before I have to."

John nods stiffly, his mind racing. The weight of Sasha's words feels like a noose tightening around his neck.

As John rises to leave, Sasha picks up his phone, his tone indifferent. "Oh, and John? Keep laundering that arms money. Dmitri's absence changes nothing. Remember, you work for us now."

John opens his mouth slightly to respond but thinks better of it and exits the room. The door clicks shut behind him.

Sasha speaks into the phone, his voice low but commanding. "John is too weak to be trusted or clean things up."

The soft clink of silverware against plates fills the cozy Italian restaurant, underscored by the faint hum of conversation around us. Across the table, Aiden's warm brown eyes meet mine, grounding me in the moment. "So, tell me more about your plans as school winds down," he says, his voice genuine and tinged with curiosity.

I take a sip of wine, the rich flavor lingering as I gather my thoughts. "Well, nothing special. I'll finish my degree this semester. Just a few more exams to go, then graduation."

"That's fantastic," Aiden replies, leaning forward slightly, his enthusiasm contagious. "You must be excited."

"I am," I admit, though the word feels heavy. A mix of determination and anxiety churns in my chest. "It's been a long road."

Aiden's expression softens, his open and supportive gaze steady. "And I want you to know, I'm here if you need anything."

The pang of guilt that follows his words feels almost reflexive. I glance down at my plate, my voice quieter. "About that… I'm sorry for imposing on you, staying at the farmhouse."

He waves off my apology with an easy gesture. "Don't even think about it. I'm happy to help. And I promise, I'll respect your privacy. The guest room is yours as long as you need it. Plus, it gives me an excuse to spend more time with you."

I study his face, searching for cracks in the sincerity, but there are none. Just Aiden, uncomplicated and earnest. A rare thing in my world.

"Thank you," I say softly, letting the words carry more weight than usual. "It's been a long time since… well, since I've been able to lean on anyone. I've been on my own for so long. No father, no family except my mother until she passed."

Aiden's lips curl into a warm, reassuring smile. "Your mother must have been an amazing woman. Dragging you to church, raising such a wholesome girl."

My stomach twists at the word "wholesome." If only he knew. "Well," I mutter, trying to deflect, "I'm not that wholesome."

His eyebrows lift, amusement flickering across his face. "Oh? So, what rebellious streak are you hiding?"

I meet his gaze briefly before focusing on my plate, hoping he can't read too deeply into the cracks. "It's not about rebellion. It's just… people. Everyone has their own agenda. Everyone has their own view of what defines wholesome. Regardless, I'm not sure anyone is perfectly wholesome by any definition."

"You don't give yourself enough credit," he says after a moment. "You see people so clearly. You notice things most don't. That takes more than intelligence. It takes insight."

The compliment catches me off guard, but I let a small smile escape. "I've always been good at noticing what's not said. Words are easy to manipulate. Intentions, not so much."

He leans back, studying me like a puzzle he's determined to solve. "You're like Sherlock Holmes but with a love for language and thought. Isn't that a contradiction? Loving words, yet fascinated by what's left unspoken?"

"Maybe," I reply, a light laugh escaping. "But words and silence are two sides of the same coin, aren't they? Both tell a story."

Aiden chuckles, shaking his head. "You're something else, Dara."

I lower my gaze to my plate, suddenly aware of the warmth spreading through my chest. His admiration feels real, untainted by ulterior motives. He thinks he sees me for who I am, but does he? Do we really know anyone? In my view, all of us need redemption at some level. For a fleeting moment, I wondered what it would be like to tell him everything; to be seen, wholly, and unmasked, but not tonight.

Later that evening, the farmhouse is still, the quiet broken only by the occasional chirp of crickets. The day's weight presses on me as I pick up my phone. My thumb hovers over Jillian's number momentarily before I hit call.

"Dara," Jillian answers, her voice tight with concern. "How are you holding up?"

"I'm ready to come back," I say, trying to sound confident. "I can't hide forever."

There's a long pause, the static of her hesitation almost audible. "Are you sure?" she finally asks. "Things are still… complicated."

I close my eyes, steadying myself. "I need to finish school. And I need to bank a bit more money before graduation."

"Dara…" Jillian sighs heavily. "It's not safe right now."

"Then limit me. Only the safest clients," I insist, the edge in my voice betraying my nerves. "I can't just stop my life."

Another pause, longer this time. I hold my breath.

"Alright," Jillian concedes reluctantly. "But only carefully vetted clients. And you can see George on Tuesday. He's safe."

Relief washes over me like a wave. "Thank you, Jillian."

"Be careful, Dara. Please."

"I will," I reply, my voice softer now. When I hang up, my thoughts already leap ahead to Tuesday. The thought of George steadies me, even as the rest of my world threatens to spiral.

The soft hum of the city buzzes faintly outside George's penthouse windows. The room is immaculate, just like him; clean lines, polished surfaces, and a view that speaks of power and privilege. I often wonder if this meeting place is his real second apartment as it lacks something. George greets me with his usual warmth, but tension is beneath the surface.

"Dara," he says, his voice calm but weighted. "I'm glad you're here."

I force a smile that turns into a smirk. "I really had no choice. You're the safest of my clients. At least that's what Jillian thinks."

George smiles and gestures toward the plush leather couch. "Sit. Let's talk."

I settle into the couch, its luxury almost making me uncomfortable. George remains standing, his posture stiff, his hands clasped behind his back like a commander preparing for battle.

"Dara," he begins, his tone serious, "you shouldn't return to this work."

My instinctive reaction is to push back, but the firmness in his voice gives me pause. He raises a hand, preempting my argument.

"It's too dangerous," he continues. "You don't need to do this anymore. Not with everything going on."

"I can take care of myself," I say, a flicker of irritation creeping into my voice.

He sighs, the weight of his concern evident. "I know you can. But sometimes, it's okay to accept help. You've done enough, Dara."

I study him, my mind swirling with questions. Who is this man who's so invested in my life? What is it he's not telling me? Why does he always seem to know so much more than I ever expected?

"George," I say carefully, "I appreciate your concern. But I need to finish my degree. I'm so close."

"Your safety is more important than—"

"Than my independence?" I snap, cutting him off. "This is my life, George. I've been on my own for years, and I'm not stopping now."

His brow furrows, but he doesn't interrupt. I press on. "Aiden's letting me stay at his farmhouse. It's safe. He's... safe."

His eyebrows lift slightly at the mention of Aiden. "Aiden. The professor. Yes, I understand you've been spending time with him."

The way he says it, casual yet knowing, sends a ripple of unease through me. I don't press him on how he knows so much because I sense it between his words. Instead, I nod. "He doesn't know about... this. My work."

George exhales, running a hand through his silver hair. "It's your last few weeks of class. You've saved enough money. Escorting now is unnecessary. And dangerous."

I narrow my eyes, suspicion threading through my thoughts. There's something in his tone, something he's not saying. George is an enigma, and for all my skills at reading people, I've never quite been able to crack him. He has been the only one I could never decode. And I know, without knowing how, that he has secrets of his own. Not being able to read him has never felt accidental.

"What do you know about Dmitri's murder, George?" I ask, my voice sharp.

He stiffens, barely, but enough for me to notice. "Only what's been in the news."

I don't believe him. Not for a second. But I let it slide, for now.

"I'll be careful," I say instead, my tone softer. "But I need to finish this on my terms. You still have the note?"

George nods reluctantly. "It's safe. And so will you be, as long as you stay at the farmhouse. If you need anything, you know you can call me."

I study him, gratitude warring with unease. George is the closest thing I have to a constant in my life, but even constants cast shadows. I nod and agree to consider cutting back.

Later that evening, I sit at the farmhouse desk, my laptop glowing softly in the dark room. The faint hum of crickets filters through the window. The world feels still, but my mind races.

"What's my next move?" I mutter, fingers hovering over the keyboard.

I open my bank account, the numbers blurring as I stare at them. Enough for tuition. Enough to finish school. But is it worth the cost of staying in this life for even a moment longer? Maybe George is right. My independence feels like both a shield and a burden, and its weight presses against my chest.

My phone buzzes, breaking my thoughts. Leslie's name flashes on the screen.

"Hey, Les," I answer, trying to sound cheerful.

"Dara! Are you okay? I haven't seen you in days," she says, her voice tinged with worry.

"I'm fine," I lie. "Just... studying. What about you?"

"Worried about you," she admits. "When are you coming home?"

Home. The word sticks in my throat. "Soon," I promise, though the word feels hollow. "How's the apartment?"

Leslie chats on, her words fading into the background as I glance at my email. Another request from a regular client stares back at me. My finger hovers over the delete button, indecision gnawing at me.

"Dara?" Leslie's voice cuts through. "Are you even listening?"

"Sorry," I mumble, "just distracted."

We hang up, and the silence of the farmhouse wraps around me. The weight of my decisions is heavier than ever. Safety or independence? Security or freedom?

I close my laptop and glance out the window. The moonlight casts long shadows over the yard, and for a moment, I think I see movement. A shadow slipping just out of sight.

I take a deep breath, my chest tightening. Sometimes, it's hard to tell the good guys from the bad.

Chapter 9

"…genius doesn't make you immune to the world's cruelty." – *Dara*

The fire crackles softly, casting flickering golden light across Aiden's living room. I sink into the plush armchair, letting its warmth envelop me. The room smells faintly of cedarwood and tea, a comforting mix that feels both foreign and strangely inviting. Across from me, Aiden leans forward, elbows on his knees, his warm brown eyes alive with curiosity. It wasn't the time of year for a fire, but fireplaces were new to me, the evenings could be chilly, and Aiden insisted that in the country, sitting around a fire was always appropriate.

"I have to say, Dara," he begins, his tone both admiring and teasing, "your academic record is... well, it's impressive, to say the least. I've been finishing up final grades for class."

I tilt my head, feigning casual indifference. "Have you been researching me, Professor?"

He chuckles, a faint blush creeping into his cheeks. "When you have a student who's clearly exceptional, it's hard not to be curious. Your transcripts leak that you're a bit of a genius. You should seriously consider graduate school."

"Genius might be overstating it," I say, shrugging, though I can't stop the corners of my mouth from twitching into a small smile. "I've always tested well. That's all."

"No, it's more than that," he counters, his voice earnest. "Your work isn't just smart. It's insightful. Creative. You have a rare mind, and I'm not biased when I look over these class papers."

The compliment warms me, but I feel exposed as if Aiden is seeing through the carefully curated version of myself I show the world. "Well," I say, trying to steer the conversation, "I suppose the governor's school helped. Summers spent with other overachievers. It was a whole new world from my small high school."

Aiden's brow lifts in interest. "Summers spent at Governor's school? Advanced courses, peer pressure of the good kind... Tell me more."

I take a deep breath, allowing myself a small glimpse into the past. "It was transformative," I admit. "For the first time, I was surrounded by people who got it, who got me. There was no pretending, no need to downplay anything. We had access to advanced coursework and research opportunities. It wasn't just academic but about embracing your potential without fear. My mom was my biggest cheerleader."

"She must've been proud," Aiden says, his voice soft.

I nod, my throat tightening slightly. "She was. She worked so hard to make sure I could go. A scholarship made everything possible. After she passed, finishing school became more than a goal. It was a promise. Even if I had to do it alone."

His expression shifts, thoughtful and intent. "And here you are, close to keeping that promise. But with everything you've said... your focus on language, your love for unraveling what's not being said. It's almost... Sherlockian."

"Sherlockian? That's a word?" I echo, raising an eyebrow.

He grins. "You love words."

I laugh softly. "Maybe it's just my way of understanding the world. People rarely say what they truly mean. Their words are the surface; the truth is underneath."

Aiden leans back, his gaze steady. "And yet, here you are, opening up a little more. It's nice. A contradiction, sure, but one that works."

The fire pops, breaking the moment, and I glance at the flames. The room feels heavier, like we've stepped into uncharted territory. I'm not used to this, being seen, being understood.

Aiden shifts slightly, a faint smile playing on his lips. "Your last name, Keene. And you're smart. Any relation to Elliot Keene? I'm joking, of course, as I know from his biography that he didn't have any children. But he did have ancestors and other family. "

I blink, startled. "No, not directly. I've gotten the question before, though."

"He's always fascinated me," Aiden says. "A pioneer of computer science. Codebreaker. Math genius. One of the quiet architects of modern intelligence."

I nod, my thoughts racing. "He developed the first ideas for computers decades before they were realized. Formulas that are still relevant today. Maybe even more so."

"Absolutely," Aiden agrees, his eyes lighting up. "His insights on artificial intelligence, the ethical questions he raised... decades ahead of his time."

"And yet," I say quietly, "despite all he gave to the world, his personal life was... devastating. He was persecuted for who he was, and his secrets regarding his personal life and sexuality overshadowed his brilliance. It's a reminder that genius doesn't make you immune to the world's cruelty."

Aiden's gaze softens. "A dark chapter in history. But even in tragedy, his legacy endures. It was a time when there was much suspicion if a man didn't marry. He was judged heavily despite his brilliance and overlooked for Nobel Prizes as a result. I know his story from a computer language course I took in college."

The silence stretches between us, comfortable yet charged. I feel his eyes on me, not with fleeting desire but with a depth I'm not used to.

"You know," Aiden says, his voice barely above a whisper, "I can't decide if I'm more drawn to your beauty or your intellect."

Heat rises to my cheeks. "I hope it's both," I say, surprising myself with my boldness.

He smiles. The kind of smile that reaches his eyes. "Definitely both."

For a moment, the world outside fades away. No secrets, no shadows, just the crackle of the fire, the weight of his words, and the quiet possibility of something real.

The crackling fireplace in Aiden's cozy living room feels distant now, its warmth unable to compete with the chill spreading through my chest. His words of admiration still linger in the air, but they knot my stomach tighter instead of comfort. His sincerity and belief in me are everything I've ever wanted, yet everything I fear. The weight of my secrets presses down on me like a heavy stone, making this connection feel fragile, and fleeting. Just as one of the world's great minds was judged for what he hid, I carried my own hidden life.

My gaze drifts to the window, where the late afternoon shadows stretch long across the farmyard. How long can I keep this up? A life I desperately want but feel I don't deserve. The thought gnaws at me: will this, too, be discarded with my past when I graduate? Is Aiden simply a chapter, or something more? I could lose more than a Nobel Prize for what I did in the bedroom with men every night. Society can be a harsh judge, as times haven't changed that much.

"Dara?" Aiden's voice pulls me back, his concern unmistakable. "Are you alright?"

I force a smile, hoping it's convincing. "Just lost in thought."

Before he can ask more, the crunch of tires on gravel snaps both our attention to the driveway. My body tenses instinctively.

"Expecting someone?" I ask, trying to keep my voice steady.

Aiden stands, peering out the window. "Looks like a delivery truck."

Panic blooms in my chest like wildfire. "Don't answer it," I blurt, the urgency in my voice startling even me.

He hesitates, then moves toward the door despite my protest, caution etched into every step. "Dara, it's just a delivery. Are you still worried about-"

"Please," I cut him off, hating the edge of desperation in my tone. "I just… I have a bad feeling."

Aiden hesitates, the conflict plain on his face. Reassure me or trust his instincts? Finally, he nods. "Okay, I won't open the door. But Dara, we need to talk about this. The break-in at your apartment… it's understandable that you're shaken. But you can't keep living in fear."

I nod, unable to explain the real source of my fear. If only he knew about the tangled web of lies I've spun, the shadows that cling to my life. As he moves to draw the curtains, my stomach churns. How much longer can I keep this act together before it all unravels?

The doorbell chimes, slicing through the silence like a knife. My heart leaps into my throat. Aiden's eyes meet mine, questioning.

I nod reluctantly, my pulse pounding in my ears.

He approaches the door with measured caution. "Who is it?" he calls out.

Silence. Then, another impatient ring.

Aiden reaches for the handle, and I want to scream at him to stop. My voice is trapped, doubt and fear battling for dominance. Am I just being paranoid?

The door creaks open. "Can I help—"

A blur of motion. The delivery man lunges forward as soon as the door cracks, something metallic glinting in his hand. Aiden stumbles back, his face a mix of shock and disbelief.

"Aiden!" I scream, frozen in terror.

Before I can react, another figure materializes on the porch, moving swiftly. The cold barrel of a gun presses against the delivery man's temple.

"Drop it," the new arrival commands, his voice calm but unyielding.

The delivery man freezes, his eyes wide with surprise. The weapon in his hand wavers before the second man smoothly disarms him. The entire exchange happens in seconds.

Aiden scrambles back toward me, his body instinctively placing itself between me and the unfolding chaos. My mind spins as I catalog details about the second gunman holding the attacker at bay: military bearing, a concealed holster, a discreet communication device in his ear. Every detail screams professional. But whose side is he on?

The second gunman's eyes flick to me. "Ms. Keene," he says evenly, not lowering his weapon. "Are you alright?"

Aiden turns to me, his face etched with confusion. "Dara, do you know this guy?"

I shake my head, my voice caught in my throat. "No, I… I don't think so."

The man's next words chill me to my core. "I'm part of your protective detail, ma'am. We've been monitoring the situation. You're safe now. Call the police."

Protective detail? My mind whirls. Who could have arranged this? And why?

"What's going on?" Aiden's voice breaks through my spiraling thoughts, equal parts concern and frustration.

I wish I had answers. But all I have is the weight of secrets, the sting of half-truths, and the unnerving realization that the shadows in my life might not be as distant as I'd hoped. As the stranger steps further inside and orders the attacker to remain still, a million questions race through my mind. But one thought rises above them all: are these shadows here to save or bury me?

The wail of sirens tears through the tense silence, growing louder as two police cruisers barrel into the driveway, tires screeching to a halt. Officers spill out, weapons drawn, their movements sharp and deliberate.

"It's okay, guys!" shouts the man holding the delivery man at bay, his voice cutting through the chaos. "Situation under control!"

My heart races as I watch the officer's approach cautiously, their eyes darting between him and the subdued intruder. One of them, a gruff-looking sergeant with salt-and-pepper hair, nods in recognition.

"Michaels," the sergeant says, his tone carrying both respect and curiosity. "What've we got?"

Michaels doesn't lower his weapon, keeping it trained on the would-be intruder. "Attempted home invasion. Subject armed and dangerous."

The officers spring into action, cuffing the delivery man with swift precision. Their efficiency and unspoken coordination suggest this isn't their first encounter with Michaels.

"Russian passport in his wallet," one officer calls out, holding up the identification. "And there's a cache of weapons in the van."

A chill washes over me, tightening my chest. Russian? Weapons? This is no random break-in.

The sergeant turns back to Michaels, a flicker of unease in his otherwise composed demeanor. "Good work. Your team's intel was spot on."

My analytical mind reels, questions stacking faster than I can process. I step forward before I can stop myself, my voice breaking through the controlled chaos. "Excuse me, but who exactly are you? And who do you work for?"

Michaels finally holsters his weapon, his expression unreadable. "I'm not at liberty to disclose that information, Ms. Keene."

The sound of my name on his lips makes my stomach drop. "But you know who I am," I press, the frustration and fear bubbling over. "Is this... is this George's doing?"

Michaels hesitates, a flicker of recognition crossing his face at the mention of George. He doesn't confirm it, but his silence speaks louder than words. The unspoken signals are all there.

"Please," I plead, my voice cracking. "I need to understand what's happening."

For a moment, something softens in Michaels' steely exterior. "I'm sorry, ma'am. I truly can't say more. Your safety is our priority. But I would advise you to remain here at the farmhouse as much as possible. It's easier to protect you here outside of your studies at school."

I nod, but it's an empty gesture. Are there men assigned to protect me? Why the flicker of recognition when I mention George? That's the obvious reason they are here. The unanswered questions hang heavy in the air as the officers lead the intruder away. My world feels like it's unraveling, every thread connected to George, the enigmatic man who seems to know far more about my life than I ever understood. I wondered if that was a good thing as the unknown still nagged at me. George obviously knew who I really was, where I lived, and who I dated. How much more does he know? How long has he known? George knows my real name.

Aiden's hand on my shoulder jolts me back to the present. His touch is warm and steady, but his eyes are searching, filled with questions I'm not ready to answer.

"Dara," he says softly, his voice calm but firm. "What's really going on here?"

I glance away, the weight of his gaze too much to bear. "It's probably nothing," I lie, my words hollow. "Just a random robbery attempt." My eyes squint slightly, knowing the explanation isn't believable.

Aiden raises an eyebrow, his skepticism clear. "A robbery attempt with a Russian passport, a cache of weapons, and a protective detail outside? Dara, come on."

"I..." My voice falters. The lie feels like sand crumbling in my mouth. "I was piling lies upon lies with Aiden."

He sighs, raking a hand through his hair. "Look, clearly, there's more to this than you're letting on. And that's okay. I just want you to know you can trust me. And you definitely need to stay here if you're in trouble. For your safety."

His words hit me like a blow, unexpected and overwhelming. **Trust.** It is such a simple word, but it feels impossibly heavy at this moment.

"I know," I whisper, the admission scraping against my carefully constructed defenses. "I know I need to tell you more. And I'm not really in trouble. It's just... complicated."

Aiden takes my hand, his thumb brushing slow, deliberate circles over my palm. "I understand. And I'll wait. However long it takes. Let me help protect you from whatever those men outside think you need protecting from because obviously someone wants to hurt you."

The sincerity in his gaze undoes me. For the first time in so long, I feel truly seen, not as a puzzle to solve or a role to play, but as a person. And I suddenly feel safe.

"You trust me?" I ask, my voice barely audible, almost childlike in its vulnerability.

"Without question," he says, the certainty in his tone unwavering.

The room seems to close around us, the weight of the moment pressing down. Outside, the red and blue lights of the police cars fade as the cruisers soon pull away. Inside, the silence stretches, broken only by the crackle of the fireplace.

I meet Aiden's gaze, a thousand unspoken fears and desires swirling in my chest. The thought of dragging him into my tangled, dangerous world terrifies me. But the idea of pushing him away feels even worse.

Something's got to give. Secrets like mine can't stay buried forever. I just hope when the truth finally surfaces, I don't lose the one solid connection I have left. I need to take control.

The next morning, the door clicks shut behind me as I step into the apartment, the familiar scent of vanilla candles and Leslie's perfume wrapping around me like a memory. It's been days since I've been here, but it no longer feels like home. Not after everything. Not after the invasion. The attack at the farmhouse. The way my life has been split into before and after.

Aiden waits by the door, his presence steady as I move through the space, grabbing what little I need; clothes, my laptop, a few books. I should feel more attached to this place, but I don't. The farmhouse feels safer now. George's men have made sure of that.

Leslie's voice calls from the living room. "Dara? That you?"

I step out, tucking my hair behind my ear. "Yeah, just grabbing some things."

She's curled up on the couch in leggings and an oversized sweater, the glow from her phone lighting up her face. News alerts flicker across the screen. Then, she spots the men outside the door standing just beyond Aiden as he moves to shut it. Her brows knit together, glancing from them to me.

"So… who are the guys in the hallway?"

I follow her gaze. George's men. At least, I think they are George's men. They are at least protective. Their presence no longer startles me, but I see the flicker of unease in Leslie's expression.

I force a casual shrug. "They're with me, I guess." Tossing a duffel bag onto the couch, I try to downplay it.

Leslie arches an eyebrow. "I knew you attracted men, Dara, but this is next level. Since when do you travel with bodyguards? They *are* bodyguards, right? Because they *look* like bodyguards."

I sigh, rubbing my temple. "Since people started trying to kill me."

Her mouth falls open. "Wait. What?"

"It's complicated." I drop onto the couch beside her, feeling the weight of it all pressing down on me. "I'll be safer at the farmhouse with Aiden. You'll be safer if I'm not here. I'm attracting too much attention from the wrong kind of men."

Her expression shifts, concern flashing behind her usual warmth. "Dara… what the hell is going on?"

I don't answer. Instead, my gaze drifts to the TV. A news segment scrolls across the screen, the bold headline pulling me in:

'FBI Investigation Expands in Russian Businessman's Murder – International Links Suspected.'

Leslie follows my gaze. "It's everywhere. They keep talking about Dmitri. Saying he had serious American ties. Some anonymous sources even hint that *local businessmen* could be involved. The FBI won't comment, but they even asked the Chief of National Intelligence about it at a press conference in DC today. The guy was friends with former Russian leaders. Even a Russian president."

I blink. "Dmitri had connections to a former Russian president?"

Leslie nods. "Yep. And apparently, this whole thing is a *lot* bigger than just some nightclub scandal gone wrong."

I exhale slowly. "I didn't know any of this."

Leslie studies me, then smirks. "You wouldn't, would you? You and Aiden have been busy. Not taking time to watch the news?"

I roll my eyes but don't argue. She's right. The past few days, I've been wrapped up in him, talking, unraveling our thoughts together, letting my guard slip, piece by piece. We watch as Aiden heads for the bedroom to find another suitcase.

Leslie nudges my knee. "So, Professor Aiden, huh? Is he the real deal?"

I hesitate, glancing toward the bedroom where he will be waiting. "I keep looking for flaws. For warning signs. But…"

Leslie tilts her head. "But?"

I exhale, shaking my head. "I can't find them. Surely, there's no such thing as the perfect man."

She studies me for a beat, then grins. "Wow. This is new for you."

I smirk. "Tell me about it." I shift gears. "What about you? How's Jake?"

Leslie's smile softens, a light blush creeping onto her cheeks. "I like him. A lot. It's… different. We're getting more physical."

I nod, watching her carefully. "And you feel good about that?"

She hesitates just slightly before nodding. "I think so. I'm trying not to give mixed signals. I want to take things slow, but sometimes I just—" She exhales, looking conflicted.

I reach for her hand, squeezing gently. "Les, you only ever need to give as much of yourself as you're willing. Emotionally. Physically. It's okay to want someone, to explore what that means. But don't give more than you're ready for. Ever."

She bites her lip. "What if I mess it up by overthinking?"

"Then it wasn't meant to be." My voice is firm and steady. "A real connection? It won't fall apart just because you take your time. If it's meant to last, it will. And if not, you'll be glad you gave yourself the space to walk away."

Leslie exhales. "You always sound so sure about these things."

I smile wryly. "You don't sit across from men for years, studying them, learning their tells, their intentions, without learning a thing or two. Desire and love are different things, Les. It's a dance, but one where *you* can lead, not them."

She nods slowly, letting my words settle. "I trust Jake. But… yeah. I'll take it slow."

I give her a knowing look. "Good. Protect your heart, Leslie. Guard it until the right person earns it."

She watches me carefully. "Is that what you've been doing? Guarding your heart?"

I hesitate, my thoughts drifting back to Aiden. To George.

I exhale, shaking my head. "I thought I was. But lately? I'm not so sure anymore."

Leslie frowns. "Are you talking about Aiden… or the *George* mentor you've always talked about? You talked about hiding your identity from your regular client to keep him out of your real world, and now you're guarding Aiden from your escort world?"

I blink at her, surprised by the insight. "Yes, both, maybe. I'm just learning about Aiden. But I'm learning more about George than ever before too. Some of it's confusing. And… unsettling."

Leslie's brows knit together. "Unsettling how?"

I hesitate, then shrug. "I always felt safe with George. It was natural, instinctive. I never questioned it. I trusted my instincts. Never pried about where he came from, what he really did. Didn't even ask if his first name was real. He was just… George. The only man I ever let get close. Because I sensed I could."

Leslie tilts her head. "But now?"

I sigh. "Now I see more. Things I overlooked. Jillian won't even fully talk about him. It's like I'm peeling back layers of a puzzle I didn't even know I was holding. And I'm not sure I'll like what I find. I just realize there's things about George I can't figure out yet despite knowing him for so long. He's more of a mystery than I thought."

Leslie bites her lip. "Dara… do you trust him?"

I open my mouth, then close it. My answer isn't as clear as it should be.

I force a small smile instead. "Let's just say I'm paying attention."

Leslie studies me, then nods. "Fair enough. But Dara… just like you told me, protect your heart. Protect yourself. With both Aiden and George. Don't let your heart be betrayed by either."

I smirk, standing up. "I'll try."

Leslie glances toward the hallway, where the bodyguards still linger outside. She crosses her arms. "And the security detail? What's next?"

I sling my bag over my shoulder. "Hopefully, the last steps of this mess."

Leslie raises an eyebrow. "That sounds… vague."

I flash her a cryptic smile. "Nothing with George is ever straightforward. I'm also taking it slow with Aiden. There's a lot of things I need to unravel."

She watches me carefully, sensing the weight behind my words as Aiden exits the bedroom with a suitcase that we then pack.

Finally, Leslie nods as we turn to leave. "Just be careful, Dara."

"I'm trying."

And as Aiden and I walk out the door, I know, some parts of my past I'm leaving behind. Others? They'll follow me. Ready or not.

Chapter 10

"…for the first time in forever, it feels like enough." – Dara

The neon sign of Mom & Pop's Diner buzzes faintly, its flickering light casting an uneven glow across George's face as I slide into the booth opposite him. His crisp navy suit and perfectly knotted tie look almost out of place against the diner's worn red vinyl seats and laminated menus. Yet George, composed and deliberate, seems at ease.

"John's in deeper than we thought," George says, wasting no time with pleasantries. His tone is low, measured, and laced with urgency. "He's always used his real first name with Jillian. John is common enough to sound like an alias, especially to agency girls."

I wrap my hands around the ceramic coffee mug in front of me, the warmth grounding me. "How deep are we talking?"

George leans slightly forward, his eyes sharp. "Blackmail. Arms dealing. Dmitri wasn't just a client. John was orchestrating his moves. They were tied at the hip in this mess. John's mistake was greed. He wanted a bigger cut. Which makes him more dangerous. He's in over his head."

The words land like a punch. My mind races, fitting this revelation into the chaotic web of information I've been unraveling. John, a slick attorney, moonlighting as a criminal puppet master? It's both plausible and utterly chilling. I study George's face, searching for any cracks in his calm demeanor.

"You know a lot of details about the scandal, George. And I just learned that you obviously know my real name, who I am, and where I live. How do you know all this?" I ask, forcing my voice to stay even as my eyes narrowed.

His eyes flick toward the window, drawing mine with them. A black sedan idles across the street, its silhouette illuminated by a street lamp. A man in a dark suit sits behind the wheel, his posture alert.

"You always seem to have a driver," I remark, my tone sharp. "Sometimes, there's more than one in your entourage. You've never revealed how much you've always known about me, and I know so little about you. Want to tell me why?"

A faint smile tugs at George's lips. "I operate with a measure of caution, Dara. It's a habit I've never broken."

A habit, or something more? I hold my tongue, filing away this observation. George always seems a step ahead, his knowledge cutting through layers of secrecy like a scalpel. How long has he known my real name? Who does he think I am to take such an interest in me? But his protectiveness and connections beg a larger question: Who exactly is he?

"Dara," George's voice pulls me back, firm and deliberate. "This isn't just about John. It's about the larger picture. This world is dangerous, and you're caught in the middle of it. There are international elements involved here much bigger than John."

I meet his gaze, his genuine concern evident. But there's something else, an undercurrent of knowledge he's not sharing. It is always disconcerting if I cannot decipher a man's deeper intentions, even if they seem sincere. "I appreciate the warning," I say cautiously. "But I can handle myself."

George leans back, studying me as if calculating the weight of his next words. "I don't doubt your strength. But Dara, you're navigating waters far murkier than you realize. John and these Russians aren't amateurs, they're sharks. And when sharks smell blood..."

He doesn't finish the sentence, but the implication is clear. I shift uncomfortably, the weight of his words pressing down on me. I look around the diner we both adored.

"Thank you for the intel," I say, my voice steady despite the turmoil in my chest. "But I need to see this through. There's too much at stake. I need to step in to put a stop to the uncertainty. I'll take care of him myself. I've looked into his eyes before."

George's lips press into a thin line, his disapproval evident. "Dara, you can't seriously mean to confront him."

"I need answers," I insist. "For myself. For clarity."

George's gaze narrows. "If you confront him, you risk more than just answers. You risk drawing attention from the wrong people. The kind who don't care about collateral damage."

I hold his gaze, unwavering. "I'll be careful. I operate with a measure of caution, George. It's a habit I've never broken."

The corners of George's mouth twitch, not quite a smile but something close. "I see. Well, careful isn't always enough. John is being watched by people far more dangerous than you can imagine. And let's not pretend that your sudden proximity to him hasn't raised eyebrows."

I arch an eyebrow, leaning forward. "Raised whose eyebrows, George? Yours? The FBI's? Or someone else's?"

He sighs, running a hand through his silver hair, his confidence faltering for a fleeting moment. "There are men... keeping an eye on you. For your protection."

I grip the coffee mug tighter. "Are they yours?"

He doesn't answer directly. "If I told you yes, you'd push them away. And if I said no, you wouldn't believe me."

"So, you're admitting it." I study his face, watching for subtle lies betraying his poker face. "You don't want me to ask questions. You just want me to follow your lead. Even if you have the best intentions. I've met the men on that detail. Your detail. They knew my real name. You know my real name. It wasn't hard to figure out."

George exhales slowly, leaning closer. "Dara, I've spent my life navigating the kind of world you're only just beginning to glimpse. Trust me when I say that stepping back from all this isn't a sign of weakness. It's survival."

His words hang in the air, heavy with unspoken truths. For a moment, I wonder if I've misjudged him. He isn't just a protective figure in my life; he's a man who knows the game better than anyone else at this table. But what game is he playing, and where do I fit?

"You keep saying you know what's best for me," I say, my voice quiet but firm. "But what about what I want? My independence matters, George. If that's even your real name."

His eyes soften, a rare glimpse of vulnerability breaking through his stoic exterior. He doesn't respond to my emphasis on his name. "And I respect that. But independence won't mean much if you don't live to enjoy it."

The conversation stalls as the server refills our coffee. George waits until she's out of earshot before speaking again. "Dara, one last thing. There's more to John's involvement with Dmitri. He has connections to international arms deals and American companies. Russian mobsters are involved. John tried to blackmail Dmitri with your photos in those deals. That got Dmitri killed when another Russian faction just stepped in, seeing an opportunity. John didn't expect it to escalate."

I nod slowly, absorbing his words. "Then why are you telling me to stay out of it? If he's that dangerous, doesn't that make confronting him even more urgent?"

"Because," George says, his voice dropping to a near whisper, "there are people watching him already. People who don't need you adding to the complexity. People he upset by interfering with their competition with Dmitri as it got messy. Stay out of their way, Dara."

"Who's watching him?" I press, my curiosity outweighing my caution.

He doesn't answer, his silence more telling than words. Instead, he reaches into his pocket and places a small, sealed envelope on the table. "For emergencies," he says simply.

I hesitate, then pick it up, tucking it into my purse. "What's in it?"

"Cash. Don't use the bank for a while. Cut your phone off if you leave the farmhouse. Keep it on for school. Off when you move. When you leave predictable routes. Date the professor and stay at the farmhouse until graduation." George replies cryptically. "And there is one more thing, Dara, I've been thinking about something," George said, his tone casual but carrying an undertone of seriousness.

I raised an eyebrow, leaning back slightly. "You're always thinking about something, George. What's it this time?"

He swirled his coffee, then leaned back as if weighing his words. "You've worked so hard to carve out a future for yourself, finishing school, setting up your next chapter. But there's one thing you've neglected."

I didn't mean to frown and a faint smirk tugged at my lips. "Oh? What's that? My taxes? My thrilling social life?"

George smiled faintly. "Your relationships. Real ones. The kind that has nothing to do with your past or your work."

I'm sure my expression darkened, and I shifted uncomfortably in my seat. George seemed to also be able to read people, so I hoped I didn't look too upset by his observation. "I've had enough people trying to 'fix' me, George. If this is your segue into a lecture on dating, spare me."

"This isn't about fixing you," George replied, his voice soft but firm. "It's about giving yourself permission to have what you deserve. You've spent so long keeping everyone at arm's length, holding your worlds separate. But sooner or later, Dara, you're going to need to let someone in."

I stared at my own coffee, the steam rising between us. "That's easy for you to say. You don't know what it's like, being judged, hiding who you are because you're terrified of losing what little control you've managed to claw back."

"I do know what it's like," George said quietly. He leaned forward, resting his elbows on his knees, his eyes holding mine. "And I've seen you. You're stronger than you give yourself credit for. But strength isn't about standing alone forever. It's about knowing when to let someone stand with you."

I laughed. I was afraid it sounded bitter as the sound was sharp in the quiet diner. "Who would want to stand with me, George? You've seen the mess of my life. The lies, the secrets..."

"Enough," he said, his tone sharper now. "Don't sell yourself short. You're brilliant, compassionate, and capable. A man would be lucky to stand beside you. But you have to believe that, too."

I looked away, my fingers tightening around the mug. "I'm not sure I know how to let anyone in."

"You've already started, haven't you?" George asked, his voice softening. "With Aiden."

I froze. I could feel the color rising in my cheeks. "That's... different."

"Different, how?" he pressed. "Because he doesn't know everything about you yet? Or because you think he won't accept you once he does?"

My gaze fell to the dark liquid in her mug. "Maybe both."

George took a slow sip of coffee. "You won't know until you try. And if you're serious about leaving your escort world behind and transitioning into the life you've worked so hard to build, then you need to let yourself have that life. That includes love, Dara. Real love."

I let out a slow breath, staring into the skyline. "What if I fail? What if I ruin it?"

"Then you pick yourself up and try again," George said simply. "But you can't keep running from what you deserve. You're not that girl anymore. The one who had to fight for every scrap of independence and safety. You've built something better for yourself. It's time to live it."

I glanced at him, my eyes softer now, the hard edge in my voice dissipating. Just when I was ready to be paranoid about George's intentions, he leans back in with introspective advice. "You really think I deserve all that?"

He smiled warmly, leaning back in his chair. "I don't just think it. I know it. And deep down, so do you. Now, go on. Give that professor of yours a chance. He might surprise you. And who knows? You might surprise yourself."

I managed a small, almost shy smile, a flicker of something hopeful breaking through my guarded demeanor. Could I really have a future that leaves my past behind? George was one of the people I dreaded leaving in the past. But part of me was hoping I could even push George into that past, as I now learn he has a shadowy side that I can't discern. I would miss discussions like this as he has always given me hope for the future as well. He was right, though. He has always been able to read me. I have been keeping Aiden at arm's length despite the tug I felt. George knows me well and understands I will be slow to let anyone in. I nod in consideration of his observations as we get up to leave.

I glance back at the black sedan across the street as we exit the diner. The man inside briefly meets my gaze before looking away. I take a deep breath, resolving to keep moving forward, even as shadows close in around me. My confusion over my feelings about George continues to swirl.

The cool night air bites at my skin, but it does little to settle my nerves. I need answers, and there's only one place I can start. John. His face, his expressions. Those would tell me if George was truly on my side or playing his own game. John doesn't have a poker face; I've seen enough men lie to know how to read it when they do.

The next morning, the familiar buzz of campus life provides a fleeting sense of normalcy. Aiden's class is a sanctuary of sorts, even if just for an hour. Aiden and I had agreed to keep things casual while at school to maintain appearances. But the distance feels strange after the quiet intimacy of the farmhouse. Reflecting on George's observation that I tended to throw up barriers of letting anyone get close, I realized that intimacy was moving slowly because of my own fears.

As I slide into my seat, Aiden's warm gaze catches mine. His concern lingers, unspoken but palpable. "Dara," he says softly, leaning slightly closer. "How are you holding up?"

I force a smile. "I'm fine. Really. Just a bit shaken."

His brow furrows, and for a moment, I think he might press the issue, but the arrival of other students pulls him back. Still, his quiet patience wraps around me like a comforting embrace. He doesn't push, doesn't demand, just waits. My chest tightens at the thought of all the things I haven't revealed to him. George is right. I have to let someone in at some point to move on.

After class, Aiden catches up with me in the hallway, weaving through the crowd with that effortless charm of his. "Hey, Dara," he says, his tone casual but laced with unmistakable care. "How about dinner tonight? Just to get you out of the farmhouse for a bit."

I hesitate, the familiar tug-of-war pulling at my chest, the deepening desire to be close to him, battling the fear of letting him in too much at the same time. To this point, Aiden has been nothing but respectful of my space. Patient. Thoughtful. We've only held hands, shared laughs, and enjoyed each other's company. But the more time we spend together, the more I feel the walls I've carefully built starting to crack. The closeness I crave with him is terrifying because it feels real.

His hopeful smile breaks through my defenses like sunlight cutting through clouds. It's warm and sincere, and I know I won't say no. "That sounds perfect," I say softly.

Aiden's face lights up, and the sight makes my heart skip a beat. "Great. Let's say seven? I'll even let you pick the place."

I smirk, trying to hide the flutter of nerves and anticipation bubbling inside me. "You're brave, giving me that much power."

"Always," he replies, his tone teasing but his eyes steady. "I trust your judgment."

The words settle over me, simple but powerful. Trust. It's a word I don't take lightly, especially not now. As Aiden's gaze lingers just a second longer, I feel that same war inside me. The desire to let go, to let him in completely, against the fear of what he'll see if I do. But tonight, maybe I can let myself enjoy the moment, for both of us.

A prickle of unease creeps up my spine as we exit the building. My eyes instinctively scan the area, landing on a man in a dark jacket leaning against a tree, his casual pose just a little too deliberate. Aiden notices my tension immediately.

"Everything okay?" he asks.

I tear my gaze away. "Yeah, I just thought I saw someone I knew."

But as we walk, another figure catches my eye. This one pretending to be absorbed in his phone. My pulse quickens, and the knot in my stomach tightens. They're not even trying to be subtle anymore. Or maybe I'm being too observant.

"Dara," Aiden's voice cuts through my spiraling thoughts. He had been watching me scan the area and spotting the men who seemed out of place on campus. "Those men... they're following us, aren't they?"

I stop, staring at him. "You noticed too?"

His jaw tightens. "Of course I did. There's been too much happening lately for me not to notice. Are those the men that watch the farmhouse? At some point, you have to tell me why you have a protective detail watching you."

The urge to spill everything rises in my throat, but years of keeping secrets clamp it down. "It's... complicated," I manage.

"Complicated how?" he presses gently, his tone more patient than accusatory.

I exhale sharply. "I'm handling it, Aiden. I just need to figure some things out on my own."

His lips press into a thin line, and I can see the battle in his eyes between respecting my boundaries and wanting to protect me. "You realize," he says finally, "there's no way I can abandon you knowing you might need someone. Especially since we've already had one incident at the farmhouse."

His words stop me in my tracks. "Is that why you've been so patient? Letting me stay at the farmhouse? You think I just need someone?"

"No," he says firmly, meeting my gaze. "You're overthinking it."

"I just don't want you to feel guilty. Like you have to take care of me," I say, my voice quieter now. "I don't need anyone."

Aiden steps closer, his expression serious but soft. "Dara, that's not it at all. What I mean is, you can depend on me. I'm here because I care about you; not out of guilt, not out of obligation. I care about you, Dara. Surely, you know that."

I study his face, every line and nuance. His voice, steady and unwavering, carries no sign of deceit. Over the years, I've honed the ability to spot a lie; pitch changes, verbal hesitations, even subtle facial twitches. But there's none of that here. His words flow naturally, his sincerity clear in his tone and body language.

For a moment, the weight of his truth overwhelms me. I'm so used to navigating deception, to parsing what's said and unsaid. But Aiden is something else entirely. His honesty feels foreign, yet it's the most grounding thing I've ever encountered.

"I do know," I say finally, my voice barely above a whisper. "And I'm sorry. It's just... it's been a stressful few weeks."

Aiden reaches out, his hand brushing mine. The touch is light but deliberate, his thumb grazing my knuckles. "I get that. And I'll be here. However long it takes."

His words settle over me, a soothing balm to my frayed nerves. I squeeze his hand lightly, my chest both aching and hopeful. For the first time in a long while, I let myself believe, just a little, that someone might truly care for me, not the persona I've crafted, not the image I project, but the real me. Someone who doesn't just want something from me, but sees me. And that terrifies me more than anything.

Aiden continues to walk with me across campus, his presence steady yet charged with an undercurrent of something unspoken. My mind swirls with thoughts, and I can sense he is doing the same. When his hand brushes against mine, a hesitant touch, I respond by gently taking it. The warmth of his palm against mine sends a shiver through me, and though our words have fallen silent, the air between us is heavy with anticipation.

We reach a secluded corner of the campus garden, surrounded by the soft rustle of leaves and the calming scent of jasmine. Here, away from the noise and the world, Aiden stops and turns to face me. His eyes search mine, their intensity almost making me forget how to breathe.

"Dara," he begins, his voice quiet but full of meaning. "I... I need to tell you something."

My mind races, analyzing, calculating. But none of my scenarios prepare me for his next words.

"I care about you," he says, his voice raw. "More than I probably should."

My breath hitches. The space between us crackles with energy. It's a feeling I've encountered before, yet this time it's different. It's unguarded. Real. My carefully constructed defenses feel flimsy like they could crumble at any moment. When his hand brushes a stray strand of hair from my face, his thumb grazing my cheek, a surge of warmth floods me. I can read his thoughts. I know his intent.

I remain still, savoring the moment, letting it sink in. My heart races, and I meet his gaze, letting him see the emotion I can no longer hide. "I feel the same way, Aiden," I say softly, my voice steady despite the whirlwind inside me. Usually, I'd help close the space between me and the man staring lovingly into my eyes, playing my part as an escort. But I wasn't an escort to Aiden. This was real.

For a heartbeat, time seems to stop. Aiden hesitates briefly, as if afraid to move too quickly, to break the fragile spell between us. I place my hands lightly on his waist, grounding us both and signaling I'm not going anywhere. He leans in slowly, giving me every opportunity to pull away. But I don't.

The charged air thickens as his face moves closer to mine. Time stretches, each second weighted and deliberate. Just as our faces are mere inches apart and his eyes begin to close, I place my hand on his chest, stopping him. His eyes suddenly snap open, his expression a mixture of confusion and apology.

"I'm sorry," he says quickly, his voice tinged with regret. "I didn't mean to be too forward or assume—"

"No," I interrupt, my voice soft but firm. "It's okay. I just...want it to last."

His brows knit as he processes my words, and I use the moment to grab his shirt lightly, pulling him closer toward me. Slowly, I press my lips to his, barely a whisper of a kiss at first, a tentative exploration. The softness of his lips sends a jolt through me. I tease his lips with mine, drawing him in before fully committing to the kiss.

Aiden responds, his lips pressing against mine with gentle yet firm intent. His hands find my waist, steadying us as my hand slips behind his head, fingers threading through his hair.

The kiss builds, passion intertwining with the vulnerability of the moment. His arms tighten around me, pulling me closer, and for the first time, I let myself be fully present. Every sensation, his warmth, the pressure of his hands, the way his lips move against mine, is vivid, unfiltered by calculation or control.

When we finally break apart, it's slow and reluctant. We both draw in needed breaths, our foreheads resting lightly against each other. I look into his eyes, finding them filled with the same awe and emotion coursing through me.

A startling realization strikes me. This is my first true romantic connection. There are no agendas, no performances, just us. The raw honesty of it thrills and terrifies me in equal measure.

He studies my face, his expression shifting between relief and a flicker of confusion. I take a deep breath, the words balancing on the edge of my lips, daring to tumble out.

"That was...my first kiss that felt real," I admit, my voice steady but vulnerable.

Aiden's eyebrows shoot up in surprise. "Really? But it felt so... I mean, you seemed so..." His words trail off, and I catch the hesitation in his tone.

A sudden flare of defensiveness rises in me, but I quickly suppress it. "What? Experienced?" My voice is sharper than I intend, laced with an edge of self-consciousness.

"No, that's not—" Aiden stammers, clearly flustered. His sincerity is evident, but the unspoken question lingers in his eyes.

"You're wondering about my past," I say flatly, more as a statement than an accusation. My analytical mind races to dissect his reaction, though the truth is simpler: I'm self-conscious. Self-conscious about the paradox of my life, the experience I carry that feels hollow, disconnected from any emotional truth and self-conscious to the point of defensiveness. My analytical tendencies simply make it worse.

Aiden exhales, running a hand through his hair, his expression softening. "I'm sorry, Dara. I'm overthinking it. It's not my place to ask. It doesn't matter."

His willingness to let it go catches me off guard. I brace for more questions, for the probing curiosity I've faced countless times. But instead, he smiles. A gentle, understanding smile that feels like a balm to my frayed nerves. He truly wants to find my boundaries so as not to cross them.

"Whatever your past is, it's yours," he says softly. "I trust you. You don't owe me any explanations until you're ready to give them."

The knot in my chest loosens slightly. His words resonate, not because they dismiss my secrets but because they respect them. His freely given trust feels heavier than I anticipated as if it comes with the weight of my unspoken truths. He actually is careful not to push me away.

"Thank you," I murmur, my voice barely above a whisper. For once, the gratitude I feel is genuine and unfiltered. I wanted to tell him that my body simply remembers movements that my heart never felt. How could I possibly explain that although it wasn't my first kiss, it was the first one that meant anything? My lips had memorized the choreography of seduction long before they knew what affection felt like. Sure, I had mastered the art of the kiss, the bedroom, and erotic gestures. But they were all calculated and performative. I'd have to explain why the experience I had was simply transactional, while this was the first that wasn't about control, power, or illusion. I should tell him. But I couldn't.

We stand there in the quiet, the evening breeze playing softly around us. The world feels suspended as if this moment exists outside of time. I can see the conflict in his gaze, the tug-of-war between curiosity and respect. And yet, he doesn't push, doesn't pry. He simply lets me exist as I am, secrets and all.

The weight of my past hovers in the periphery, ever-present. But for now, in this fleeting moment, I let myself breathe. I let myself be seen, not as a collection of stories or experiences, but as simply Dara. And for the first time in forever, it feels like enough.

My phone buzzes, slicing through the delicate quiet of the moment. Jillian's name lights up the screen.

"I need to take this," I say to Aiden, stepping away. His eyes linger on me, filled with quiet understanding.

"Jillian?" I answer, my voice steady despite the sudden pounding of my heart.

"Dara, honey. I've got news about Susan," Jillian's voice crackles through the line, tinged with both relief and caution.

My grip on the phone tightens. "Is she okay?"

"She's still in the hospital," Jillian begins, her tone measured. "But they've reduced her watch. The doctors think she might be released soon."

Relief floods through me, but it's fleeting, overtaken by the gnawing edge of unease. "That's good, right? But…"

"But she's not out of the woods yet," Jillian finishes, mirroring my own fears. "Listen, Dara, you need to be careful. Things are... complicated."

The weight in her words isn't lost on me. I nod, even though she can't see it. "I understand. Thanks for letting me know, Jillian."

"Take care of yourself, Dara. And keep your guard up," she adds before the line goes dead.

As I turn back to Aiden, I slip my phone into my pocket. His eyes meet mine, filled with unspoken questions. He doesn't press, and I appreciate that more than he could know.

"Everything okay?" he asks gently, his concern evident.

"Yeah," I reply, though the word feels hollow. "Just... something I need to handle."

He doesn't push further, offering a small nod instead. His restraint and willingness to let me process things on my terms make me ache with a mixture of gratitude and guilt.

As we part ways, a quiet determination hardens within me. Susan is still vulnerable, and the web I've stumbled into grows darker by the day. I need to confront John. I need answers, about Susan, about Dmitri, about the chaos creeping ever closer to my carefully guarded life. In my mind, the best way was to confront the source directly. But how to do it without dragging Aiden into danger? Without jeopardizing the fragile peace, I've found in his presence?

And then there's George, a man I trust but can't entirely read. His motives hover just out of reach, leaving me to wonder whether he's protecting me out of genuine care or for reasons I've yet to uncover.

One thing is certain: I can't keep dancing on the edge of this storm. I need to take control.

Squaring my shoulders, I push aside the doubt that is threatening to creep in. My analytical mind kicks into gear, piecing together the steps of a plan. The first step is clear: I need to see John. I need to look him in the eye and read the truth, or the lies, etched across his face.

It's time to stop reacting and start acting. Whatever awaits me on the other side of this, I'll face it head-on. No more waiting. No more wondering. It's time to rewrite the rules of the game.

Chapter 11

"…un-fuck this up" – *Dara*

It wasn't hard to find him. It took a ten-minute internet search looking at photos of area attorneys. I knew it was reckless walking in alone. But predators don't expect prey to knock on the front door.

The polished marble floor amplified the sharp staccato of my heels as I strode into the law office. The receptionist looks up, her professional mask faltering just enough to betray her assessment of me. I'd dressed the part deliberately, a sleek, tight-fitting dress with a revealing slit up the leg and high heels that made every step feel purposeful. I wasn't here to blend in, and I knew what role to play.

"I have an appointment with John Mitchell," I say, my voice smooth but firm.

The receptionist's brows knit together as she checks her computer. "I'm sorry, I don't see—"

"Tell him Dara Keene is here." I hold her gaze, unwavering. "He'll see me."

For a moment, there's a flicker of recognition, or maybe just curiosity. She picks up the phone, murmuring into it. Seconds later, she nods curtly. "Mr. Mitchell will see you now."

I step into John's office, taking in the ostentatious display of power: dark wood paneling, rows of leather-bound books, and a hulking desk that seems to swallow the room. John sits behind it, his forced smile a thin veneer over his obvious discomfort. His shoulders are stiff, and his hands grip the armrests as if they anchor him to his seat.

I sit across from him, crossing my legs deliberately, holding his gaze. I can almost see the gears turning in his head. He didn't expect me here, not on his turf. The silence stretches between us, heavy and unyielding. I'm content to let it.

Finally, he clears his throat. "Dara. What can I do for you?"

"Interesting choice of words," I reply, my tone icy. "Especially after you threatened me."

His face hardens, though he leans back in his chair, trying to feign nonchalance. "Threatened? Come now. I was merely looking out for you. You're in over your head."

A wry smile curls my lips. "I think you've got that backward, John. You're the one who's drowning."

His smile falters, and for the first time, I see it—fear. A bead of sweat glistens on his temple, and his breath hitches ever so slightly. This isn't the confident man who once cornered me, his arrogance oozing like cheap cologne. The balance of power has shifted. He knows it, and so do I.

John's eyes flick to his desk drawer, a calculated move. He opens it slowly, pulling out a checkbook. His pen hovers over the first blank check, his movements deliberate but betrayed by a nervous tremor.

"Let's be practical, Dara," he says, his voice smooth but strained. "I'm willing to compensate you generously for your... discretion. Consider it a non-disclosure agreement. Attorneys do this all the time."

I tilt my head, watching him like a predator sizing up its prey. He's choosing bribery over intimidation, an interesting tactical choice.

He continues, sensing an opening. "I have a reputation to uphold as an honest, upstanding attorney. Our previous... encounters were regrettable. A lapse in judgment on my part, all for your protection, of course."

"Of course," I echo, leaning forward. My gaze locks onto his. The twitch in his left eye, the rhythmic tapping of his fingers against the desk.

He seems to be slowly unraveling. I imagined he was feeling heat from many directions.

"And the note?" I ask, keeping my voice even.

Relief flits across his face, too fleeting to hide. "I'll pay for it. Whatever you think it's worth. Just hand it over, and this whole unfortunate situation goes away."

I study him, the subtle shift in his tone when he mentions the note. The desperation that hums beneath his carefully constructed façade. He's fishing, testing the waters, hoping to buy my silence and secure his escape.

"An honest attorney," I repeat, letting the words hang between us like a challenge.

His smile tightens, his composure slipping. "Yes. My career is built on integrity. I have powerful clients. International leaders. Business executives."

Liar. The thought snaps through my mind like a whip. But the question remains. What is he so desperate to hide?

I let the silence stretch, watching him squirm under its weight. The truth, I know, lies in the unspoken spaces. His discomfort tells me more than his words ever could. John Mitchell isn't just a pawn in this game. He's a pawn trying desperately not to tip over. And I'm here to watch him fall.

John leans forward, his mask slipping for a moment. "One piece of advice," he says, his voice dropping to a dangerous whisper. "Stay away from George. He's not who you think he is."

I arch an eyebrow, letting the weight of his words hang in the air. I don't respond, inviting him to keep talking. I tilt my head slightly and lean forward, a silent cue for him to continue. The bait works.

"You two..." he says, his tone quickening, almost desperate. "You can't trust each other. You're worlds apart. He hasn't told you about his past, who he really is, what he does."

"Sounds like you don't want us to trust each other," I reply coolly, keeping my voice level and my face unreadable.

John shakes his head, a flicker of agitation betraying his polished demeanor. "On the contrary. I know the truth. And let me remind you, Dara if you don't cooperate; you could very well be implicated in Dmitri's death along with everyone you care about."

My heart skips a beat, but I refuse to show it. "The photos," I say, cutting through his theatrics. "The ones you tried to use to blackmail Dmitri. The photos that exposed his weaknesses, making him a liability to whatever deal you had."

John smirks, regaining a shred of his usual arrogance. "Yes, the photos. But you're in them, Dara. That's the point. Dmitri ends up dead after those photos surfaced. Do you think it matters why? It's you who looks guilty. Who's to say you didn't have him killed or someone you know killed him? To protect you?"

My mind races, threading through the possibilities. Why was Dmitri killed? I speak my suspicion aloud, my voice calm, measured. "Or could it be your blackmail attempt backfired? You got tangled in Russian rivalries, pushing an already volatile situation over the edge. Maybe the mob saw those photos as an opportunity to eliminate a competitor."

John's veneer cracks just a little more. "It doesn't matter," he snaps. "You're in those photos. That's all that matters to you."

I feel the weight of his threat settle over me, thick and suffocating. But I'm not powerless. Not by a long shot.

"I have a fail-safe, John," I say, my tone as calm as his is agitated. "Think of it as a dead man's switch. If anything happens to me or to anyone I care about, it activates automatically. The note, your reputation, your entire carefully constructed life… it all comes crashing down. No effort is required on my part. You don't think I keep that note on me, do you? The note with your DNA on it? Your directions to a murdered man, in your handwriting."

The color drains from his face, his confidence evaporating in an instant. I lean in closer, my voice dropping to a whisper, each word laced with icy precision. "So much for an honest attorney, right?"

John's jaw tightens, his eyes flashing with fury. "You think you're clever, don't you? Got it all figured out?" He leans forward, narrowing the gap between us. "Ever heard of mutually assured destruction, Dara?"

A chill runs down my spine, but I don't flinch. His threat is clear. He's ready to expose my escort work, drag my name through the mud, and ruin everything I've worked for. The precarious balance of power between us sharpens, teetering dangerously.

"Sounds like we understand each other, then," I say, my voice steady despite the storm raging inside me. My poker face is better than his, and I know it.

John nods, a humorless smile tugging at his lips. "Perfectly."

I rise, smoothing my skirt with deliberate ease. "I'm trying to reform my language," I say lightly. "But listen to me carefully as sometimes in my line of work there just isn't any other way to say it to be clear." I lean forward across his desk, my voice dropping to a sultry whisper. "Go, un-fuck this up."

His face flushes red, anger surging beneath his forced composure, but I'm already turning toward the door. The tension in the room hums like a live wire as my hand closes around the doorknob. I've dropped my plan that for the note and his DNA to remain hidden meant that I was untouchable.

Just as I'm about to leave, John's voice stops me. Of course, he wants the last word. Typical. His ego won't let him stay silent.

"When I learned your real name," he says, his tone almost smug, "I did some digging. Keene isn't exactly a common name. Tell me, Dara. Do you like math?"

I turn back slowly, meeting his gaze with a calculated coolness. I let the silence linger, just long enough for his curiosity to fester. "If you're wondering whether brilliance runs in the Keene lineage, I'll let you figure it out for yourself," I say, my voice soft but laced with steel. "By blood… or by inspiration. You do the math."

I hold his gaze for a beat longer, then walk out, leaving him to stew in the uncertainty I've planted.

The hospital corridor is a world away from John's opulent office. Antiseptic scents replace the richness of leather and wood, and muted conversations echo against sterile walls. I push open the door to Susan's room and find Jill sitting by her bedside, her expression soft but tinged with worry as Susan rests.

"Dara," she says, looking up as I enter. "You look shaken. What happened?"

I sink into a chair, exhaling slowly as I grip the armrests. "John happened. He's... dangerous, Jill. More than I realized. Dangerous like a cornered animal."

Jill narrows her eyes. "He's always been a snake. You saw him?"

I hesitate, gauging how much to share. "Dmitri's death. He's trying to tie me to it. But it's more than that. He's terrified of George and me trusting each other."

Her lips press into a thin line. "George is... powerful," she says carefully. "More powerful than even John likely understands. John just thinks he knows. He was a lawyer who was involved with government contracts at one time. He had to deal with George in that capacity. But let's be honest, even I don't know the full scope of George's power and influence."

"Then why is John so scared?" I press, leaning forward. "You said he doesn't even know George's real identity. He acts like he does."

Jill leans back, exhaling through her nose. She takes a moment, choosing her words deliberately. "John did contract work in international law. George represented the government during that time. But John never knew George's true identity, only his authority. He knows enough to be afraid but not enough to act intelligently. And John's a gambler. He's playing this hand blind. He's bluffing, and he's only going to bluff if it benefits him."

"What kind of role did George have with the government?" I ask, sitting straighter.

Jill hesitates. Her body language shifts as if she's navigating a minefield of classified information. "John's work put him in contact with... questionable clients. Let's just say George wasn't just another bureaucrat. He operated in the intelligence world. George was interested in John's clients who posed national security risks. "

My brow furrows. "And John?"

"More like an informant," Jill says, a faint smirk on her lips. "I doubt he was trusted with anything major. He probably fed George information on his sketchier clients, for a price, of course. That's how John operates."

"And George?" I press.

Jill shrugs, her gaze turning distant. "George? He represented the U.S. intelligence community. But that's what he let people see. Who knows his real role. You've seen how he operates, Dara. He's a master of staying in the shadows. John only knows George by his first name and isn't even sure if that is real. Even now, I can't tell you where George's alliances lie. Sometimes, I wonder if even he knows. It's a shadowy world he operates in."

I sit back, letting her words sink in. "So, John doesn't really know George. He's just bluffing with what he does know. But in their world, who's to say who's good or bad?"

Jill sighs. "Exactly. John's far more terrified of Sasha. And for good reason. Sasha's ruthless in ways George could never be. If George is a shadow and works within US law. Sasha is a storm and lawless. But Dara," she adds, her voice dropping, "it's not always as simple as good guys and bad guys in their line of work. There are shades in between."

I shake my head, processing. "John's caught between Sasha and George. No wonder he's unraveling. But what about me? Why am I suddenly the thread they all seem to want to pull?"

Jillian leans forward, resting her hand on mine. "Dara, you've become a collateral problem in their game. But you're smart and resourceful. You can navigate this. And George, he'll protect you, whether you realize it or not. That's one thing you can trust. It's the one thing I'm sure of."

I nod slowly. "I trust George. He's never given me a reason not to trust him," I say, as much to convince myself as Jill. "Even though he's the only man I've never been able to read completely."

Jill smiles faintly. "Maybe that's for the best. Some people aren't meant to be figured out entirely. George is one of them."

I stand, glancing at Susan, sleeping but stable. "I should let her rest."

Jill nods, her expression softening. "Be careful, Dara. And trust your instincts."

As I step into the hallway, something catches my eye. A man in a lab coat walking toward Susan's room, his pace measured, intentional. He moves too deliberately, his eyes scanning the corridor with practiced precision. My stomach tightens. His shoes are caked in mud, strange for a hospital.

My gaze locks on his ID badge. Pediatrics. Why would a pediatric doctor be on an adult floor? My pulse quickens, my senses on high alert. Something isn't right.

I glance over my shoulder toward Jill, who hasn't noticed him yet. My mind races. Friend or foe? It's becoming harder to tell.

Adrenaline surges through me. My heart pounds as I pivot, scanning the hallway. Spotting a nurse nearby, I grab her arm, my grip firm but urgent.

"Call security. Now," I hiss, my voice low and intense. Her eyes widen in alarm, but she nods quickly and hurries toward the nurses' station.

I glance down the corridor, my pulse racing. Relief floods me when I see George's familiar silhouette. His calm, commanding presence is exactly what I need as he too seems to be walking toward Susan's room.

"George!" I call out, rushing toward him. My voice catches his attention immediately. "There's a man—"

George's posture changes in an instant. He is alert and focused. "Where?" His tone is clipped, and he is ready for action.

I point back toward Susan's room, where the man is walking ahead of us, his movements too deliberate. "Lab coat. Muddy shoes. He's not supposed to be here."

George's eyes narrow, his body taut with readiness. Without hesitation, he strides past me, his voice sharp. "Hey!" he shouts, his steps quickening. "Stop right there!"

The man freezes for a split second, his eyes darting toward George. Then he bolts.

George takes off after him with surprising speed. I stand rooted for a moment, stunned by the sudden chaos. When I finally move, my heels click loudly against the linoleum as I follow. My breath catches as I round the corner in time to see George reach under his tailored jacket and place his hand on a holstered weapon.

A gun. George is armed?

Who *is* he? CIA? FBI? The questions tumble through my mind like a storm, but I don't have time to process them. I then see hospital campus police join the chase, their voices echoing through the corridor.

"Dara!" Jillian's voice pulls me back to the present. She's standing at Susan's door, her expression tight with concern. Together, we watch the commotion that's drawn the attention of staff and patients alike as doors fly open and the chase lengthens down the hall.

"What happened?" she asks, her eyes darting between me and the fleeing man.

"He seemed out of place," I say, still catching my breath. "When I pointed him out and asked a nurse to call security, he ran. Then George... George just *took off* after him."

Jillian's lips press into a thin line. "George has been covering Susan's medical expenses. He stops by regularly."

I glance toward the corridor where the chase disappeared as Jillian continues. "You think that man was dangerous?"

"Well, he ran," I reply. "And Susan can identify Dmitri's killer. She's not safe, is she?"

"The police think she's fine. They believe she wasn't a target," Jillian says, but there's doubt in her voice.

"Of course they think that," I mutter, rolling my eyes. "In their eyes, she's just a prostitute. What do they care?"

Jillian's silence speaks volumes.

A bit later, after the chaos has subsided, I find George in a quiet alcove. He's leaning against the wall, looking more weathered than I've ever seen him.

"We need to talk," I say, my voice steady despite the turmoil swirling inside me.

George exhales heavily, rubbing the back of his neck. "I suppose we do."

I cross my arms, stepping closer. "Who are you, really? Government? Still active? I thought you were retired from... whatever it is you did."

He studies me for a long moment, his expression unreadable. "Dara, there's so much I want to tell you," he says finally. "But some truths... they're dangerous."

I scoff, meeting his gaze head-on. "I can handle dangerous, George. I think I've proven that."

He hesitates, his eyes flickering with a mix of pride and regret. "Let's take it one step at a time," he says. "For now, you should know we caught him. Russian. Armed. The police are questioning him."

"And you?" I challenge, raising an eyebrow. "You're armed too, George. Care to explain?"

He doesn't flinch. His voice is calm and steady. "Yes, I am."

I wait for him to elaborate, but he doesn't. The weight of his secrets presses down on me like a physical force.

“George,” I say, my tone softening, “I trust you. But if I’m going to stay safe, I need to know what I’m up against. What *we’re* up against.”

For a moment, I think he might finally open up. But instead, he places a hand on my shoulder, his grip firm but reassuring. “You don’t have to trust me completely yet,” he says. “Just trust that I’m on your side.”

The farmhouse kitchen glows with the soft warmth of lamplight as Aiden and I return from our latest date. The looming weight of exams still lingers in my mind, mingling with the whirlwind of the day’s events. Yet, in Aiden’s steady presence, a grounding comfort quiets the chaos. We linger near the stairs, reluctant to part, his hand in mine.

Every evening with Aiden feels like a refuge. Gentle kisses, thoughtful conversation, and his unwavering respect for my boundaries. He doesn’t press or pry into the corners of my private life, even when he must sense the shadows I’m navigating. He still feels... real, in a way that still catches me off guard.

"I had a lovely time," Aiden says, his smile sincere and unguarded.

I nod, returning his smile, but there’s a question burning in my chest. I hesitate, then decide to push through the uncertainty. "Aiden," I begin cautiously, "can I ask you something?"

"Of course," he says, his brow creasing slightly in curiosity.

I take a breath, my analytical mind racing even as the words tumble out. "Why haven’t you tried to sleep with me?"

His eyes widen in surprise, a faint flush creeping up his cheeks. "What?" he stammers.

I press on, my voice steady, but my heart pounding. "We've been dating. We've kissed. We're literally staying in the same house. Most men would've taken advantage of that situation."

Aiden's blush deepens, and he glances away briefly as if searching for the right response. Then, he turns back to me, his hand tightening gently around mine. "Dara, I..." He pauses, taking a steadying breath. "It's not that I don't want to; it's just that…well, I think I'm falling in love with you. I don't want to mess that up."

The words hit me like a jolt. My heart skips a beat, and for a moment, I'm unsure how to respond. "That wasn't what I expected," I admit softly, my voice almost a whisper.

Aiden chuckles nervously, rubbing the back of his neck. "It's not like I'm not attracted to you. I just don't want to take our relationship lightly."

"Do you feel like you'd be taking advantage of the situation? Is that what you mean?" I ask.

He steps closer, his expression earnest. "Dara, it's not about taking advantage. It's about doing this right. You're not just someone I'm drawn to just physically. You're so much more than that."

His words disarm me. Then he speaks again, his tone soft, deliberate as he studies my eyes. "Love is patient, love is kind. It does not envy, it does not boast, it is not proud. It does not dishonor others, it is not self-seeking, it is not easily angered, it keeps no record of wrongs."

The familiarity of the words pierces through me, pulling at buried memories. My mother's voice reading from the Bible. Long-forgotten studies bubbling to the surface. 1 Corinthians 13. It's as though he's reached into the depths of my guarded soul and offered a balm I didn't know I needed from my childhood.

"You're quoting scripture," I say, half incredulous, half amused. "To explain why you haven't slept with me?"

He nods, his gaze unwavering. "I want to do this right, Dara. You're worth more than a casual fling. You're worth... everything. I know you're going through a lot right now. Everything will work out in due time, as I'm attracted to everything about you. You're very special. I don't want us to rush or ruin what we seem to be building in a relationship."

Something deep inside me stirs, something warm, unfamiliar, and terrifying all at once. I've never been treated like this before. In my world, physical attraction was often a currency, a game to play. But with Aiden, it's different. His sincerity is jarring but in the best possible way. I almost feel guilty as part of me would bed him in a minute, and I sensed he would as well. It was something I had to work out in my analytical mind as this felt different.

"I don't know what to say," I admit, my voice thick with emotion.

"You don't have to say anything," Aiden replies gently. "I just want you to know that I care about you. Deeply. And I'm willing to wait, however long it takes."

His words resonate in a way I can't fully articulate. This moment feels like an anchor for all the chaos swirling around me and all the secrets I carry. Like safety. But it also feels fragile as he has yet to find out who I really am, and that scares me the most.

"Thank you," I whisper, barely able to meet his gaze. "For seeing me. The real me."

I lean in, pressing a soft kiss to his cheek. His stubble grazes my lips, grounding me in the present. He smiles, his warmth enveloping me like a shield against the storm.

"Goodnight, Aiden," I murmur, retreating toward my room. I force myself not to look back, afraid he'll see the tears welling in my eyes.

Once inside, I close the door and lean against it, my heart heavy and full at the same time. Sliding down to the floor, a single tear escapes and then streams down my cheek.

Chapter 12

"If I do lose you. I understand." - Dara

The sharp knock on Jillian's office door drew her attention, her practiced calm momentarily giving way to tension. Smoothing her silk blouse, she straightened in her chair as the door opened to reveal two men in dark suits.

"Ms. Foster?" the taller of the two asked authoritatively as they both displayed government credentials. "I'm Agent Davis, and this is Agent Thompson. FBI."

Jillian nodded, gesturing toward the chairs across from her desk. "Gentlemen, what can I do for you?"

The agents exchanged a glance before sitting, their postures rigid and imposing. Agent Davis leaned forward as he sat, his penetrating gaze locking onto Jillian's. "We need to discuss your agency's connection to Dmitri Voronov."

Jillian forced a measured smile though her pulse quickened. "Of course. What would you like to know?"

Agent Thompson pulled a manila folder from his briefcase, sliding a photo across the desk. "We have evidence that in addition to the young lady injured during the hotel room murder of Mr. Voronov, that one of your other escorts, Dara Keene, met with him as well. We understand this meeting was arranged through your agency."

Jillian glanced at the image of Dara seated across from Dmitri in a plush hotel room. She remained calm, her years of experience handling high-pressure situations serving her well. "Ms. Keene is a college student who works with us part-time to fund her education. We provide a legal, high-end service for clients seeking marketing models, event companions, and the like."

Davis raised an eyebrow. "And how did Ms. Keene end up paired with Mr. Voronov?"

Jillian chose her words carefully, maintaining her composed demeanor. "We match clients based on their stated preferences and compatibility. Mr. Voronov specifically requested an intelligent companion for a business event."

Thompson's lips pressed into a thin line. "These photos get a bit more graphic. Do you know how these photos were obtained?"

Jillian met his gaze evenly after viewing the blackmail photos. "No, but I'd be very interested to find out. Where did you get them?"

Davis ignored the question, his tone turning sharper. "Are you familiar with an attorney named John Mitchell?"

Jillian's smile didn't falter. "My client list is confidential, Agent Davis."

"So, he is a client," Thompson said, jotting a note. "You realize we can subpoena those records if necessary?"

Jillian's voice remained even. "He may have been a client at one point. My discretion is part of my business, not protection of illicit activities. We welcome your subpoena."

Davis leaned forward. "It's no secret Mr. Mitchell had a professional relationship with Dmitri Voronov. He likely recommended the meeting between your escort and Dmitri. We're just asking if you can confirm it."

Jillian's expression grew more cautious. "It's possible. Dmitri valued our services. John may have facilitated introductions, but I'd need to check our records."

Thompson tapped his pen on the desk. "So, Mr. Mitchell was involved in the arrangement with Ms. Keene. Was Mr. Mitchell also involved with the escort who was with Mr. Voronov at the time of his assassination?"

"Susan?" Jillian asked, her tone clipped. "I'll have to review our documentation, but I severed ties with John Mitchel when complications arose."

Davis pressed. "Complications like endangering the women under your agency's care?"

Jillian stiffened. "Something like that. I take the safety of my escorts very seriously, Agent Davis."

The agents exchanged another glance. Davis sighed. "A man recently attempted to enter Susan's hospital room. A Russian who was armed. He's in custody, and his testimony is proving valuable."

Jillian's mask of calm slipped slightly. "I understand Susan may have been able to identify Dmitri's killer. I hope she is safe now that you have someone in custody."

Thompson nodded. "She's safe for now, and the hitman's confession is far more damning."

Jillian exhaled, regaining her composure. "So, you've determined he was indeed a hitman. Good. But I'm also worried about Dara. If you're protecting Susan, you need to protect her too."

Davis leaned back, "Our next step is to interview Ms. Keene."

"She's been through a lot," Jillian said firmly, jotting down Dara's contact information.

Agent Thompson stood, collecting the folder. "We appreciate your cooperation, Ms. Foster."

As the agents left, Jillian's polished exterior remained intact, but her mind churned. She was walking a dangerous line, balancing the safety of her women against the unpredictable tides of powerful men like John

Mitchell and shadowy forces like Sasha's network. And at the center of it all was Dara, unknowingly caught in a storm Jillian was struggling to control.

Sasha's gloved fingers worked the lock on Dara's apartment door with meticulous precision. The soft *click* echoed in the quiet hallway, drawing a cold smile to his lips. He slipped inside, his movements silent and deliberate, a predator entering its prey's den.

His icy eyes swept the room, taking in the tidy, modest space. Everything was in its place, too neat, too organized. It was the kind of order that hid secrets.

He began his search methodically and unrelentingly. Drawers were pulled open and upended, their contents spilling onto the floor like discarded debris. Cushions were sliced open with a blade, white stuffing spilling out like entrails. He tapped on walls, his ear attuned to any hollow resonance that might betray a hidden compartment.

The chaos around him mirrored his growing frustration. The silence after the chaotic search was deafening. Each overturned piece of furniture, each scattered paper, each gutted cushion brought him no closer to the item he and John demanded. The key to untangling this intricate web of deception still eluded him. The key that connected trouble to John and ultimately to Sasha.

Sasha paused, surveying the havoc he'd wrought. The room looked like a hurricane had hit it, but he knew better. Someone else must have been here before him. Sasha allowed himself a dry chuckle. The wolves were circling the same prey, but none had yet sunk their teeth into the prize. John would have said something if his hired guns had found something earlier though.

With a resigned sigh, Sasha stepped back, scanning the destruction one last time. He adjusted his gloves, ready to retreat and regroup. His work here was incomplete, but it did not turn up what he hoped.

Suddenly, the sound of keys jingling in the hallway jolted him. He froze, every muscle tensing as adrenaline surged. He took a measured step back from the door, his hand instinctively resting on the concealed weapon at his side. He closed his eyes briefly, exhaling slowly to steady himself.

The door creaked open, revealing a young woman with wide, startled eyes; Leslie. Her presence was unexpected, and her innocence radiated even as fear clouded her face. She stood frozen in the doorway, her gaze darting between Sasha and the chaos behind him.

"Who... who are you?" she stammered, her voice trembling.

Sasha's lips curled into a predatory smile, his accent thick and deliberate. "A friend of Dara's. We have unfinished business."

Leslie's eyes flicked over the wreckage, her expression shifting from shock to confusion, then to fear. "What happened here? Did you do this?"

Sasha's smile didn't waver. He took a step forward, his presence overwhelming. "Tell Dara I came looking. And if she values her life, she'll hand over what I want."

Leslie's brow furrowed as she instinctively stepped back, her hand gripping the doorframe for support. "This isn't the first time someone's broken in. Was that you too?" Her voice grew steadier, though her fear was evident.

Sasha's grin widened, a cold gleam in his eye as she confirmed his suspicions. "Interesting. Seems I'm not the only one after her little secret. But don't worry sweetheart. I'm far more... effective." His words dripped with menace.

Leslie flinched as Sasha brushed past her, his movements casual, almost leisurely. He paused at the top of the stairs, turning back to deliver his final warning.

"Remember my message," he said, his voice low and cutting. "Dara's life depends on it."

He descended the stairs without a backward glance, leaving Leslie standing frozen in the doorway. Her trembling hand covered her mouth as the weight of his threat sank in. The scent of fear hung in the air long after Sasha disappeared.

The phone's vibration jolted me from my thoughts, Leslie's name flashing on the screen like an alarm.

"Leslie?" I answered quickly, tension already coiling in my gut.

"Dara, oh God," Leslie's voice trembled, barely holding together. "Someone broke in again. He… he said he knew you."

My blood went cold. "You saw who broke in? Are you okay?"

Her shaky recounting of the encounter made my pulse race. Beside me, Aiden watched intently, his eyes full of questions he didn't ask. His hand found mine, warm and comforting, as though he could sense the storm inside me.

"I'm coming back," I said firmly. "Call the police and stay with a neighbor until I get there."

Hanging up, I met Aiden's gaze. "My apartment was broken into. Again."

His jaw tightened. "I'm coming with you. No arguments."

I wanted to protest, to shield him from the darkness that seemed to close in around me, but the determination in his eyes melted my resolve.

He wasn't going to let me face this alone, and for once, I allowed myself to lean on someone else's strength.

"Okay," I whispered. "Let's go."

As Aiden and I drove, my fingers trembled over my phone. I dialed George's emergency number that he had given me, the familiar click in the line signaling he'd picked up after just two rings.

"Dara?" George's calm, steady voice cut through the tension, soothing me like Aiden's hand had.

"My apartment's been broken into again," I said, surprised at how steady my voice sounded despite the chaos inside me.

A pause. "Are you safe?"

"For now," I said. "But I'm scared, George. What do I tell the police?"

George's tone softened. "The truth, my dear. It's your best shield. Tell them about John, Sasha… everything. The note you gave me is being tested for DNA by Feds. It will confirm who gave it to you. I'm sure you apartment intruder are still looking for it."

I hesitated before asking, my curiosity piqued. "You gave it to authorities already? And you actually have John's DNA to test against the note?"

There was a moment's silence before George answered. "We do."

"We? You never cease to amaze me," I said, letting out a dry laugh. What I didn't tell George was that by using the word 'we' and the space between what he didn't say, made it clear he was an active participant rather than just a bystander or informant defending me. I sensed he knew I analyzed every word. "What other tricks do you have up your sleeve, George?"

Another pause. "Well, Dara, since you ask... I promised I'd reveal more when the time was right."

"You mean when you thought I could handle it," I countered, a wry smile tugging at my lips.

"True, and you deserve to know some things," George admitted. "For instance, I've known your real name long before this scandal broke."

"Well, I figured that out long ago," I said, my voice softer now. "It's why I never questioned it when you gave me your number and seemed to know so much about me."

"And I've tried to pay your tuition more times than I can count," he added.

"Tell me something I don't know. And I've always fought you on it," I replied.

George hesitated before speaking again. "I also had my driver follow you the night your first apartment was broken into. I couldn't risk anything happening to you."

"Yep," I said gently. "And I know you've been asking Jillian to fire me for years, to push me out of the business, and I understand. Way ahead of you, George. But thanks for sharing."

George sighed, his voice carrying a weight that made my chest ache. "I'm sorry for not always being upfront, Dara. But everything I've done has been to protect you, even if I wasn't as forthcoming as I should've been. But it was for the best. My work has always required me to have a great deal of discretion."

I nodded, a small, understanding smile breaking through. George was trying. "It seems we've both known more than we let on. We're both just… observant. We both have required…discretion. That's ok. I've figured out more than you realize. A lot more."

The silence between us wasn't empty. It was heavy with unspoken truths, with an understanding that didn't need words. It was almost as if we both knew what each would say next.

"George," I began, my voice resolute, "it's time. I'll quit the escort service. I realize now it's time to leave that life behind. But when this Russian mess is over, I have to leave all of it behind, including you. As painful as it will be. I've thought about it despite the things I've come to realize. And you know why."

George's silence spoke volumes. Finally, he said, "I understand. And I'll help you get this Russian situation behind you. But Dara…" His voice faltered slightly, uncharacteristically hesitant. "If you ever need anything after this is over, after graduation, you can always call me. I understand your reluctance."

I took a shaky breath, emotions tangling in my chest. "Thank you, George. But after this, I need to leave all of it behind. The work, the chaos… everything. That includes you, even though it pains me to say it. It's even harder to say it now." I bit my lip. I knew I'd have to say those words one day. I took a deep breath as soon as the words escaped.

George paused. I wondered what he was feeling after spending so much time together these past few years. Sadness? Regret? He finally spoke. "I see," he said softly.

I hesitated, searching for the words to explain what I was feeling, and added, "Unless you can somehow create a family that has never existed, George… there's no place for any of my old life in my future. I have to start fresh. Even from you," I paused as my voice dropped. "Especially from you. You understand."

"Understood," he said finally, his voice steady. Too steady.

George was an enigma. His emotions were always carefully controlled, and I could almost feel his pain and emotion over the phone.

"I'll do everything I can to make sure you start fresh on that new life, Dara," he said quietly, almost to himself.

"Thank you, George," I replied, a lump forming in my throat. Hanging up, I left the words hanging between us, unaware that they meant more to him than I could possibly imagine.

My hand lingered in midair, clutching the phone long after the call ended. A single tear slipped down my cheek, quickly followed by another. I wiped them away, startled by the unexpected surge of emotion. I wasn't one for tears, never had been. But the weight of everything pressed down all at once: the FBI, the break-ins, my decision to quit the agency. Yet another invasion into my apartment was the last straw. I had to put it all behind me. It wasn't just about leaving my old life behind; it was about leaving all of it behind, even the few good parts I wished I could hold on to. Even George as I loved and hated who he was and what he was trying to do at the same time. What he had been trying to do for three years.

The thought of never seeing him again after graduation tightened my chest. I had known this day would come. I'd prepared for it, steeling myself against the inevitable. But now that it was here, the finality of it hit harder than I'd imagined. What's more, losing Aiden could be next.

Taking a deep breath, I forced the emotions back down. There was no time for this. I needed to tell Aiden what was coming. He deserved to know, especially with graduation looming and the looming chaos threatening to break. The question gnawed at me: would Aiden, like

George, become another casualty of my old life? Would I have to leave him behind too, once he knew the real me?

There wasn't much to do at my old apartment. There was another police report, and there were more questions. Leslie described Sasha perfectly. Then Jillian texted about the FBI. Things were coming to a head.

Before long, we were back at the farmhouse, and Aiden retreated to his study to finish grading papers. I paced the floor in deep thought. I knew I'd have to walk away from George one day. The recent chaos simply made that decision more difficult. Aiden may be the next unexpected casualty of my decisions. But he had to know, and as it was, I may have waited too late anyway.

I found him in the study, bent over a stack of papers. He looked so composed, so absorbed in his work, everything I wasn't in that moment.

"Aiden," I said, my voice barely above a whisper.

He looked up immediately, concern flickering across his face. "Dara? What's wrong?"

I hesitated, the words sticking in my throat. "The FBI is coming," I finally managed, watching his expression shift from concern to sharp focus.

"The FBI?" He set down his pen and turned fully toward me. "Why? What's going on?"

I sank into the chair across from him, my fingers nervously tracing invisible patterns on the armrest. "There's... so much I haven't told you," I admitted, my voice trembling. "I'm sorry."

Aiden leaned forward, his gaze steady, intense. "I've been patient, Dara. But you know I'm starting to worry."

"I know," I whispered, my chest tightening. "And I appreciate that more than you know. But you don't understand. I've never had this before.

Someone who actually cares. Someone real. And I'm terrified that once I tell you everything, it'll all change."

He reached across the desk, his hand enveloping mine with a warmth that threatened to undo me. "Dara, if the FBI is involved, I know this must be serious. But nothing you tell me will change how I feel about you. Do you understand that?"

I looked into his eyes, searching for even the smallest flicker of doubt. But there was none. Just the same quiet, steady care he'd shown since the beginning. A lump rose in my throat.

"How bad can it be?" he asked gently, his voice a soothing balm against my fraying nerves.

A bitter laugh escaped me before I could stop it. "Oh, Aiden," I said, shaking my head. "You have no idea." I felt a tear begin to well up.

His hand tightened around mine, grounding me. "Then let me help," he said softly.

I hesitated, fighting the urge to retreat. "Let me talk to the FBI first," I said. "Maybe after that, I'll have the courage to tell you everything. We'll have more time then."

He nodded, standing and pulling me into his arms. His embrace was firm, reassuring, and heartbreakingly kind. I clung to him for a moment longer than I should have, soaking in the safety of his presence.

But as he held me, all I could think was how different things might be once the truth was out. How much would he change once he knew the whole story of my life? And how much would I lose if he couldn't handle it? It would be more for him to take in than he realized. I was more to take in than he realized.

One way or another, I knew the answers were coming. And I wasn't sure I was ready for them.

The crunch of tires on gravel pulls my attention to the window. Two black SUVs roll to a stop outside the farmhouse. My heart thunders as four agents in dark suits step out, their faces impassive, their movements precise.

I spot Michaels, our bodyguard, striding toward them. He exchanges clipped words with the lead agent, gesturing toward the house. One of the agents glances directly at the window where I'm standing. I instinctively step back, the weight of their presence settling in my chest.

"They're here," I say to Aiden, my voice steadier than I feel.

He squeezes my hand. "I'm right here with you."

The doorbell chimes, echoing through the quiet farmhouse. Each step down the hallway feels like I'm walking toward a reckoning. At the door, I take a breath and open it, summoning a polite smile I don't feel.

"Miss Keene?" the lead agent asks, his voice clipped but not unkind. I nod.

"I'm Agent Carlson. We'd like to ask you some questions."

"Of course," I reply, stepping aside. "We can use the study."

As I lead them down the hall, I glance at Aiden over my shoulder. His concerned eyes meet mine, offering silent reassurance. I don't deserve his unwavering support, but I cling to it anyway.

The study door closes behind us, isolating me with the agents. Agent Carlson takes a seat across from me, his partner standing by the door, a silent sentinel.

"Miss Keene," Carlson begins, "we need to discuss your connections to John Mitchell and Dmitri Voronov."

I steady myself with a deep breath. There's no room for half-truths. Honesty is my best defense now, recalling George's advice.

"I met John through my work as an escort," I say, carefully watching their faces. "He introduced me to Dmitri at a party."

Carlson nods, his pen moving methodically across his notepad. "And the nature of your relationship with Mr. Voronov?"

"Professional," I state firmly. "I was hired to accompany him to events. Nothing more."

Carlson glances up. "You said John Mitchell introduced you to Mr. Voronov?"

"Yes," I say, the knot in my stomach tightening. "After John and I met, he left me a note asking if I'd accompany Dmitri and show him a good time. At the end of the evening, I was to say something to him in Russian: 'Vorovskoy Zakon.'"

The agents exchange a brief look, and Carlson leans forward slightly. "Do you know what that phrase means?"

I nod. "It translates to 'Thieves' Code.' It's a term tied to organized crime in the Soviet Union. I learned it was a formal status that carries authority over other criminals. I didn't know the significance of the phrase until later."

"Do you know the punishment Russian mobsters give to other mobsters for violating the Thieves' Code?" Carlson presses, his tone probing.

I swallow hard. "Death," I say quietly. "I assume John wanted me to deliver a message that only Dmitri would understand. I now know it was a threat."

Carlson's pen halts mid-note. He studies me, his expression inscrutable. "Did you know about the compromising photos taken of you and Dmitri?"

I suppress a bitter laugh. "Yes. Naked photos of me and a Russian mobster weren't exactly a career choice. Sasha Petrov showed them to me."

The other agent speaks for the first time, his voice sharp. "Sasha Petrov is a competing Russian mobster. Did he tell you why he showed you the photos?"

"To intimidate me. He wanted to know who I worked for and what I told Dmitri," I reply.

"And what did you tell him?" Carlson asks.

"I played dumb," I admit. "At the time, I didn't understand what was happening."

Carlson nods, then shifts gears. "Your colleague, Susan. She was with Dmitri when he was killed. You're aware of that?"

"Yes," I say, my voice barely above a whisper. "I first saw it on the news."

The agents exchange another glance. "Where is the note John left you?" Carlson asks.

I hesitate, but only for a moment. "I gave it to George. He's a longtime client."

Both agents seem to stiffen ever so slightly at the mention of George's name. Their reactions confirm what I've suspected: George's name carries weight or at least they expected me to use his name.

"Why did you give it to him?" Carlson asks.

"For protection," I say. "I knew it had John's DNA on it. If something happened to me, it would prove my story. My apartment has been broken into twice by people looking for it. The local police have the reports. I gave the note to George as I knew it would physically connect John to the threat on Dmitri. You'll have to ask George where the note is currently."

Carlson's expression remains neutral, but his eyes flicker with recognition. My analysis of their responses, nonverbal cues, and monotone patterns is clear. I've not provided them with any new information To my relief, it seems the visit was a formality confirming what they already knew. The agent looks up from his notes. "We may be in contact again, Ms. Keene."

It was clear at this point that they weren't going to pursue any line of questioning that involved George. They seemed to know or at least assumed to know which George I was talking about. How many George's do they know? I take a breath, steadying myself. "Before you go... do you know George?"

Carlson's face hardens. "We can't discuss details of an ongoing investigation, Ms. Keene."

Of course not. I nod, letting the question linger in the air as they rise to leave. I didn't expect them to answer. I just wanted to see their reaction to the question. Their unspoken words told me everything I needed to know. I catalogued those unspoken cues.

Their departure feels abrupt, almost anticlimactic, but the tension they leave behind lingers a bit even though I'm now reassured.

As the door closes, I lean back in the chair, exhausted but oddly relieved. They know more than they're saying. They always do. But now, I've given them everything I know. And I can only hope it's enough to keep me one step ahead of whatever's coming.

The door closes behind the FBI agents, leaving the house eerily quiet. I exhale slowly, my shoulders sagging under the weight of exhaustion and relief. The momentary stillness feels fragile, as though it could shatter at any second.

Footsteps echo in the hallway. Aiden appears in the doorway of the study, his brow furrowed, his eyes full of concern.

"Dara?" he asks softly. "Are you alright?"

I force a smile, though it doesn't quite reach my eyes. "I'm fine," I say, my voice brittle.

He crosses the room in a few strides, his presence solid and reassuring. When he places a tentative hand on my shoulder, the warmth of his touch sends a rush of conflicting emotions through me. Comfort. Fear. Longing. I want to lean into him, to let him share the weight of everything I've been carrying. But I can't, at least, not yet.

"What did they want?" Aiden's voice is gentle, but there's an undercurrent of worry.

I hesitate, the truth hovering on the edge of my lips. The words feel sharp, like glass, threatening to cut both of us if I let them out. My heart pounds, torn between my desire to confide in him and the fear that he won't look at me the same way once he knows everything.

"It's... complicated," I finally say, my voice faltering.

Aiden crouches slightly, bringing himself to my eye level. His gaze searches mine, patient and steady. "Whatever it is, Dara, we can face it together."

His words hit me like a gentle blow, breaking something inside me. The walls I've spent years constructing, brick by painstaking brick, start to crumble.

"It's not just about what they wanted," I whisper, barely able to meet his eyes. "There's so much you don't know about me."

Aiden doesn't flinch. Instead, he takes my hand, his fingers warm and firm around mine. "Then tell me," he says simply. "I'm here. I'm listening."

I swallow hard, the lump in my throat making it difficult to speak. His unwavering support feels like a lifeline, but it also terrifies me. What if this changes everything?

"Okay," I murmur, my voice steadier now. "But you have to promise me something first."

"Anything," he says without hesitation, his sincerity disarming.

"Promise me you'll hear me out completely before you make any judgments," I say, holding his gaze.

His nod is slow and deliberate. "You have my word."

"And you'll try not to be shocked," I continue.

"Dara, whatever you've been holding back to tell me. It can't be that bad," he says as he sits beside me, holding my hand. His eyes are full of support and encouragement. For now, at least.

I close my eyes for a moment, inhaling deeply as I gather the courage to step over the threshold of truth. When I open them, I meet Aiden's gaze head-on.

"It started after my mom died," I begin, my voice barely above a whisper. "I promised her I'd finish college. It was the last thing she asked of me, and when she was gone, it felt like all I had left. But there was no money. No family. Nothing. I was desperate."

Aiden's hand tightens around mine, a silent gesture of support. His expression remains open, free of judgment, and it gives me the strength to continue.

"I made some choices... choices I'm not proud of. But at the time, they felt like my only option." My voice trembles, and I have to pause to steady myself.

Aiden doesn't interrupt. He doesn't look away. The quiet understanding in his eyes is like a balm on my frayed nerves, but it also deepens my fear. When he knows the whole truth, will that warmth still be there?

"I just..." I trail off, my words faltering. "I don't want to lose you, Aiden. Not because of this. But if I do lose you. I understand."

He lifts my hand, brushing his lips gently against my knuckles. "Dara," he says, his voice firm but kind. "Whatever you're about to tell me, it doesn't change who you are. And it doesn't change how I feel about you."

My breath hitches at his words, the sincerity in his tone overwhelming. For the first time in a long time, I allow myself to hope.

"Alright," I say, my voice barely audible. I was about to reveal to Aiden the life I wanted to leave behind. The question would be if Aiden would be part of my new life after the revelation.

Chapter 13

"I understand if this changes things" – Dara

My hands tremble as I clasp them together, trying to steady myself. This is it. No more half-truths. No more hiding.

Aiden leans forward, his face a mixture of concern and patience. "Dara, you don't have to rush. Take your time."

I take a deep breath and reach for his hands, steadying myself in his warmth. His concerned gaze encourages me, silently promising that he'll listen.

"There's something I've needed to tell you," I begin quietly. "And it doesn't start with the FBI. It starts with my past. How I paid for school, rent…how I survived after mom died."

Aiden nods once. "Okay."

"You already know my mom died when I was eighteen. Cancer." My voice tightens. "With her last breath, she made me promise that I'd finish college. She insisted I transfer to the University."

He squeezes my hands. "That must have been unbearable."

"It was," I admit. "After she died, I had nothing. I was alone. There was no family. No safety net. Just debt and that promise. I tried everything. Waited tables, retail, tutoring. None of it came close to what I needed.

I force a humorless breath. "Then I saw an ad for modeling."

Aiden doesn't interrupt.

"It led to other offers. Higher paying ones." I lift my eyes to his. "Eventually…I became in escort."

The word lands between us like a held breath.

Aiden leans back slightly, running a hand through his hair, not recoiling, not angry. Just recalibrating. I could see him turning the word over in his brain trying to grasp the depth of what I was saying.

"Okay," he says after a moment. "I…wasn't expecting that."

I nod. "I know."

He looks at me again, searching. He doesn't appear to be judging, but figuring out his next words. "Were you safe? I mean, I assume all that has been happening is because of what you do."

The question nearly undoes me. *What you do*, echoed in my brain.

"Yes," I say quickly. "As safe as something like that can be. Jillian, who runs the agency, screened clients. It wasn't what people imagine. Not always." I pause. "But it still changed how I learned to relate to people."

Silence stretches. Heavy, but not cold.

"That first kiss," he says quietly. "You weren't lying?"

"No." My voice softens. "It was my first kiss without expectations. Without a role. Without transaction. Just…real. I promise."

He studies me for a long moment, then nods. "I felt that."

Tears burn, but I don't let them fall. "I understand if this changes things."

"It does," he says honestly.

My chest tightens.

"But not how you think," he continues. "I just need a minute to absorb it. But I don't see you differently. I see what you survived."

Relief hits so fast I almost laugh.

"I'm done with that life," I say firmly. "For good. I'm graduating. That chapter is over."

Aiden exhales slowly. "Good."

I lean in, kissing him. Slow, deliberate, unguarded. When we part, his forehead rests against mine.

"Still different?" I murmur.

"Still different," he says. "Good different."

I allow myself to hope, just for a moment.

Then I inhale. "You probably think the FBI and men outside were the biggest secrets."

His brow furrows. "I assume they were connected to…that."

"They are," I say carefully. "But it gets worse."

He stiffens slightly. "Okay."

"There's a Russian mobster. And an attorney named John Mitchell." I don't rush. I don't soften it.

Aiden exhales sharply. "The one on the news?"

"Yes."

I explain cleanly this time. The note. The phrase. The photos. The murder. Susan. The break-ins. The FBI. And a bit about George helping me.

When I finish, he's quiet.

Finally: "Are you safe right now?"

"Yes…I think so."

"Then I'm not going anywhere," he says simply. "We'll deal with the rest together."

I close my eyes, leaning into him.

Chapter 14

"Some secrets aren't hidden out of fear. They're hidden out of love." — *Dara*

The next morning, the sharp aroma of coffee greets me as I step into Mom & Pop's Café.

George is already there, immaculate, composed, impossible to read. "I met with the FBI," I say, sitting down.

His eyes flicker. "And?"

"They knew you," I reply. "The interview practically stopped when I mentioned your name."

A faint smile. "I'm known in certain circles."

"That's all you're going to say?"

He sips his coffee. I study him, the man who has always known more than he should.

"Our time together is changing," I say quietly. "I need to understand who you are."

He sets the cup down. "That's fair. You deserve answers."

He speaks carefully. Intelligence field has been his lifelong work. Government operations that don't make it into history books. Technology that doesn't appear in public records. Intellectual property.

"Technology. You mean patents?" I ask.

"Yes. Some public. Many under secrecy orders."

"So… NSA?"

He smiles thinly. Then shrugs with a non-answer. "The CIA has better marketing."

"There must be a hundred ways people are afraid of you. You've always known everything about me then." I shake my head. "Why me, George?"

His gaze softens. "You needed someone."

The answer comforts and unsettles me all at once. But I push questions out of my mind that I don't want answered. I pause then exhale.

"I'm quitting," I tell him. "The escort work. For good."

"I'm glad," he says. "You were always meant for more."

"But after graduation," I add, "this ends. Us. I need a clean life. My escort past can't follow me. You admit you operate in the shadows because of your work. I'll have to be one of those shadows."

He nods slowly. "I understand."

"Coffee until then?" I offer.

A pause. Then his eyes crinkle with warmth. "I'd like that."

Not being able to read George was always unsettling. But at that moment, I saw something I wasn't ready to understand.

I left the café with the unsettling sense that I hadn't learned something new. I'd merely brushed against something I had always known. Some secrets aren't hidden out of fear. They're hidden out of love.

Chapter 15

"I'm quitting." — Dara

The door to Jillian's office creaks as I push it open, my heart thudding harder than it should. The familiar scent of vanilla candles drifts through the room, usually calming, now suffocating.

Jillian looks up from her desk, her sharp eyes narrowing as she takes in my expression.

"I'm quitting," I say. My voice is steadier than I feel.

She studies me for a long moment before setting her pen down. Slowly, she leans back in her chair, lips curling into a knowing half-smile.

"Well," she says quietly, "I wondered when you'd finally say it."

Finals. Graduation. A line I can't keep straddling. I nod. "It's time. After graduation, I'm moving forward."

She exhales, something unguarded flickering across her face. "You've been one of my best, Dara. I won't pretend I'm not losing something. But I knew this day would come."

There's pride in her voice. It surprises me.

"There's more," I say. I step closer to her desk, lowering my voice. "I need you to be honest with me. About George. About you. Why I ended up… with him."

Jillian stills.

The pause is brief. But it's enough. It speaks louder than anything she says next.

"George requested you," she says finally. Her tone is measured. Controlled.

"I knew it wasn't random," I reply. "But why? How did he even know about me?"

Her eyes flick to the door. Then she stands, closes it quietly, and turns back to me with a seriousness I've never seen before.

"I knew George before I opened this agency," she says. "Long before."

My stomach tightens.

"I worked in intelligence," she continues. "Government. The escort agency began as a front. One of several. Collection. Access. Observation."

The words hit me harder than I expect. I sink into the chair across from her.

"And George?" I ask.

"He's been in intelligence his entire adult life," she says. "Still is, in his own way. He helped build systems, networks, ways of seeing what others miss. He's a very smart man."

I let out a breath I didn't realize I was holding. Pieces fall into place. Too many of them.

"So he watched me," I say quietly. "Paid to see me once a week. That was his way of guiding me?"

Jillian hesitates. "He wanted you safe. Away from the worst of it. He hoped you'd focus on modeling, conventions. He accepted, reluctantly, that your time with him was at least one night you weren't elsewhere."

The truth stings because it fits.

"And the Keene name?" I ask. "Did that matter?"

Jillian nods slowly. "You know about Elliot Keene. A pioneer of artificial intelligence. George's field so he has an interest." She pauses again before continuing. "George notices patterns. He always has. Your aptitude. Your instincts. Your resistance to control." She pauses. "He does suspect you have a connection to Elliot Keene's family. Not proof. A theory."

I shake my head. "Even if it were true, I don't want that life. I don't want to be studied like some kind of pet project."

"I know," Jillian says gently. "And I don't believe George ever saw you as a project. Whatever else he is… he cares."

That might have been the hardest thing she said. I knew all along. All the dots were there. I was just too afraid to allow them to connect. I look at the ceiling as those dots fell into place. I then shook my head slowly.

"I'm done," I say, standing abruptly. "After graduation, I leave all of it. The agency. George. Everything. I don't want to be watched anymore."

Jillian nods once. "I understand."

As I turn for the door, she adds, quietly, "You know, Dara…you were never invisible."

The drive back to the farmhouse barely registers. Jillian's words loop in my head, stacking unease on top of revelation. Why had I not allowed myself to see everything that was clearly obvious?

When I pull into the driveway, something feels wrong as I step out of the vehicle.

The air is too still. The porch light flickers. I catch movement behind the living-room curtain. Aiden's face appears, then vanishes.

"Aiden?" I call.

A twig snaps in the woods.

My pulse spikes. I turn slowly, scanning the tree line. Shadows press in where light should be. My breath sounds too loud.

"Who's there?" I call toward the darkness as I ease toward the porch.

Silence.

Then gunfire explodes.

I hit the gravel instinctively as glass shatters overhead. The farmhouse windows burst inward, alarms screaming through my senses.

"Dara! Get down!" Aiden shouts. His silhouette at the doorway.

I crawl toward the steps as another shot cracks through the night. Aiden grabs my arm, hauling me inside just as movement surges from the trees. The shots seem to be coming from different directions.

A man suddenly breaks from the darkness, weapon raised, charging the door.

Time fractures.

Aiden lunges at the gunman. The gun discharges. They collide hard, bodies slamming into the ground. The weapon skitters away. Aiden fights. But I can see it immediately.

The man is trained. He soon is overpowering Aiden.

"Aiden!" I scream.

The attacker gains leverage, fist rising. Then suddenly, a blur of motion slams into him.

George's bodyguard tackles the man with brutal force, pinning him in seconds.

Sirens then wail before I can even process it.

Too fast.

Police flood the property and promptly take custody of the attacker from George's bodyguard.

"How did you get here so quickly?" I ask numbly.

"We intercepted a credible threat," the detective replies. "Federal coordination."

Of course they did.

Later, as officers secure the scene, Aiden finds me inside the shattered living room. The farmhouse feels hollow. I could only imagine what federal agencies were tracking every cell phone around me. How many more were they tracking?

"What is this, Dara?" he asks quietly. "Who is coming after you?"

I swallow. "A lawyer. A mobster. Men who don't like loose ends. My former life that I told you about following me. A note."

His hand tightens on my shoulder. "You're safe here. But we can't pretend this isn't our present life, Dara."

I nod, resolve hardening. "I know. I'm done being a pawn in somebody's game."

Chapter 16

"Why does it feel like I just made a deal with the devil?" — Dara

The bell above the café door chimes as Aiden holds it open for me. Warm air, thick with coffee and cinnamon, wraps around us, familiar, comforting. For a moment, it almost feels normal.

Almost.

My eyes scan the room out of instinct, landing immediately on two men in dark suits near the window. George's security detail. Always present. Always watching. One of them glances our way, cataloging, assessing, before returning to his practiced indifference.

We'd grown used to this routine, checking in whenever I left the farmhouse, the quiet shadow of protection following me through final exams, across campus, into places that should have felt safe on their own. It was supposed to reassure me.

Instead, it reminded me I was still a pawn.

"After you," Aiden says lightly, gesturing toward a corner booth.

I slide in just as he nearly trips over his own feet. A laugh escapes before I can stop it.

"Graceful as ever, Professor."

He grins, settling across from me. "I'll have you know I was a champion stumbler in college."

"Ah, yes," I smirk. "Clearly fast-tracked to faculty for athletic excellence."

The banter creates a fragile bubble, normalcy we both pretend can hold. But I catch the way his eyes linger on me now, more searching than before.

"Dara," he says quietly, setting the menu down. "Now that you've told me about your past you can trust me… I want to know more. Not about the chaos. About you. Your childhood. Your life before all this."

The question hits harder than I expect. No one's ever asked me that, not without an agenda.

"You know the things that matter. It was… complicated," I say carefully. "After my mom died, everything changed. No siblings. No father. She was all I had. That's it. I felt alone in a way nobody should."

Aiden's expression softens. "That kind of loss leaves a mark."

"It does," I agree. "The only thing that stayed consistent were the stories she took me to hear every Sunday. Sunday School. They were… grounding. A connection I still had to her."

He studies me. "Faith?"

I shrug, a sad smile forming. "More like memory. Those stories felt stable when nothing else did."

"Did you have friends?" he asks gently.

I laugh softly. "Not really. I was too analytical. Too curious. So I hid in books. Scripture, philosophy, things far beyond my age."

He reaches across the table, his hand covering mine. "You grew up fast."

"Yes," I say quietly. "And alone."

I hesitate, then add, "I've always felt drawn to certain women in those stories. Rahab. The woman at the well. They were outcasts. I could relate."

Aiden leans in. "Because they were judged?"

"Because they were seen," I say. "And still chosen."

The word hangs between us.

"Do you think you need redemption?" he asks softly.

I look down. "I think I've always believed I do."

His grip tightens. “We all need a second chance. But you’re stronger than you realize.”

For the first time in a long time, I let myself hope that might be true.

Later, alone in the car, my thumb hovers over George’s number.

I need control. I need answers.

I call.

“Dara,” George answers on the second ring. “Are you alright?”

“I want to help the FBI set up Sasha.”

Silence.

“That’s dangerous,” he says finally. “Sasha isn’t impulsive. He’s calculating.”

“I know,” I reply. “That’s why it has to be me.”

Another pause.

“Very well,” George says. “I’ll make the arrangements.”

Hours later, the FBI office is sterile and quiet, designed to strip emotion from decisions. Two agents sit across from me.

“You understand the risks,” the older one says.

“I do.”

The younger agent slides a small device across the table. Jewelry. Undetectable listening device.

“We need proof,” the older agent continues. “A direct link between Sasha and the U.S. supplier.”

"So I'm the bait," I say calmly.

"Essentially."

The older agent's face turns grave. "We've intercepted communications mentioning a codename: **Agnes**."

My mind snaps to attention. Agnes. Too clean. Too ordinary. The kind of word you choose when you don't want it to sound like a code.

"In what context?" I ask.

The younger agent flips open his notebook. "It shows up the same way every time. Short messages. One line. Always paired with a time window and a location, never a name. Example: *Agnes confirmed. Thursday. 21:00. Port.* Or: *Agnes delayed. Two days.*"

I stare at him. That isn't a person. Not the way they're using it.

"It's a trigger," I say quietly before I can stop myself. "A green light."

The older agent's eyes narrow, interested. "Meaning?"

"Meaning Agnes isn't who," I reply. "It's *what.* A phase. A status. Maybe a shipment. Maybe a handshake condition, like a verified channel, or an authentication step."

The younger agent's mouth tightens. "We've tried the obvious. Saints. Russian diminutives. Acronyms. Nothing fits clean."

Agnes. I turn it over in my head like a coin, feeling the ridges.

I murmur, mostly to myself, "It has to be symbolic. Or linguistic."

The younger agent straightens. "You're familiar with codebreaking?"

I shrug, keeping my voice light even as my brain accelerates. "I've read a few books."

But I'm not reading books now. I'm hearing patterns.

Agnes. My mind runs through associations, fast, ruthless:

- **Agnus Dei -** Latin. "Lamb of God." Too on the nose… unless it's meant to sound harmless.
- **Saint Agnes**—martyr, purity, a symbol. Again: *harmless.*
- An **acronym** wearing a human name like a mask. *Maybe.*
- **Agniastra** – Ancient Sanskrit for fire weapon. *Possible.*
- Or a word chosen because it travels well across languages—easy to say, easy to text, hard to flag.

Then a more unsettling thought surfaces: *Agnes* might not be a codeword at all. It might be a signal of trust. A reference only insiders recognize. But it has to be symbolic or linguistic in meaning.

I look up. "How often does it appear?"

"Only around key movement," the older agent says. "Before meetings. Before transfers. Before contact with the American supplier."

A pulse of cold clarity goes through me.

"They're using it like a latch," I say. "A confirmation that the next part of the chain is safe. Like, *Agnes is live.*"

The older agent studies me for a beat, then nods once. "That's… consistent with what we're seeing."

"I'll give it more thought," I say carefully. "But if I'm right, you won't crack Agnes by translating it. You'll crack it by catching what happens *after* it's said."

The older agent's gaze hardens with resolve. "We will definitely follow that lead."

I slide the listening device back across the table, my fingers steady now. "Tell me exactly what you need me to do."

Because I know one thing for certain. If I fail, I won't get another chance.

The café buzzes with life, easy conversation, the clink of cups, the hiss of steam. I sit at a corner table, hands wrapped around a latte, forcing myself to look at ease. Casual. Normal. Just another college student on a coffee break.

Not someone wired for sound, about to sit across from a predator.

Every nerve in my body is coiled tight.

I spot Sasha before he sees me. He moves through the café with predatory grace, scanning the room with cold calculation. When his gaze lands on me, it feels like a blade against my skin.

I straighten my spine and meet his eyes with practiced indifference.

"Ah, Dara," Sasha says as he slides into the chair across from me. His voice is smooth, cultured, but every syllable carries a veiled threat. "So good to see you again."

Men settle into seats around the café at nearly the same moment. His people. Silent. Watching. Across the room, a few patrons linger too long over their coffee, FBI, posing as ordinary customers. Maybe Sasha knows and doesn't care.

I offer a polite smile. "Likewise, Sasha. I hope you're well."

He leans back, studying me. "Let's skip the pleasantries." His fingers drum lightly on the table. "I'm curious about your… relationship with Dmitri and John. Is that why you had John set up our little meeting?"

A careful opening. He's testing me.

I keep my voice light, even. "Dmitri and I had a mutually beneficial arrangement. You know that. Nothing more, nothing less." I shrug. "And John?" A soft laugh. "He tries to screw everyone around him. How was he screwing you?"

Sasha's lips curl into a shark's smile. He leans forward, voice dropping. "Careful, Dara. Curiosity can be dangerous." Then, casually: "I wonder what your friend George would think of your… inquisitiveness."

George.

My blood goes cold. I keep my muscles loose, my expression amused. Bluff or trap?

"George is a client," I say mildly. "Nothing more. I'm not sure why he's relevant."

Sasha chuckles, humorless. "Misplaced trust can be deadly." His eyes sharpen. "And your friend Susan? It would be a shame if something happened to her."

Threat confirmed.

I sip my coffee slowly, giving him nothing. "I appreciate your concern. But my trust is well placed."

Before he can push further, one of his men leans in, murmuring in Russian.

I follow Sasha's gaze to the window.

The FBI. Damn it.

An undercover agent stands just a little too close. Too obvious. A rookie mistake.

Sasha's hand shifts toward his jacket.

A gun.

I smile smoothly. "That's my bodyguard."

His eyes flick back to me.

"George insists on protection," I continue easily. "Given the nature of his work. You understand. That's why you brought him up, right?"

I watch his pupils. No sudden dilation. No spike. His mind is already slotting George into the category of shadow operators. The intelligence community he dodges. It fits his worldview.

He buys it.

Sasha exhales, easing back. "George's paranoia knows no bounds." Then, coldly: "But involving the law would be unwise. They wouldn't believe a prostitute anyway."

Prostitute.

I swallow the sting and let it work for me. "Of course not," I say with a bitter laugh. "Prostitutes don't like the cops."

Approval flashes in his eyes.

"We both seem to know Dmitri and John," I add.

"I had business dealings with them," he says.

"And yet you confronted me before Dmitri was killed," I reply. "You had compromising photos of us together."

Sasha tilts his head. "Do you want the photos? Or do you know something I should know?"

I mirror his posture. "Why did you agree to meet me?"

A smirk. "Tell me."

"You and I both know why," I say evenly. "Susan saw the man who killed Dmitri. Was it you or one of your men?"

I raise a hand. "Doesn't matter. I'm not a cop. I don't even want to know."

His expression flickers. The first crack. But it lowers his guard further.

"I'm concerned about collateral damage," I continue. "John tried to screw Dmitri. It wrecked your deal. Now you're wondering what I know and whether I'm a loose end."

I see it land.

"Sounds like Susan should be concerned," he says sharply.

I lean in. "I have a note."

Sasha freezes.

"It has John's DNA on it," I say quietly. "It connects him to the setup. To the photos. And if law enforcement ever gets involved, I can testify that I first saw those photos in your possession."

The balance shifts.

I soften my tone. "Neither of us wants this to spiral."

"But you went to George," he says.

I gesture vaguely toward the window. "George isn't law enforcement. He operates in the shadows, like you. No jurisdiction. No badges. Whatever he knows, he can't use against you."

Sasha studies me, weighing enemies.

"You should be careful trusting George," he says at last. "He isn't always who you think he is."

Bluff. Or warning.

"How so?" I ask.

He shrugs. "He works in the shadows."

The words land heavier than they should.

For the first time, I wonder how much George always knows and never says.

Sasha stands, tossing bills onto the table. "Let's hope John isn't picked up for questioning before I leave the country."

A non-admission that says everything. Got him.

"Before you go," I say. "Susan stays out of this."

He pauses. "Why should I agree?"

"Because I'm holding up my end," I say. "The note stays buried as long as she's untouched."

A long beat.

"You're stubborn," he mutters. Then: "Fine. Your friend is off-limits. For now."

Relief washes through me. I don't show it.

"See?" I say calmly. "That wasn't so hard."

He leans in, voice low. "You play a dangerous game."

"So do you."

Sasha disappears into the crowd.

I sit still, hands wrapped around my cup, forcing my breathing to slow.

I got what I needed.

So why does it feel like I just made a deal with the devil?

Chapter 17

"I'd played a role without love so many times that the lines between performance and feeling had blurred" - *Dara*

The farmhouse kitchen feels smaller tonight, the walls pressing in as Aiden and I sit at the worn wooden table. The warm glow of the overhead light does little to ease the tension thickening the air between us. I study Aiden's face. The furrow of his brow, the quiet intensity in his eyes. My heart pounds. It's now or never.

I take a breath, steadying myself. "Aiden, there's something I need to tell you." My voice is barely above a whisper.

He leans forward, his gaze locking onto mine. "What is it, Dara?"

I hesitate for only a second before forcing the words out. "It's about Sasha. When I met with him... I wore a wire for the FBI. He made threats. Against Susan. Against me."

Aiden's face darkens instantly. "Why? What kind of threats?"

"The kind that makes you question whether you'll wake up tomorrow." My hands tighten around my mug, fingers pressing into the ceramic. "He's more dangerous than I realized. More dangerous than I was prepared for. I could see it in his eyes. You can sense it exuding from him."

I see the shift in Aiden's expression, concern morphing into something sharper. His jaw clenches, his protective instinct kicking in.

"Dara, you need to get out of this," he says, his voice low, urgent. "It's not safe."

I shake my head. "It's not that simple."

"Why not?" His fingers brush over mine, warm and soothing. "Your safety matters more than anything. Just walk away from all of it. The FBI shouldn't need your help."

For a moment, I let myself imagine it. A life without threats, without secrets, without the weight of my past pressing down on me. A future with Aiden, where I'm just Dara, just a girl finishing school, laughing with him over coffee, not analyzing every shadow for danger.

But reality crashes back in.

"It's more than just me," I say, thinking of Susan, the FBI's case, and the tangled web I've been dragged into. How can anyone walk away until it is over?

Aiden's grip on my hand tightens. "I care about you, Dara. You know that, right?" His voice is softer now, more pleading. "And I hate watching you put yourself at risk."

I swallow the lump forming in my throat. "I appreciate that, Aiden. More than you know." And I do. But what if I don't deserve it?

I pull my hands back, glancing away as I steel myself for the next revelation. "Then there's George." My voice is quieter now, measured. "He's... influential. And I can't shake the feeling that he knows more than he lets on. I've sensed it but could never pinpoint why I felt it."

Aiden's brows knit together. "What do you mean?"

"It's like he's always one step ahead. He's always been supportive. But I can never tell how much he's actually controlling behind the scenes. Jillian hinted at it. Sasha practically spelled it out."

Aiden's fingers drum lightly against the table. "That sounds... manipulative."

I shake my head. "No, it's not like that. It's more... protective. But unsettling at the same time. I can read men, Aiden. I know when someone is lying. George's deception feels different. There has always been this sense of sincerity. But there's something he's not saying at the same time. Maybe it's because he's an intelligence professional.

Silence falls between us, thick with questions neither of us knows how to answer. My fingers trace patterns on the table, a nervous habit I didn't realize had resurfaced.

Aiden finally exhales, nodding slowly. "If you trust him, then I'll trust your judgment. He's given you no reason to doubt him, even if he's holding something back."

His faith in me sends a strange warmth through my chest, but I know I'm not done. There's one more truth I need to share.

I look up, meeting his gaze. "There's something else, Aiden."

He nods, patient. "Go on."

I hesitate, then take a breath. "I might be related to Elliot Keene." The words sound surreal even as I speak them.

Aiden blinks. "The Elliot Keene? The father of artificial intelligence? Computer guru and codebreaker? Genius? I've read about him. But he never married, as I recall."

A dry smile tugs at my lips. "Apparently, Keene had a brother. Jillian told me. It's not definite, but she thinks my intellect and possible lineage are part of why George took an interest in me. I'm sure there's a picture on the wall of Elliot Keene in an intelligence building somewhere. George may have been planning to recruit me into the intel world the whole time, figuring it was in my genes. Who knows?"

Aiden leans back slightly, absorbing this. "That's... incredible."

"Is it?" I let out a breathy chuckle. "Because to me, it feels like just another layer of a life I never asked for."

He studies me. "Have you looked into it?"

I shake my head. "I don't want to. Not now. It's too much, and honestly, it doesn't change anything. If it's true, Keene's brother would be like a great-grandfather. That's the way I figure it anyway."

Aiden watches me carefully. "And what if it is true?"

I shrug, forcing a casualness I don't feel. "Then I guess I have a legacy I never knew about. But it doesn't define me, Aiden. Just like my past doesn't define me. What I do now, the choices I make, that's what matters."

He nods, reaching for my hand again. This time, I don't pull away.

"You're right," he says. "But Dara... you're meant for something big. I can feel it."

I let his words settle over me, unsure if I believe them. Because at the moment, I don't feel meant for anything. I feel like I'm barely holding on.

The farmhouse is still, the quiet stretching between us as we sit across from each other, continuing our discussion. It's our quiet time together to discuss our day. Aiden leans forward, his fingers tracing lazy patterns on the table as well. His eyes brighten with an idea.

"You know, George might be able to help you uncover more about your ancestry. With his connections—"

"No," I cut him off, sharper than I intended. I see the flicker of surprise in his expression and take a steadying breath, softening my tone. "I'm sorry. I just… I can't involve George in my private life."

Aiden's brow furrows. "Why not? This could be a chance to—"

"To what?" I interrupt again, the frustration in my voice edging too close to something raw. "To introduce myself to potential relatives as the college student who paid her way through school as an escort? To drag them into this mess, I'm still untangling?" I shake my head firmly. "No. I need to leave my past behind, Aiden. Not dig it up."

He watches me carefully, his fingers flexing slightly against the worn table before reaching for my hand. The warmth of his touch is steadying, yet it sends an unexpected jolt through me. I sense his response before it comes. Aiden seems to know when to push me and when to pull back.

"I understand," he says gently. "I just thought..."

"George already offered to look into it," I admit, my voice quieter now. "I declined."

Aiden says nothing, his thumb brushing lightly over my knuckles. Silence settles between us, thick with unspoken thoughts. His presence is a steady pull, drawing me in like gravity, and I suddenly realize how close we are. How close I want to be.

Our eyes meet. The space between us narrows until I close the distance, pressing my lips to his. The kiss is slow, unhurried, and yet it consumes me. I lose myself in the comfort of his embrace, in how he holds me as if I'm fragile yet unbreakable.

Then, something shifts.

A deep, familiar tug stirs inside me, primal, electric. I want more of him. My body responds before my mind can catch up, an instinctive hunger blooming in my chest. It's a feeling I know too well. All too well.

I hesitate.

Why do I want this?

Is it real? Or are these just old habits dying hard, echoes of my past bleeding into my future? I distorted physical and emotional intimacy so many times. I don't trust my own instincts.

I pull back slightly, my breath uneven. "Aiden, I—"

He searches my face, concern etched in every line. "What's wrong? Are you okay?"

I struggle to articulate the tangle of emotions clawing at my chest. "I don't know if my feelings are real or just... reflex. It's not you, it's me." My mind reels. This should be an intimate moment between two people falling in love. But I'd played a role without love so much that the lines between performance and feeling had blurred. Can I trust my emotions when I've faked them so many times?

Aiden's eyes soften with understanding. He doesn't push, doesn't question. Instead, he cups my face gently, his touch impossibly tender. "Dara," he murmurs, "whatever you're feeling, it's real. And we don't have to rush anything. I understand."

His words wash over me, soothing the raw edges of my doubt.

"I respect you," he continues, his voice steady and low. "And I respect your boundaries. We'll take this at your pace. I'm not going anywhere."

I search his face, the habit of reading men too ingrained in me to ignore. My entire life has been spent looking for ulterior motives, for deception lurking beneath kind words.

But all I still see in Aiden's eyes is patience. Sincerity.

"Thank you," I whisper, my throat tight with emotion.

Aiden squeezes my hand, his fingers threading through mine. "I care about you, Dara. That's not going to change, no matter what pace we move at."

His words settle over me like a warm cloak, wrapping around the cold places I didn't even realize were still there.

I lean in again, not out of hunger but something softer, something quieter. Our lips meet again, tentative and slow, full of things we aren't yet ready to say out loud. And yet, somehow, it says enough.

As we part, I exhale shakily. "I care about you too," I admit, the words barely above a whisper. I run my hand through his hair briefly.

Aiden's lips curve into a small smile, but he doesn't say anything. He doesn't have to.

We sit in the quiet for a moment, the air between us charged with something new, something fragile and real. My mind races, analyzing every aspect of this shift between us. Is this desire rooted in my past, or is it a sign of my future? The question lingers, unanswered.

I sink into the worn couch, exhaustion pressing down on me. Aiden settles beside me, his arm draping over my shoulders, a quiet reassurance. We don't speak. We don't need to.

The silence surrounds us like a protective cocoon, a space where neither of us has to pretend.

My eyelids droop, heavy with the weight of the day. Aiden shifts slightly, drawing me closer, and wraps his arms around me.

"Is this okay?" he murmurs, his breath warm against my hair.

I nod, the tension draining from my body. Words feel unnecessary.

I should tense. I should pull away. But I don't.

Instead, I let my head rest against his chest, listening to the steady rhythm of his heartbeat. And for the first time in a long time, I feel safe.

The next morning, light filters through the curtains, casting soft golden hues across the room. Aiden's steady breathing is a calming sound beside me, but my mind is already racing. Codes, patterns, hidden meanings, pieces of a puzzle waiting to be solved.

I sit up abruptly, reaching for the notepad on the side table, flipping it open as my fingers fly across the page. I sense Aiden slowly rustling from his sleep.

"Aiden," I say, my voice cutting through the quiet. "The FBI is struggling with a codename, 'Agnes.' I've been thinking about it."

Aiden blinks awake, rubbing his eyes as he adjusts to my early-morning intensity. "Interesting," he murmurs, shifting up onto his elbows. "Ancient languages are often used in codes. Greek? Latin? Maybe something even older?"

I nod, already sketching out linguistic roots, cross-referencing sounds and meanings. Aiden leans in, scanning the notes, his brow furrowing in concentration as he rubs his eyes.

"So, you're thinking if 'Agnes' is a codename, we need to break it down into a pattern, identify substitutions, and reconstruct the meaning?"

I tap my pen against the notepad. "Exactly." My brain began to whirl. My thoughts recalled operatives in World War II cracked the Enigma code machine because they knew the code wasn't random. It followed structure and repetition. If 'Agnes' is built on a linguistic pattern instead of an anagram or a common name, we must consider phonetics, transliterations, and symbolic references. Something that refers to who they are talking about but is not obvious. A name that resonates with those who understand that name's meaning.

Aiden watches as I flip to a fresh page, my handwriting quick and precise. My thoughts still racing. I start thinking out loud. "'Agnes' is a Latinized form of the Greek 'Hagnē,' meaning 'pure' or 'sacred.' But that's too obvious. We need something obscured through translation if they're using an ancient root. Sasha knows multiple languages. He wouldn't make it easy. But he would be familiar with European forms of words. And the FBI said their messages reference weapons and an arms company, so we know they were probably referencing a specific arms dealer, merchant, or US arms company, right?"

"Right," Aiden agrees, his eyes alight with intrigue. "So, we tie it to military terms, armament, or historical figures associated with warfare. Maybe even a phonetic shift?"

I hesitate momentarily, letting my mind filter through possibilities before whispering the word aloud. "Agniastra." The word felt wrong in my mouth. Too clean. Too deliberate.

Aiden blinks, then leans forward. "Sanskrit?"

A small smile tugs at my lips. "Yes. 'Agni', fire. 'Astra', weapon. Fire weapon. It was an ancient projectile weapon in Hindu mythology, said to be blessed by the fire god Agni. A literal 'firearm' in ancient terminology. Agnes is the closest modern form of the word."

Aiden exhales sharply, realization dawning. "So, they're not naming the company outright," he murmurs. "They're hiding it in plain sight. 'Agnes' is a symbolic stand-in for 'Agniastra', a company tied to weapons manufacturing, specifically firearms or military-grade technology. They've buried the reference in historical language to make it look innocuous."

I nod, my pulse quickening. "But also makes it easier to discuss in conversation. And if we search for defense contractors with branding tied to fire, heat, combustion, or ancient warfare, we might be able to narrow it down. A cross-reference of patents, marketing materials, and even trade filings could make the connection to the word that they may have just shortened."

Aiden shakes his head in admiration. "Dara, that's brilliant. You've reduced infinite possibilities into a controlled pattern and let logic do the rest. If Elliot Keene were your ancestor, he'd be proud."

A slow smile spreads across my lips, but my mind is already three steps ahead. "George has pioneered artificial intelligence methods for intelligence gathering. He's coy about it, which means his AI capabilities are probably better than anyone realizes." I tap my pen against the page. "If anyone can cross-reference and find this company, it's him. If we give him the right lead."

Aiden watches me work, the wheels in my mind spinning faster than he can keep up. He reaches out, his fingers brushing against my cheek.

"Dara, you're not just sharp, you're extraordinary. With your knack for this, maybe you really are a descendant of a math genius."

I snort, shaking my head. "Hardly. These skills? Honed by years of reading men, deciphering their true intentions. Not exactly a noble lineage."

His face softens, his expression filled with something deeper than admiration. "Dara, your past doesn't define you. Your intelligence, your resilience, that's all you."

A lump forms in my throat, but I swallow it down. There's no time for sentimentality now. "So, 'Agniastra' means 'Fire Weapon' in Sanskrit. That actually fits. It could be a code name for a weapons company or a hidden defense contract that Sasha and John used to move arms under the radar. We agree."

Aiden nods, his hand finding mine. "And now? You just give this to George?"

I take a deep breath, steadying myself. "I need to tell George. This could be crucial to the investigation. The FBI won't take me as seriously. But George will."

Chapter 18

"His gaze meets mine, and for a fleeting second, something unreadable flickers across his face." — Dara

The familiar bell chimes as I push open the door to Mom & Pop's, the scent of freshly brewed coffee and warm pie wrapping around me like something I almost trust. The small-town hum of conversation fills the space, but my eyes go straight to the corner booth, our booth. I catch the subtle presence of his men scattered around the room, pretending they aren't watching.

George is already there, silver hair neatly combed, suit impeccable as always. His coffee sits in front of him, loaded with sugar and cream, just as I've ordered it for him countless times over the years. His favorite.

I slide into the seat across from him, my pulse quickening. Before he can even greet me, the words tumble out.

"I quit the escort service."

George's eyebrows rise slightly, but there's no shock, no hesitation. He sets his cup down with a quiet clink. "Finally," he says, calm and measured. "And how do you feel about that decision, Dara?"

I exhale, willing my emotions to stay in check. "Relieved. Scared. But mostly… grateful." I meet his gaze, searching for any sign of reaction, though I'm sure he already knew. "I'm grateful for everything you've done for me these past few years. I couldn't have made it through college without you."

A small smile tugs at the corners of his mouth. I think I even see his eyes glisten. "You've worked hard," he says. "What's next?"

I swallow, gathering my thoughts. "Med school, actually. It feels like the right step. I actually toyed with the idea of Law school after all this."

He nods, considering. "Admirable pursuits. You certainly have the intellect for either." He signals the waitress for a refill, movements precise and deliberate.

I watch him, memorizing the familiar lines of his face, the set of his jaw, the way his eyes soften ever so slightly when he listens. He's been my constant, my safe harbor in a storm I barely navigated. But tonight, something in him feels different. A quiet melancholy that mirrors my own. The unspoken knowledge that our Tuesday meetings are numbered.

"You know," I say softly, tracing the rim of my cup, "these past few years… these meetings… they've meant a lot to me. More than I can put into words."

George reaches across the table and pats my hand briefly, his touch light but steady. "I'm glad I could provide that for you, my dear. You've done quite a bit for me as well. You must realize, you have a gift. Don't ignore it." His eyes hold mine. "And don't look back."

A lump rises in my throat. How do I explain what his presence has meant? That in a world where I had to constantly read between the lines, where every interaction with a man came with expectation, George was different, the only man who never wanted anything from me except for me to be my best.

"Thank you," I whisper. "For everything."

A comfortable silence settles between us, one of those rare moments where words are unnecessary.

Then a thought crashes into me like cold water.

"Oh God, Leslie." My stomach twists. "I haven't checked on her in a week."

George tilts his head slightly. "Leslie?"

"My roommate." I sigh, rubbing my temple. "She's got this new boyfriend. She's been bouncing between his place and ours."

George studies me, expression neutral but attentive. "You sound concerned."

"I am." I chew on my bottom lip. "Leslie's… innocent. The kind of girl who believes in saving herself for marriage. But when she falls, she falls hard. She sees what she wants to see in people."

George blows on his coffee, waiting. I appreciate that about him, his silence is never empty; it's permission to speak freely.

"She doesn't read men well," I admit. "Or maybe she overreads them. She thinks if a guy looks at her a certain way, it means he loves her. And I don't know anything about this boyfriend. That's the problem. I should check in."

George nods, and his silence prompts me to go deeper. And I do, because with him, I always do. It occurs to me I spent years hearing men's problems as an escort. But George mostly let me unload mine.

"I worry about her," I confess. "But I also know I have to focus on my own path now."

His lips curve in quiet understanding. "Indeed. You've made some big decisions recently."

I inhale deeply. "Yeah. Med school applications. Quitting the escort service. It's… a lot."

He doesn't offer advice or tell me what to do, just watches me with the patience of someone who's always seen my potential, even when I didn't.

I look down at my hands, then back at him. "I'm scared," I whisper. "But also… excited. I feel like I'm truly in control of my life for the first time in years."

George's smile is small but full of something deeper, pride, maybe. "You've always had that strength within you, Dara. I'm merely honored to have witnessed your journey. It's been a highlight of my life watching you grow these past few years."

The words settle deep, an anchor in the shifting tides of my life.

I lean forward, hands clasped on the worn wooden table. The comfortable routine we've shared for years suddenly feels heavier, weighted with unspoken truths. We seem to be having a long goodbye.

"George, there's something else we need to discuss."

He lifts his cup, expression calm, unreadable. "Oh?"

I don't hesitate. "Jillian told me about your CIA connections."

The words tumble out, my heartbeat spiking. I know I'm prying into something deeper, something carefully kept in the shadows.

George's face remains unchanged, but there's the slightest flicker in his eyes, barely noticeable. He takes a measured sip before responding.

"Yes," he says simply.

His answer is unceremonious. I exhale sharply. "So all this time…"

"Intelligence is gathered in unexpected places, Dara," he says, voice even, as if discussing the weather. "Including the bedroom. Secrets emerge when people think they're safe." His gaze stays steady. "You, of all people, understand that."

My stomach twists. "Were you… was I…?"

"No." His voice is firm, cutting through my unspoken fears. "Never. My interest in you was never about recruitment."

I study his face, searching for any cracks, any deception.

"Then why?" I demand, low and edged. "Why take an interest in a college student turned escort?"

George leans back slightly, folding his hands on the table. "What I said was true. I recognized your intelligence and your need for guidance. Nothing more." He pauses, measured. "Jillian saw it too. A young girl with no family when you needed one. Someone with extraordinary talent standing at a crossroads. You needed something stable." A knowing smile flickers. "And, well… you're not exactly easy to steer, are you?"

A small huff of laughter escapes me, despite myself. "No. I suppose I'm not."

His expression sobers. "But I never intended to pull you into that world, Dara. If anything, I wanted to keep someone like you away from it."

I frown, still feeling the gnawing weight of doubt. "Someone like me?"

"Someone with your potential," he clarifies. "You see patterns, connections, codes in places others don't. You can read people." He lets that land. "People with that gift benefit the intelligence community… but at a price. Relationships. Family. Peace. That gift deserves a different path."

I sit back, digesting his words. I want to believe him, I really do. But Jillian and George both moved through the shadows of a world I wanted no part of, a world that had tried to drag me under. Was George really a lifeguard and Jillian a referee all this time?

Then his expression shifts slightly, something calculating behind his gaze.

"That being said," he adds, "there is something that has always intrigued me about you."

A sliver of unease creeps in. "What?"

George sets his cup down carefully, studying me. "Your last name. Keene."

I pause, my coffee hovering midair. "What about it? I declined your offer to look into my family. I don't want to know."

"It's not exactly common," he says, watching me closely.

A sharp chord of recognition strikes in my mind, but I feign ignorance. "Who is Elliot Keene? That is who you think I'm descended from, right?"

George leans in slightly, lowering his voice. "Keene was a mathematician. A pioneer in computer science. Code work in World War II. Later, early artificial intelligence, the kind of mind governments don't forget." His eyes narrow slightly, as if weighing how much to say. "The name is… respected in my world."

My mind races, connecting dots at an alarming speed. "And you think I'm related to him? I've discussed this with Jillian. I know you two talk."

"Not him directly," George clarifies. "Elliot Keene had no children. But possibly his brother's descendant." He pauses, then says it anyway: "Your name was flagged in some intelligence files. It caught my attention."

A chill ripples through me. "You looked into my background?" The sting of betrayal sharpens my words. "Even if it's true, I told you I didn't want any part of my father's family."

George sighs, expression softening. "I knew before you asked me not to dig, Dara. I didn't pry beyond what I already knew."

I let out a hollow laugh, shaking my head. "So our little game, about never using real names was never just a game to you, was it?"

For the first time, George looks almost guilty. "Not entirely."

I should be furious, but a strange amusement rises in me instead. "All this time, I thought we were just teasing each other."

"We were," he says with a smirk. "Mostly."

I shake my head, an unwilling chuckle escaping. "You're incorrigible, you know that?"

His smile lingers, but then his expression turns serious. "Dara, my interest in you was always about you, your intelligence, your resilience, your safety."

I study him again, searching for deception. "Not even a little bit about my ancestry?"

"When I saw your name, it caught my attention," he admits. "But what kept my attention was your mind, your ability to adapt and analyze. You had no one. You needed someone." His gaze holds. "That's what mattered. You weren't ready to know about who I was. You would have pushed me away if I revealed who I was and what I did. You know that's true."

Warmth flickers at his words, but I push it down, unwilling to fully accept it. "Well… that's reassuring, I guess."

George watches me carefully before speaking again, voice softer now. "Dara, do you at least want to know what happened to your father?"

My jaw clenches. "No."

"Understanding his actions—"

"I don't care, George." The words come out sharp, but I don't take them back. "I don't care about his actions. Or his family. That chapter is closed. I want nothing to do with them." I inhale, steadying. "I know our time together is almost over, and I have to accept that." I sit my cup down, decisive. "Just like I don't pry so I can never track you down later, I want the same courtesy. I have to move forward. Every part of this life has to be left behind." I nod once. "Even my father. Especially my father."

George exhales slowly, watching me with something unreadable in his eyes. "I understand. But sometimes confronting our past is the only way to move forward."

I shake my head. "Not this time."

We sit in silence, coffee cooling between us. I know he thinks he's right. Maybe, in time, I'll wonder if he was.

But not today.

I turn the revelations over in my mind. I should pry more into George, his motives, where he lives, where he goes when he vanishes from my life. But I probably know more than I should already. Knowing more won't make anything better now. Besides, I sense he wouldn't tell me, though I do know more when I study his face. I always do. So I shake the feeling.

I lean forward, letting the thoughts pass, and tap my fingers against my cup.

"There's something I need to run by you, George. The FBI intercepted some of Sasha and John's communications. They used the name 'Agnes' when referring to a U.S. arms dealer. I don't think it's a person."

George lifts his cup, pausing mid-sip. His sharp eyes narrow slightly. "A code name, then."

I nod. "Exactly. And I have a theory."

George sets his cup down, gesturing for me to continue.

I take a breath, gathering my thoughts. "Language can be a weapon, especially in espionage. Names and symbols are layered with meaning. Sasha was a translator for the Russian government at one point, according to the FBI. He knows how to conceal information in ways that aren't obvious. And John, being a lawyer, thrives on precision and misdirection." I swallow, then commit. "'Agnes' could be a linguistic mask. Something hiding in plain sight. A reference they both understand."

George tilts his head. "Go on."

I flip my notepad open, sketching the name in different phonetic variations. "'Agnes' is too clean, too obvious for this kind of operation. But if you strip it down to origins, it shifts. In Greek, 'Hagnē' means pure or sacred, but that doesn't fit. If you go older, Sanskrit, it resembles something else entirely."

I underline the name and write beneath it.

"Agniastra."

George's eyebrows lift slightly, his mind already catching up. "The mythical fire weapon."

I nod. "Yes. 'Agni' means fire. 'Astra' means weapon. Fire weapon. It fits the reference. And if this arms dealer is using a codename, wouldn't it make sense to hide it in a name that describes what they do?"

George sits back, rubbing his chin. "So instead of naming the company outright, they refer to it by a linguistic equivalent, a term only someone well-versed in ancient languages, like Sasha, would recognize."

I point at him. "Exactly. Think Enigma. Codebreakers didn't solve it through brute force alone, they found patterns. Here, the pattern isn't numbers or symbols. It's language."

George exhales slowly, nodding. "And the FBI hasn't figured this out yet."

"Not as far as I know," I say. "They just know Sasha and John keep referring to an 'Agnes' when discussing weapons shipments. But this isn't a random female codename, it's a cipher. A stand-in."

George's expression darkens slightly, mind already working. "If you're right, and this is a reference to a U.S. defense contractor supplying weapons illegally, then we can cross-reference companies with branding tied to fire, combustion, mythology. Anything that connects."

I nod eagerly. "That's what I was thinking. We can narrow the list if we combine that with Sasha and John's known contacts."

George watches me, then chuckles softly. "Your talent is wasted outside the intelligence community, you know that?"

I smirk.

He sips his coffee and sets it down, demeanor shifting into something more serious. "I can run this through my network. One of my

AI systems can scan patent filings, defense contractor communications, and keyword references faster than any analyst. If the term Agniastra is hiding in documentation, we'll find it."

Relief loosens something in my chest.

I nod and rise from my seat, smoothing the fabric of my skirt, but the weight in my chest remains. "Thank you, George. I… I should go."

George watches me, expression unreadable yet familiar. "Take care, Dara."

I nod again, but words fail me. The weight of everything unsaid lingers between us. The bell above Mom & Pop's chimes as I step outside, crisp air filling my lungs. The cold contrast against the warmth of the café mirrors the swirl of emotions inside me.

I glance back through the window. George still sits at our booth, sipping his coffee, sugar and cream, just as I've always ordered it. A man I've always known, yet barely begun to understand.

I pull my phone from my pocket as I reach the street, sensing George's men nearby. Leslie. I should call her.

The ringtone cuts through the quiet street, and after a few beats, her bright voice fills my ear. "Dara, I was just thinking about you," she says, cheerful as ever.

I exhale, tension easing slightly. "Hey, Les. Sorry I've been MIA. Things have been… eventful."

"No worries! I've been preoccupied myself," she giggles.

I lean against a nearby lamppost, eyes flicking to the shadows where George's men linger, ever-present, ever-watchful. "Oh? Do tell."

"Remember Jake? We've been seeing each other. But I'm taking it slow this time."

I smile. "That's great, Les. How's it going?"

"It's different. I'm not rushing in. Letting him pursue me, you know? And he is!"

I can hear the excitement in her voice, and it warms me. "I'm glad you're being cautious. You deserve someone who puts in the effort instead of you putting in all the heart."

"Thanks, Dara. Your advice really helped. So, what's new with you?"

I hesitate. How much should I share? "Oh, you know. Just... figuring things out."

Leslie hums. "You always make things sound simple, but I know you. That means something bigger is going on."

I take a slow breath, grip tightening around the phone. "Actually, there's something I wanted to tell you."

"Oh?"

I let the words out in one breath. "I'm applying to med school."

Leslie's squeal nearly deafens me. "Dara! That's amazing! Why didn't you tell me sooner?"

I laugh, her excitement infectious. "I wanted to wait until it felt real. It's not public yet, so keep it under wraps, okay?"

"Of course! Oh, Dara, I'm so proud of you. This is a whole new chapter!"

My throat tightens. "Yeah, it is. I just wish..."

"What?"

I swallow. "Nothing. It's silly." I pause, then let it slip anyway. "I just wish I had family to share this with, you know? You're one of the few people I've told. You are my family."

Leslie's voice softens. "Oh, Dara. I know it's not the same, but I'm here for you. Always."

I blink back unexpected tears. "Thanks, Les. That means more than you know."

When we hang up, I stand for a moment, absorbing her words. The street is quiet now, save for the occasional passing car. But the solitude feels heavier than usual.

No family to share this with. The realization stings, though it's not unfamiliar. I've been on my own for so long it should feel normal by now.

But it doesn't. Not entirely.

I close my eyes, exhaling slowly. Then an image flashes in my mind, Aiden. His kind eyes, the gentle curve of his smile. A warmth spreads through my chest.

As if on cue, my phone vibrates in my hand. Aiden's name appears on the screen.

Hope your day went well. Come home safely. Dinner tomorrow?

A smile tugs at my lips as I type back a quick reply.

Yes, please.

I slide my phone into my pocket, letting the moment settle. Med school. A real relationship. A future beyond the shadows I've lived in for so long.

"You've got this, Dara," I whisper, squaring my shoulders. "It's a fresh start. Time to make it count."

Then, on impulse, I glance back at Mom & Pop's. The neon sign flickers in the window. Through the glass, George still sits in our usual booth, coffee in hand, the man I've only ever known as simply George. A mystery and a guardian.

I linger, watching him. The familiarity of the scene pulls at me, his posture, the slow stir of his spoon, the way he seems completely in control even when alone.

Then, as if sensing me, George looks up.

His gaze meets mine, and for a fleeting second, something unreadable flickers across his face as he sees me through the window.

Then he winks.

Not playful. Not flirtatious.

It was more like: *I know. And I know that you know.*

A quiet chuckle escapes me, and a reluctant smile tugs at the corners of my mouth. I shake my head and turn away, stepping back into the night, leaving the rest unsaid, where it has always lived.

Some truths are never meant to be spoken.

Chapter 19

"I might have sold my body… You sold your soul.
Tell me, which one of us is worse off?"— Dara

The phone vibrates against my thigh.

Unknown number.

I hesitate. I already know who it is.

"Hello, Dara."

Smooth as silk. Sharp as a blade.

Sasha.

I exhale slowly. Control. Neutral. Don't let him hear the shift in my pulse.

"How did you get this number?"

A pause. Casual, but forced. "Jillian gave it to me."

Liar.

I let the silence stretch just long enough to make him uncomfortable. "I see. What can I do for you, Sasha?"

A chuckle. "Always straight to business. I like that about you."

My mind moves quickly. Jillian would never give him my number.

"John gave you my number," I say.

Another pause. A fraction too long. Which again, told me what I needed to know.

"Does it really matter?" he replies smoothly. "We have more pressing matters."

I grip the phone tighter. "Such as?"

"Our arrangement regarding Susan," he says. "I'm thinking it may need… adjustment."

Rage coils, hot and sharp. He thinks he's in control. He isn't. He's closing loose ends and I'm one of them.

"Our deal stands," I say evenly. "Unless you'd like to clarify."

A beat. He's probing. Measuring what I know.

"Perhaps we should meet," he suggests. "In person."

A trap. Without question.

"Fine," I say, feigning impatience. "Name the place."

He gives an address. Semi-private. Controlled. His choice.

I agree anyway.

When the line goes dead, my instincts scream. He's planning something final. But sometimes the only way out is straight through.

I dial another number.

"Agent Carter," I say when he answers. "It's Dara Keene. We need to talk."

The room hums with tension. Carter sits across from me, another agent beside him, quiet, sharp-eyed.

"This could be our chance," Carter says. "If you can plant this."

He slides a tracker across the table. Sleek. Nearly weightless.

"You want me to get close enough to plant a bug on a mob enforcer," I say.

"Yes."

"And Agnes?"

"Still unresolved," Carter admits. "This gets us leverage."

"And George?" I ask.

A flicker passes between them.

"You didn't tell him," I say.

Silence answers me.

George would never have approved this. But I needed to do it despite the danger. Tracking Sasha may lead them to the arms dealer or at least keep him from leaving the country. The room felt tighter.

"Fine," I say. "I'll do it."

Carter exhales. "Backup will be nearby, but—"

"But I'm alone if it goes sideways."

He doesn't argue.

I pocket the tracker. "Not the first time I've gotten close to a man I can't stand," I say dryly. "Just the first time I'm not getting paid for it."

The café hums with life when Sasha arrives.

He scans the room instinctively. A predator's habit. His hand brushes his jacket. Weapon. Expected.

"Dara," he says, sliding into the seat. "So good of you to meet me."

I smile. Practiced. "Couldn't resist."

"I hope," he says quietly, "that you and George aren't speaking to the U.S. government."

"Oh?"

"I know things about him."

Liar. His eye twitches. He's trying to inject doubt. A desperate ploy. He clasps his hands together. I've seen him do this before during moments he's trying to hide nervousness. He's pretty easy to read.

"Do tell," I say.

"You're in over your head," he snaps. "That note—"

"Ah," I interrupt. "So John *did* give you my number."

Silence.

His pupils widen. Gotcha.

"You've complicated things," he snarls. "John interfered. Dmitri resisted. Now you—"

"And now I'm a loose end," I finish calmly. "With evidence. With testimony. With a memory you'd rather not revisit. John tried to screw Dmitri. You screwed John. Everybody getting screwed. How am I doing?"

His jaw tightens.

"You think you're a smart whore," he spits.

I smile slowly. "And yet, here you are." I pause. "A whore knows a lot about screwing men."

I lean in, voice low. "I might have sold my body, Sasha. But you? You sold your soul. Tell me, which one of us is worse off?"

The air between us hardens. He's sweating now. Glancing. Calculating.

"I'm leaving soon," he mutters. "Tying up loose ends, before I go."

A warning. A threat.

Then his hand moves, wrong. Too deliberate.

And then—

"Hello, Sasha."

George.

Sasha freezes. His hand stalls mid-motion.

Time narrows.

In that heartbeat, I move.

I grab Sasha's jacket, pull him just enough to misdirect, my lips near his ear as I slip the tracker into his pocket. His attention split between me and the sudden appearance of George.

"Men usually pay to get this close," I whisper. "You get screwed for free."

George's hand clamps around Sasha's wrist. Sasha's men leap to their feet.

Chaos explodes. Shouting erupts.

Gunfire cracks through the café. Tables overturn. Glass explodes. Agents surge in from every direction. Sasha breaks for the exit. He disappears in the confusion.

A hand grips my arm, steady and firm, pulling me up from the floor. "Easy," an agent says, voice sharp but controlled. "We had to move. He went for his weapon, just before your friend stepped in."

I nod, still catching my breath, adrenaline humming through me.

"It's okay about the tracker," he adds quickly. "You did what you could. We'll track him another way."

I meet his eyes. "I planted it."

He blinks. "You…what?"

"The tracker," I say calmly. "It's on him."

The agent stares at me, disbelief flickering across his face. "When?"

"When he thought he was in control," I reply, smoothing my jacket, grounding myself in the small, familiar motions.

"How did you get that close?"

I pause, then offer a faint, knowing smile. "Men like him lose focus when they think they have power."

A beat.

"And when they think they have me."

The agent exhales slowly, shaking his head. "Where did you put the tracker?"

"Inside his jacket. Left side. Clean."

For the first time since the chaos began, the agent actually smiles. "Damn."

When the smoke clears, I find George arguing with an agent.

"You knew he was armed," George says coldly. "You still sent her in risking her life for a tracker?"

"She volunteered," the agent says.

George turns to me. His anger fades, just enough.

"You did well," he says quietly. Then to the agent: "Be careful what you ask her to do. Because she'll do it."

The agent nods.

George opens his arms.

I step into them without thinking.

His hold is steady. Familiar. Not possessive. Not demanding. Just comfortable.

I had spent years reading men, glances, pauses, intentions. But I had never truly read George. Not because I couldn't. Because I didn't want to.

I lift my head and meet his eyes. There's no calculation there. No agenda.

Just him and that kind of look you give someone who finally gets it.

Something flickers in his face. Unspoken.

He smiles at me.

Then…

The wink.

That same damn wink.

Later, at the farmhouse, exhaustion sinks deep.

Aiden enters with a folder. "Dara," he says softly. "Are you okay?"

"I'm fine." My eyes flick to the folder. "What's that?"

"Research. Genealogy."

I raise a hand. "I don't need to know."

He hesitates.

"Family isn't blood," I say quietly. "It's who shows up. Who protects you. Who believes in you." I think of Leslie. Susan. Jillian.

And George.

"I already know who my family is."

Aiden nods. "I understand."

I touch his hand. "You're one of the few pieces of my past I want in my future."

He squeezes my fingers.

That's enough.

Chapter 20

"And at least my clients were satisfied…You're about to get screwed without the satisfaction." – Dara

The shrill ring of my phone cuts through the quiet evening. Leslie's name flashes across the screen.

"Dara, turn on the news right now!" Her voice is breathless, electric.

My pulse kicks up as I grab the remote. "What's going on?"

"It's John Mitchell's office. The FBI is raiding it, right now."

The TV flickers to life. Dark-suited agents swarm a sleek glass building, moving with coordinated precision. Boxes. Computers. Evidence bags.

"Oh my God," I murmur.

"They're saying it's tied to a massive arms deal," Leslie gushes. "International. Huge."

Relief surges, then unease snaps in behind it.

"Thanks for telling me," I say. "I need to make a call."

I hang up. Aiden is already watching me. Concern is etched on his face.

"Everything okay?"

I hand him the remote. "Turn it up. I need to call George."

The line connects after two rings.

"Dara," George says calmly. "I assume you've seen the news."

"Is it true?" I ask. "About John?"

"It is," he replies. "The FBI has been building the case for months." A pause. "You're mostly safe now."

Mostly.

"What about Sasha?"

"The codename Agnes was the key," George says. "Or rather, your Sanskrit insight."

I straighten. "Agniastra."

"Exactly. I ran it through my system, cross-referenced patents, filings, corporate language. It appeared in one place. A weapons manufacturer John helped register. Their mission statement referenced *fire weapons in the ancient tradition.*"

"Hiding in plain sight," I murmur.

"Yes. John used 'Agnes' as a linguistic stand-in. Not a name. A signal. He was the middleman between Dmitri and the arms dealer. Sasha simply took Dmitri's business and kept John."

"And Sasha?"

"That's… complicated." George then explains the details as Aiden watches, searching my face for answers.

After we hang up, Aiden fills the silence. "Did they get him?"

"They tracked him to a hotel," I say. "But he bolted. Left his suitcase behind."

Aiden exhales. "He's running."

"With a fake passport. One-way ticket to Russia. They're hoping he shows up for a flight."

"And you?" Aiden asks quietly. "They'll want testimony."

I nod. "I know."

Morning light spills across campus as I head toward my final exam.

One last test, I tell myself. Then I can leave this behind.

I round the science building…

And freeze.

Sasha stands in the shadows.

"Well," he sneers. "If it isn't the clever little whore."

My pulse spikes. I'm out of sight of George's men. A surge of adrenaline floods my system.

"Sasha," I say evenly. "Shouldn't you be running?"

"Oh, I am," he says. "But not before tying up loose ends."

His hand twitches at his side. Pocket. Weapon.

Behind him, a flicker of movement. One of George's men. Not fast enough. He's still a distance away. Time to stall.

"You don't have a clean exit," I say quietly. "So what's this? Pride?"

His smile tightens. "You really think this ends in a courtroom?"

"Doesn't it?" I tilt my head. "Unless you're planning something reckless. More murders?"

His eyes darken. There it is.

He leans closer. "You still don't understand."

"Then help me," I say softly. "Explain it."

His jaw flexes. His smile thins. His hand moves inside his pocket. The decision is in his eyes.

I move before he does.

My kick lands hard to his groin. Hard, because although the target is his groin. I aimed for his chin. It's all about the follow-through.

Sasha folds, gasping. His breath a strangled wheeze.

"That," I whisper, "is for underestimating me."

The bodyguard is on him instantly. Sirens cut the air. Agents flood the scene.

They haul Sasha upright, fury blazing in his eyes.

"Whore," he spits.

I step closer, calm. "Keene. Dara Keene. Former escort actually."

I smile, slow and deliberate.

"And at least my clients were satisfied. You and John? You're about to get screwed without the satisfaction."

Confusion flickers. Then rage as they drag him away.

"Dara!"

George is already here. Concern is itched on his face as he searches mine.

"Are you hurt?"

I shake my head. But when his hand settles on my shoulder, the adrenaline fractures. Everything I've been holding in splinters at once. I lean into him without thinking.

He doesn't tighten his grip. Doesn't claim the moment.

He just lets me be there.

And that restraint, that steadiness, says more than words ever could.

For the first time in a long while, I feel safe. Not protected. Not shielded.

Safe.

My mind slows from chaos to clarity. I swallow hard, tears threatening despite my effort to hold them back. So much of my life has been noise, danger, performance, calculation.

What now?

What does a life look like when you don't have to survive it?

I pull back, steadying myself. His eyes search mine, not for answers, just to make sure I'm standing. I make a decision.

"There's one thing I do need."

He studies me. "Anything, Dara."

This chapter is closing. Not erased. Not denied. Just… finished. So, I say to him softly.

"Will you come to my graduation?"

Chapter 21

"…you know about my father. My family. Don't you?" – Dara

The farmhouse kitchen glows in the warm light of late afternoon. I sit at the worn wooden table across from Aiden, tracing the familiar grooves in the wood. The air between us is soft, expectant.

"Graduation's coming up fast," he says gently. "Have you thought about what's next?"

I gesture around the farmhouse. "This place has been safe. Steady. Part of me doesn't want to leave."

"Then don't," he says simply. "Stay."

I hesitate. "Moving in feels… fast."

He smiles. "We had our first kiss."

I laugh. "You know what I mean."

His expression softens. "I noticed you the first day of class. It took me an entire semester to say hello."

"You annoyed me," I tease. "And you tried to be smooth."

"I was intimidated," he corrects.

"I was distracted," I admit, thinking back. "That was right when…everything started unraveling." I pause and I look down at my cup. "I applied to the local med school."

His face lights up. "Of course you did."

"My grades are strong. The dean practically hinted at acceptance. There's even a scholarship application."

"You'll make an incredible doctor," he says, reaching for my hand.

I smile, but uncertainty lingers. "Starting over in the same city isn't exactly starting over."

"Your past doesn't define you," he says quietly.

I know he's right. But knowing and believing aren't the same thing.

I study the farmhouse again. "I read once that if you surround yourself with three millionaires, you'll be the fourth. But if you surround yourself with deadbeats…"

"You become the next one?" Aiden asks.

I nod. "I spent years around people who saw me as a transaction. Clients. Handlers. Men with agendas. I adapted. I survived. But I never belonged. I knew I shouldn't be there."

"And now?"

"Now I choose who shapes me."

His thumb brushes lightly over my knuckles. "So where do I fall in this analogy? Millionaire or deadbeat?"

I smile. "Your bank account might not say millionaire. But your mind? Your steadiness? Definitely top-tier."

"I'll take it."

I exhale slowly. "I need to say some goodbyes first."

"To Susan?" he asks.

"And Jillian. And…" I pause. "George."

Aiden doesn't react immediately.

"I invited him to my graduation."

His brows lift slightly, but he stays quiet.

"He's been… important," I say carefully. "There are things between us that have never been said. Things I think we both know."

"And you want him to say it?" Aiden asks.

I swallow. "I need to hear the truth."

Concern flickers across his face.

"Just be careful," he says softly. "Whatever truth you're chasing… make sure it builds you. Not breaks you."

I nod and reach for my phone.

The line rings twice before George answers.

"Dara. What a pleasant surprise."

"I saw the news," I say. "The raid."

"It was successful," he replies calmly. "And John has agreed to testify."

Relief rushes through me.

"Thank you," I say quietly. "For everything."

"You're welcome, my dear."

The words linger.

"George," I begin carefully, "you know about my father. My family. Don't you?"

A pause. Not surprise. Calculation.

"You know I have my sources," he says evenly.

Too smooth.

"If I asked," I press, "you could tell me why my father's social media account is fake. I mean, I don't look at it much. But I can tell."

Silence.

Then: "It's what's called a scrubbed account."

My throat tightens. I should let it go. But I can't.

"You think I already know," I say quietly.

Another pause.

"I think," George answers slowly, "that deep down, you do."

The air between us feels heavier. Suffocating.

I close my eyes.

"Let me finish being who I was just a little longer," I whisper. "Before the truth makes me someone else."

A quiet acknowledgment hums through the line. A silent understanding.

We let it go.

We exchange lighter words after that. Normal words. The kind we've always used to orbit what we refuse to say. I stare at the phone after the call.

When I hang up, Aiden watches me.

"Everything okay?"

I force a small smile. "Yeah. Just thinking."

Susan answers the door with a tired but genuine smile.

"You look better," I tell her.

"I am," she says, settling onto the couch, her arm in a sling. "And I have news."

"Oh?"

"I'm going back to school. George paid my medical bills. All of them. I can focus on getting my degree."

George.

Of course.

"That's incredible," I say.

"He said everyone deserves a fresh start." She studies me. "Why would he do that for me?"

"George has a habit of rescuing people," I say carefully. "Sometimes I think he's just generous. Other times…" I trail off.

"Other times?" she prompts.

"Maybe he's trying to make up for something."

She laughs softly. "Whatever the reason, I'm taking it."

"I'm glad," I say. "You deserve it."

"Jillian told me you quit."

"I did."

"You were never meant for that life," Susan says gently.

I don't argue.

"Seeing things others don't," I say quietly, "isn't always a gift."

She smiles. "It inspired me."

I hesitate, then say, "I'm applying to med school."

Her face lights up. "Dara, that's amazing."

I smile back, and don't tell her this might be goodbye.

The porch swing creaks softly when I return home. Aiden wraps an arm around my shoulders.

"How is she?"

"Hopeful."

"And you?"

I watch the sun bleed gold across the horizon.

"Maybe we don't leave the past," I say. "Maybe we decide what parts get to come with us."

"So not who you bring," he says. "But what you bring."

"Lessons. Strength. Not baggage. I've learned that every minute spent dwelling on the past steals from our future. But I don't want to leave the lessons I've learned behind either. Otherwise, that past has been wasted."

"That's my girl."

We sit quietly for a moment.

"I want to be part of your future," he says suddenly. "If you'll let me."

My mind begins to analyze.

Stop.

Not everything is a problem to solve. I smile.

"I want that too," I admit. "I'm just learning how to carry both who I was and who I'm becoming."

"Then we'll learn together."

I rest my head against his shoulder.

Graduation isn't an ending.

It's a beginning.

For the first time in a long while, I allow myself to feel it fully.

Hope.

Chapter 22

"I always knew." – Dara

The earring slips through my fingers as the news anchor's voice cuts through the room. I catch it just before it hits the floor, my pulse already racing.

Aiden moves in the background, buttoning his shirt, but I'm locked on the television.

"*Breaking news this morning: FBI indicts major players in illegal arms trade.*"

Footage flashes across the screen, federal agents flooding a courthouse, reporters shouting over one another.

"*Among the defendants is high-profile attorney John Mitchell…*"

The camera zooms in on John. He looks smaller somehow. Drained. Human.

Aiden exhales. "They actually got them all."

"For now," I murmur. "It's never really over is it?"

He squeezes my shoulder. "It's over for you."

Is it?

The anchor shifts tone.

"*In other news, recently declassified CIA documents reveal groundbreaking advancements in artificial intelligence for counterintelligence operations…*"

My breath stills.

AI. Counterintelligence. Two worlds I know better than I should. I step closer to the screen.

"*The decades-long project was spearheaded by an unnamed pioneer in the field. His identity remains redacted for national security reasons. Sources say he is set to retire and may be considered for a Nobel Prize in technology.*"

My stomach twists.

George.

His predictions. His reach. The way doors opened before anyone knocked.

The anchor continues.

"*The report also references a highly skilled CIA officer who disappeared five years ago during a covert operation. His work was closely tied to the retiring pioneer.*"

Five years ago.

That's when Dad vanished for good.

My fingers tighten around the remote.

"*The White House reports that the unnamed officer will soon have a star added to the CIA Memorial Wall.*"

The room tilts.

The pieces I couldn't force together now slide into place with terrifying ease.

"Dara?" Aiden calls. "You coming?"

I shut off the TV.

"Yeah," I answer, steadier than I feel.

Aiden notices the folded paper on the coffee table.

"What's that?"

"It's my speech."

He blinks. "Speech?"

"I'm valedictorian."

His face lights up. "Of course you are."

We step outside, but my mind stays behind eclipsed by an undeniable truth.

My father was a Keene. Of course, he was recruited. Of course, he disappeared into classified files and redacted lines.

And George…

I had been trying so hard to accept George.

Maybe I should have been trying to understand my father.

The drive to campus was a blur. The auditorium hums with anticipation when we arrive.

Aiden slips into the crowd. I take my place among a sea of black gowns.

The Dean speaks. Words continue to blur. I scan the audience looking for something. Answers. Confirmation.

"And now, our valedictorian… Dara Keene."

I rise to applause that feels distant.

Whatever secrets my past holds, this moment is mine.

I step to the podium.

The stage lights are bright, but I find Aiden's face. Then Jillian. Susan.

And in the back row…

George.

Still. Watching. That slight nod.

"We made it."

A ripple of laughter moves through the room.

"I wish my mother were here. I promised her I would finish. I promised I would finish here."

I pause.

"And for a long time… I thought that was all this was about. Finishing."

I set my notes aside.

"I came here thirsty. Thirsty for education. For stability. For purpose. Like the woman at the well in Scripture, I thought I was coming for something ordinary. Instead, I was given something that changed me."

Silence settles.

"I learned something here no syllabus could list and no professor could grade."

A breath.

"I learned that resilience isn't simply surviving. It's becoming. It's being sharpened by what was meant to break you."

I look across the graduates.

"We all arrived here carrying something. Doubt. Loss. Pressure. Expectations. Some of it visible. Much of it not."

"But it was in those unseen places that we were shaped."

A beat.

"And that shaping matters more than any line on a résumé."

The room grows still.

"I think my father was such a man. I recently overcame my preconceived ideas of who he was as I was being shaped into who I am."

A ripple of quiet.

"His past was a shadow as mine is a shadow. He chose a metaphorical wave that cost him the easy shore. I didn't always understand that. I thought he had simply walked away. I'm learning now… that sometimes the greater good asks for a life no one sees."

I steady my voice.

"And today, we stand at the edge of our own waters."

"Soon, each of us will choose our own wave. There are many waves in the ocean that we are about to embark. There are large waves and small ones. Waves that we face in public and many that we must face alone. Some will choose calm seas. Others will choose something larger, riskier, less certain."

"But once you choose your wave… you must ride it."

"You may be thrown. You may rise again. Or you may ride it all the way to shore."

"But drifting is not an option. We must choose wisely. Then persevere."

A quiet murmur moves through the room.

"As we leave here, it is less important that we know all the answers."

"What matters more is that we have learned to ask the right questions. To critically examine our own thoughts. To not only understand, but to realize how much we don't know. This is where true intellect resides."

I take a breath.

"Some of you will work in hospitals. Some in laboratories. Some in classrooms. Boardrooms. Courtrooms. Factories."

"And some will work in places without windows. Places without borders."

A subtle stir.

"Wherever you serve, serve with integrity."

"Because the world does not ultimately change through applause."

"It changes through quiet courage."

"It changes when someone does the right thing even if no one ever knows they did."

I scan the crowd.

"May we be the salt of the earth, preserving what is good, strengthening what is fragile, and leaving behind a thirst in others for integrity, truth, and courage."

"We came here thirsty."

"May we leave here able to quench the thirst of others."

A final pause.

"We made it."

"But more importantly…"

"We became."

Applause rises.

"Dara Photini Keene."

The name echoes.

Photini.

I walk across the stage and accept the diploma.

Later, outside…

"Photini?" Aiden asks. "I didn't know you had a middle name."

Before I answer—

"It means 'enlightened one,'" George says.

He approaches, composed as ever.

"Photini was the Samaritan woman at the well," George adds. "Tradition says she became a messenger of truth."

I arch a brow. "You're saying I'm enlightened?"

He smiles faintly. "I'm saying you finally are."

The words land softly. Not heavy. Just certain.

I hug him. He holds me, not tightly. Just enough.

In the parking lot, George presses an envelope into my hand.

"A graduation gift."

I look at him.

"It's the address to your grandparents."

The air leaves my lungs.

"For Dara's happiness," he says. "If she wants it."

"I always knew," I whisper.

Not accusation. Not surprise.

Just acknowledgment.

He leans closer, voice low.

"The past shaped you. It doesn't own you."

A pause.

"You were never alone."

He steps back.

"And the address is near campus," he adds gently. "Your mother chose well."

He turns toward a waiting car. The chauffeur opens the door.

He doesn't look back.

He doesn't have to.

"He cares about you," Aiden says quietly.

"He does," I answer.

More than I realized.

I look down at the envelope.

"What now?" Aiden asks.

I inhale.

"I think I'm going to visit my grandparents."

"Now?"

I nod.

"But first… one stop."

"Where?"

"Mom & Pop's cafe. I need to pick up a coffee."

He laughs. "Coffee? Now?"

"Yes. A large one. Extra sugar. Extra cream."

"That's not how you like your coffee," Aiden says.

"No," I say, watching George's car disappear at the end of the road.

"It's not."

I turn to Aiden, smiling fully now.

"But my grandfather does."

Soon we are in the car. A take out coffee in the cup holder. The envelope rests in my lap as we turn toward town.

I thought I was searching for answers.

I wasn't.

I was being led home.

Some truths don't crash into your life.

They're handed to you, strong, quiet and by someone who loved you long before you understood why.

A Note from the Author

Everyone carries a story beneath the one the world sees.

This novel was written for those who have walked complicated roads, who have been defined by mistakes, by labels, by survival, and who still choose love anyway.

Redemption does not always announce itself loudly. Sometimes it arrives quietly, in the form of a choice.

Thank you for reading.

— Carol Martin

About the Author

Carol Martin writes intelligent fiction for readers who value depth, moral tension, and emotional realism. Her stories explore love and consequence in a modern world, where strength is earned, desire has weight, and redemption is possible.

www.ingramcontent.com/pod-product-compliance
Lightning Source LLC
LaVergne TN
LVHW091118080826
845145LV00008B/1961

* 9 7 8 0 9 7 4 7 1 0 8 4 6 *